Reel LOVE

JULIE A. RICHMAN

Cover Design: Jena Brignola/Bibliophile Productions
Cover Photo: Scott Hoover
Model: Rhett Wellington Ramirez
Proofing, Interior Design & Formatting: Elaine York/Allusion Graphics
www.allusiongraphics.com

Reel
LOVE

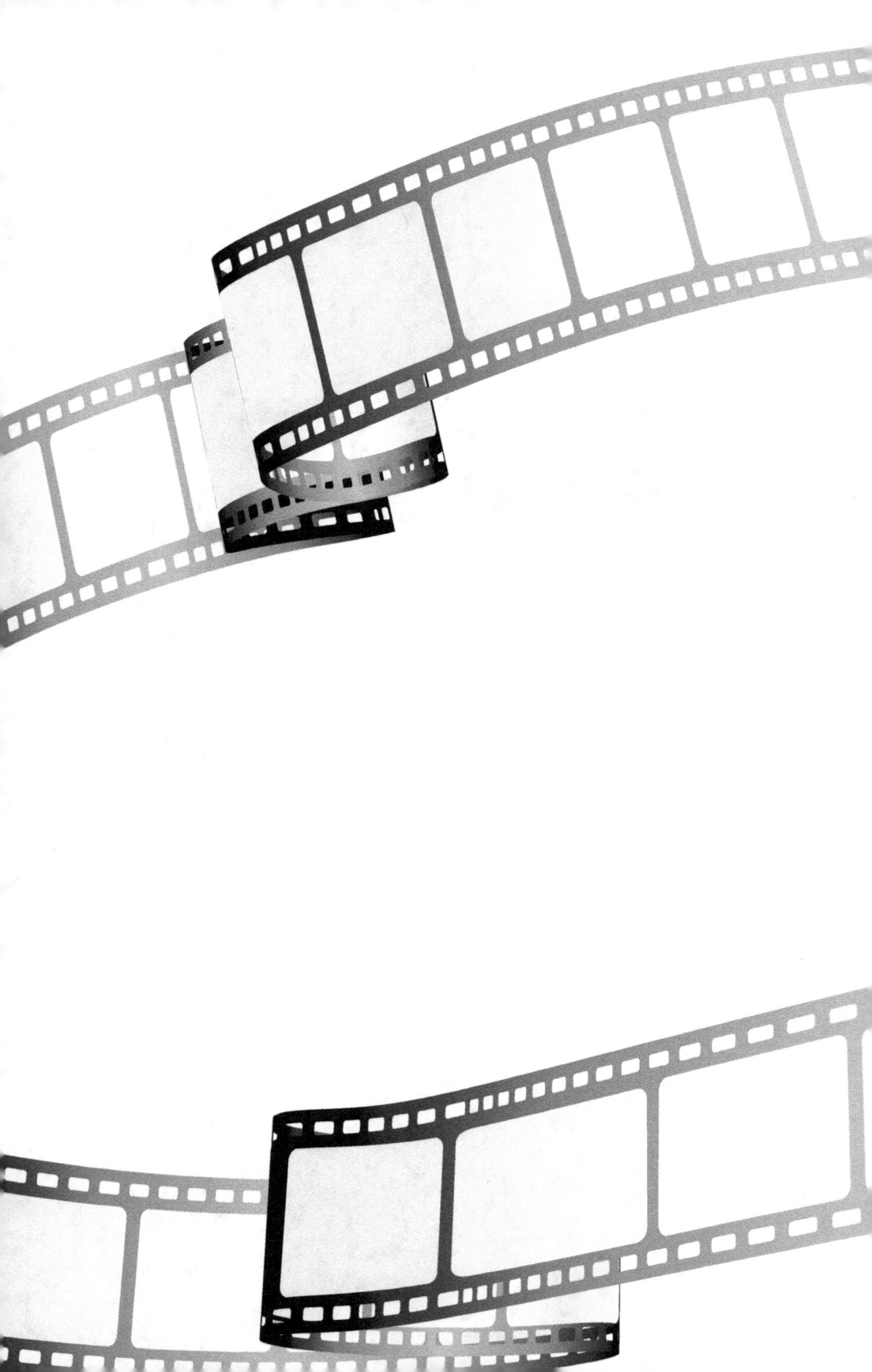

To Jake

Your heart knows what is right

Thank you for the inspiration.

Prologue

Frankie

In Flight...

Holy crap, he's perfect.

Not just like he'd be good for the role perfect, but like he stepped out of my head and onto my computer screen, perfect.

I can't believe he even exists. Well, in real life, anyway.

This is him. The guy I've been seeing in my head for over three years now. But with a picture in front of me, it crystalizes all the details in such sharp focus, for the very first time. It's like a layer of gauze was removed from the front of the lens of my mind's eye, and here he is. I am looking at the face of the hero in my biggest-selling, and let's face it, my only truly bestselling book.

Who is this man? I need to know more. I need to know *everything*. *Now*.

Finn Parker.

Good name. Obviously fake, but, nonetheless, good.

Those eyes. They are Griffin's eyes. I am finally staring into his clear blue eyes, studying the deep blue rings edging his irises, looking exactly like what I'd described the very first time Briela gazed up at him when they were just kids. Sky blue meeting a horizon line containing the ocean's power and depth was how I described them when the two meet again as adults. I have written many pages about these eyes.

Finn Parker, your eyes are killing me. Like I'm afraid to breathe, killing me.

A slight quiver in my hands radiates to my now-twitching fingertips as they hang, as if in suspended animation, just above the keyboard, choking, fearful that if I don't poke the keys with just the right finesse, he will disappear and be gone — forever. And I'm not ready to lose this flesh and blood version of the man who has invaded my thoughts for so long.

And what if I don't find him again? A moment of panic ensues as if I'm about to lose my *raison d'être.* Or maybe just lose my shit. *Or my mind.*

What the hell is wrong with me?

His freaking picture and bio are in an email sent to me by the studio's casting department. He is not disappearing into thin air, never to be found again.

Get ahold of yourself, woman.

Moving my unsteady hand from the keyboard, I grasp the stem of the wineglass on the armrest extension located between me and my sleeping seatmate, a weary-looking business traveler hitting somewhere in his late forties. With his laptop finally closed, soft snores escape a partially open mouth, assuring me he's asleep, cradled by the three gin and tonics he guzzled before the jet's wheels even lifted off the tarmac.

Taking a sip of the slightly too sweet white wine, it does nothing to quell my fear that the man staring back at me from my computer screen, Finn Parker, is merely yet another figment of my very fertile imagination.

Is this a dream? Am I asleep just like the guy sitting next to me? I always have weird, vivid dreams when I fall asleep in flight.

Maybe this is just another one of them.

Line after line of type swims before my eyes as I attempt to read his bio, letters zigzagging amorphously, out of focus, my brain not processing the words as my eyes keep veering back to his eyes, then wandering down, drawn to his asymmetrical smirk.

Damn, that is sexy.

The words don't matter. His name doesn't matter, where he's from, what movie roles he's previously had or that he's been the star of a streaming TV show that I never knew existed, does not matter. The only thing that matters is that I am staring into his eyes. Finally. And all the nuances of this stranger's ruggedly handsome face are so familiar. I've seen them in my head, as I wrote 107,000 words, living a piece of his lifetime, his heartache and failures, his journey, and finally, his triumph.

The character of Griffin Chase resonated with readers in a way I had never imagined or dared to dream. What began as a contemporary romance with a topical storyline, ended up being a call for truth, justice, and equality, with a hero who had the backbone, balls, and ethics that people were desperately searching for in their leaders. In a time of global upheaval, people worldwide needed the hope that freedom fighters, like Griff Chase, were out there in the shadows, shoring up our future, making sure the path of our choosing remained secure for all to traverse.

In all the time it took me to write *Fleeing an August Moon*, then the months of editing, my agent shopping it to publishers, the negotiations, the auction and sale, my editor's edits and my rewrites, the negotiation and sale of the screen rights, waiting for greenlighting, securing producers, development meetings, weighing in on the screenplay, the directorial selection, I have never as clearly seen Griffin's face before, not like this. Not until now. It's as if I finally focused the lens clearly and the minute details that I had imagined are exactly as I expected them to be.

Yes, I am an expert in all things Griffin Chase. I know what his hair feels like, dense and smooth. I can feel the tight muscles of his biceps unyielding against my fingertips, the texture of his skin is seared into my memory. His scent. If I breathe in deep, I can feel it excite every cell in my body. I well know the look that he gets on his handsome face in moments of anger, and that almost imperceptible squint to his eyes when something has hit home deeply in his heart. Above all else, I know every thought in his head and every word that is going to come out of his mouth.

As I look at Finn Parker, it feels like I know this man in a way I have never, ever known anyone else. But the man I know is Griff Chase, the character I created, not this Finn Parker actor guy. I know nothing about

3

the man filling my computer screen. Is he a good guy? Is he a jerk? Is he cocky and sure of himself, or is he insecure and self-doubting? Does he have a conscience or is he a handsome, soulless vessel?

This stranger whom I have never met is making me feel inexplicably out of sorts, precisely because he is a stranger. I can neither script the words coming out of his mouth, nor can I create or alter his thoughts. And I want them to be perfect. I want him to be perfect.

And, on top of that, *he doesn't know me.* I'm not an integral part of his world. Which feels really weird. It's like begging someone with amnesia to remember you. That's kind of what it feels like and that has me feeling very anxious.

And that's pretty fucked up.

Even I know that!

How much wine have I drank? The flight attendant up here in First Class has been pouring generously all flight.

Marking the page as a favorite for casting, I force myself to move on to the next actor's resume and the next after that. But, as I skim through the bios of actor after actor, I just want to go back and look at those mesmerizing eyes again.

As I finish my glass of wine, only one thought persists — I hope to God Finn Parker can act.

Finn

Holy shit, this book is a piece of crap.

But I really need to get through at least a few more chapters tonight. It would not be wise to blow this off. So, sleep is not an option. At least, not yet.

What I really need to do is get a better feel for who this character is and that is definitely going to require more info than I'm able to pull from the scene the studio provided for my audition tomorrow. By 11:30 a.m., I have to know what was in the author's head when she wrote this character. I'm reading for quite an audience tomorrow, including the director, and the freaking author herself, so I need to kill this.

This character is not my usual blood-and-gore military or shoot-'em-up action guy. The genre is very different for me. No surprise, I guess, that a chick-flick would be more emotionally complex. Man, when this book first came out, everywhere you went, women were reading and talking about it. You couldn't get onto a treadmill at the gym without every conversation you passed being about Griffin and Gabriela. And they would talk about them like they were talking about real people. *Real people they knew.* It was freaking crazy. And these women were in love with this Griffin Chase character. I'd be one rich guy if I had a dollar for every woman I heard say, "I need to find my Griffin Chase."

So, keep reading, because this is it. A breakout shot. Finally. This is the role that changes everything to leading-man status from *What-have-I-seen-you-in?* oblivion.

I'm turning thirty-five, dammit. Enough with this dues-paying crap already. I can act, I'm pretty easy on the eyes, and I just need this freaking role.

Two chapters into this book, and I'm not sure I'm going to be able to figure out what was in this author's head, because I'm not yet convinced there's actually anything in her head. I'm not sure why this book resonated with so many people, and not just here in the U.S., but all over the world. The talk was that this love story personalized real-life situations occurring all over the globe, taking place on every continent, and chronicled the human plight of immigrants everywhere. Women fell in love with this character who stood up against the prevailing winds to protect those he loved, and that made him one badass hero.

Yeah, it's topical and all, but I'm just not getting the appeal.

It's kind of amusing that I'm reading for a part that's got such strong political undertones and this guy is an ex-military, altruistic, freedom-fighter congressman (geez, author lady, did you throw in enough tropes?) who plays by his own rules. Getting into that headspace is so far off the beaten track for me, and then there's the whole romance element. Could this guy be any further away from me? Damn, I'm definitely going to have to prove my acting chops to pull off this shit.

But even I have to admit — this is it, this is what I've lived for, to act, to lose myself in a role. And who am I kidding, to be a star. Don't let any actor tell you that's not what he or she wants. That is what we *all* aspire to. We want to be household names, break box-office records, and be richer than the GNP of a small nation. *There, I said it.* We are an egotistical, self-absorbed, entitled lot. And we want it all. I want it all. Does that make me bad? Nah, it just makes me smart. And hungry. And I'm going to devour this role and spit out a performance that is going to leave everyone in that room breathless.

I just need to get into this character's head.

Setting the paperback on the bed next to me, I reach for the not-so-cold-anymore bottle and take a healthy swig of the hoppy brew. I actually bought the freaking paperback. Who buys paperbacks anymore? But I did, wanting to get the feel for this story, understand the nuances and intent that maybe didn't make it into the well-crafted screenplay scene.

Grabbing the paperback again, I rifle the pages, watching them fan and feeling the breeze they create, and as much as I'm hating this book, it's impossible not to admit that getting the part of Griffin Chase could be life-altering. And if I'm really being honest with myself, I need Griffin Chase and I really need to impress Francesca Simonelli, the newly minted, superstar author who seems to have been plucked out of obscurity with this book. Word on the street is that she will be very involved in the casting process and has final say on all roles, which is rare, especially for an author's first film project. It's not like she's a proven, not a Stephen King or a John Grisham. Two years ago, no one had ever heard of this woman, and now she's dictating her own terms.

Yeah, pretty impressive. I have to give her that.

Setting the book down for the umpteenth time, I grab my phone and hit the Google icon. Francesca Simonelli, let's learn about you.

I really want this role.

I really need this role.

2

Frankie

I can't keep my eyes open and the entrée hasn't even been served yet. I know the studio wants to give me the royal treatment and yes, the view from our table, at the Élephante Beach House here in Santa Monica, really is exquisite. The sky must've been paid off by the studio to give me such a spectacular show tonight. The sun's illumination on the water reminds me of the Yellow Brick Road with a path leading to the horizon. And I just want to bolt from this table and follow it, to escape being surrounded by the avocado toast that is being eaten by every single one of my dining companions. Clearly, by the size of these people, this is their one carb splurge of the month. Continuing to tantalize me, the sun slips into the ocean, a lover with a surprise on the other side, begging me to follow. And I really want to go.

"Francesca, you look exhausted."

I bet I do. And my face isn't pulled tight enough and hasn't been Botoxed into complacent submission to feign appearing engaged.

"Yes. I'm wiped out. Even though it's only a two-hour time difference, traveling west always kills me for the first two days. And please, call me Frankie." *And please, get these freaking entrées here like yesterday, so this long-ass day can finally end.*

"Were you able to get through the bios and headshots Sherri sent?" Marlena Gottlieb, the film's executive producer, is all business all the time, and I wonder if she ever lets loose. Maybe she only smiles when all the moving parts are nailed down, funding secured, and timetables met. Although not someone I'd want to cross, I'll bet Marlena would have your back in a pinch.

I nod, sweaty wine goblet to my lips.

"Good. We've got a long day tomorrow with two auditions scheduled every hour. And, I was telling everyone before you arrived, that I got a call from Maverick Dailey's agent yesterday, telling me Mav's interested in the part."

"Interesting." I smile brightly, hoping it conveys excitement. He's handsome and a box-office draw, that is for sure, so his fanbase will be there for opening day, whether or not they've read *Fleeing an August Moon*. It's definitely a win-win for the producers and the money people, as well as a chance for me to grow my reader audience for my next release.

But Maverick Dailey is definitely not Griffin Chase, and I suddenly have a feeling there are going to be battles, and I'm going to make some enemies if he is not my choice.

But he's just not Griff.

As the night progresses, I mostly listen. Halfway through the entrée I start counting in my head the number of times Mav's name is mentioned. We're up to seventeen.

Great first night already. Welcome to Hollywood.

This is definitely not going to be all fun and glitz, that much is becoming obvious.

We have an early call at the studio, but with my body still on Central Time, I'm up standing in front of the floor-to-ceiling windows in my hotel room looking out into the night at the shimmering lights of the Santa Monica/Malibu coastline.

From up here, it's all shimmering. Silver and gold tinsel, camouflaging the decay and broken dreams three floors below me.

My relationship with this city is classic love-hate. For me, LA is *that* boyfriend, he's a shit, he's an a-hole, he's a liar, but one look into his seductive eyes, and I just become stupid.

I wonder if there is a right outfit for watching actors audition for the lead role in a film? Covering my mouth, I laugh. Yeah, I am going to have to dress a little better than my typical writer's uniform of baggy, nasty sweatpants and three-day greasy hair. In my world, scrunchies never went out of style. But this is Hollywood and I need to do better than just presentable. And to a Texas girl, that means only one thing — ass-hugging jeans and envy-inducing cowboy boots.

I've got this. I've totally got this.

A couple of hours later, as I pass through the studio gate in the car they sent for me, I'm still pinching myself. I feel like a little kid with my nose pressed against the window, watching in awe, the people going about their everyday jobs as we drive through the lot. *You work at a movie studio,* I'm tempted to roll down the window and yell out at them. But they actually already know that.

Dropped in front of an unmarked building, I'm greeted by an assistant who leads me down a long hall. In my head, I'd always envisioned some grand old theatre or the stage in a fine arts center, but in reality, it's just a room.

I wonder what else won't live up to the visions in my head. And what sweet surprises that I never saw coming, will present themselves.

Taking my seat, there are five of us behind a table, me, the casting director, the director, the executive producer, and one of the other producers. I'm the only first-timer to this process, and it's probably just another day on the job for them. But for me, it's that first-day-of-school feeling, excitement churning in my belly as we wait to find our leading man.

An assistant delivers each of us a stainless thermal mug of coffee emblazoned with the *Fleeing an August Moon* logo.

Holy shit, this is real.

When she places a tray on the table, the excitement in my stomach turns to nausea. More avocado toast.

Ugh, not again.

Do these people eat this baby diarrhea-looking stuff three meals a day? I want breakfast tacos. I need breakfast tacos. I'm a Houston girl. The only acceptable green at breakfast are jalapeños or tomatillo green salsa —on my breakfast tacos, where they belong. Okay, yes, I know, as a Texan I should wholeheartedly embrace avocado, since guacamole is a Lone Star State staple. But I have my reasons for hating guacamole specifically, and avocados, in general, and I can sum it up in one word.

Tequila.

It seems I cannot hold my liquor.

Or my guacamole.

"Frankie, please, help yourself." Richard Lesser, the director, pushes the tray toward me. *Oh God, shoot me now.*

I need to nip this in the bud, even at the cost of coming across on day one as a diva author. But avocado toast in my presence, twice in twelve hours, on an empty stomach with only coffee sloshing around, is more than I can bear. And it needs to be stopped.

Immediately.

"Thank you, but no thank you. I can't even look at avocado without getting nauseous."

Snapping his fingers, the assistant turns on cue. This is obviously not the first time she's been snapped at. "Get this tray out of here and do not put avocado toast down in front of Ms. Simonelli again. Is that understood." It wasn't a question.

I feel bad for the girl as she scurries to remove the offending green toast, giving me a wide-eyed I'm sorry look, as she lifts the silver tray.

"What can we get you?" Richard asks solicitously, his tone with me one-hundred-eighty degrees from the tone he just used with the assistant.

As if reading his mind, I know he's thinking, *Oh, great, I've got to make nice to this author who is going to kill my movie with casting control and script approval. Fucking studio lawyers couldn't have negotiated a better deal? Useless leeches!*

"Is it possible to get breakfast tacos?" I ask sweetly, knowing I need to save my weight for the battles we are about to have. My gut tells me Maverick Dailey is going to be a royal one.

The first actor of the morning is someone I would never, ever have looked at and thought of as Griffin, at least not from a physical standpoint. I am ready to write him off, until he floors me with such a riveting performance that I'm trying discreetly to wipe the tears from my eyes as he reads the part when Griffin is saying goodbye to Briela at the border the first time she crosses on a humanitarian mission. He knows full-well that this might be their final goodbye, that she might never make it back to the United States alive, and if she does, she might be detained or turned away.

Every hair on my forearms is standing at attention, raised high and mighty to full staff from their goosebump hills. *Wow.* In my notebook I write my initial impression next to the actor's name so that I'll be able to flesh it out later. *Powerful, honest delivery. Believable Griffin, but very far from the way I envisioned Griff or the way he's described in the book. Will straying too far from my readers' mental image make my audience shut down? Try and keep an open mind – he's a talented actor!! Want to see more. He was THAT good!* Pulling out a small, pink storage container from my purse, I flip open the lid and pull out tiny scissors and a mini-stapler, then proceed to cut the photo from his bio and staple it to the page in my notebook next to my thoughts on his performance.

Without even looking up, I can feel everyone at the table's eyes on me. They're probably wondering how they are going to deal with me thoughout the process of making this film.

"What did you think?" Richard smiles at me after the actor leaves and we prepare to meet the next candidate.

"I think I need to keep an open mind. I would have never pictured him as Griffin, but his performance was riveting. He gave me goosebumps."

Richard smiles at me, knowingly. "I think keeping an open mind is important."

Yeah, I bet you do. You want your box-office busting boy as Griffin. And I just don't know if he'd make a believable Griffin.

This next actor has what I think of as classic soap opera-actor looks. He may be a little too perfect. Too pretty. Griffin Chase is ruggedly handsome. Not pretty boy handsome. Watching him tackle the scene, I can't help but to compare this actor to the first guy. He's reading the words fine, his intonation is okay, but he's not drawing emotion from the right place. He isn't there. *Can he get there? I have no goosebumps,* is the sentiment I jot into my notebook.

After the fifth actor, I stay at the table alone during the break and look back at the pages I've created. There would be no way I'd remember all of them without their pictures next to my notes. So far, the surprising first actor is at the top of my list. He is very far from standard good-looking. But I wonder if his superb acting and the role will allow him to be one of those men who become incredibly hot and sexy as people see them as the character. I can't help but think of what the role of Rick Blaine in *Casablanca* did for Humphrey Bogart or what the role of Frank Martin in the *Transporter* movies did for Jason Statham. These men, while not considered standard good looking, catapulted into sex symbol status based on nailing roles so completely that they captured the hearts of viewers.

As everyone returns to the room and takes their seats, the next actor is ushered in. I hope that none of my tablemates have taken note of my sharp intake of breath. I'm not prepared as Finn Parker enters the room, pirating what is remaining of my surrounding oxygen the moment he flashes a smile that scrambles my mind. *Oh my God, Griffin.*

I am suddenly aware that I'm staring at him, with what must be the look of someone seeing their ex walk in unexpectedly, post break-up, when you're not dressed or made up for that first meeting. I can feel my mouth moving, but nothing is coming out. And although there is a smile on his face, the look in his eyes screams confusion. *He doesn't recognize me.* And why should he? He's just meeting me for the very first time and I can't quite get that to add up in my thoughts.

He should know me.

We've been together, day and night, for three years. Three freaking years. I've known every thought in his head, every feeling sticking in his gut, every ounce of pain dripping from his heart. I know the rush he feels in the face of danger, the deep satisfaction that permeates every cell in his being when he rights the injustices of the world. I know how deeply he loves, he'd lay his life down for those he loves. For Gabriela.

"Finn Parker." He extends a hand. A big, masculine hand, with long fingers. I have a thing for hands and his pass muster.

His handshake is firm. His voice deep and manly. But it's his eyes that are so arresting. They are Griff's eyes. There are lines beginning to form on his face, and they are perfect, the way only men can age and look even better as they get older. I love the bow of his top lip. Perfect. I can't have a Griffin with a thin, or God-forbid, non-existent, top lip.

Beyond his hair being longer and the scruff on his face, this man looks just like his picture.

I merely nod. Unable to speak, still smelling his clean scent as I pull my hand back from his. Rallying a half-smile is the best I can offer. Shell-shocked and dry-mouthed, I know I must outwardly be coming across as cold and aloof, as that author who has just become quasi-famous with a book that struck the right chord with people.

I need to see how this actor stacks up against the first guy this morning. Silently, I pray this man can act his butt off.

Slay it, Finn. Please. My readers will love you.

The assistant points to the pages for Finn, who then turns his back to us before walking in a circle twice. I watch as his broad chest expands and his shoulders square, his stance physically changing, and when he turns back to us, he is Griffin Chase.

I want to stop you, you know that, don't you? Every instinct in my being is screaming at me to protect you. Which is really ironic, isn't it?

He lets out an abbreviated, sardonic laugh, and then pauses. Finn rakes his hair, his eyes cast down. Looking back up, he closes his eyes, shakes his head and lets out a slow exhale before going on.

I do know, that if I stop you, you will resent me forever and that will grow like a cancer tearing us apart.

Reaching over to the assistant that is standing in for the Briela role, he places a hand on her chin, gently letting his thumb slowly caress it. (Nice touch, Finn).

Part of me is so damn proud of you. This... this is exactly why I fell in love with you. Your strength, your fearlessness... and ironically, that is exactly what is taking you away from me. And I don't know how to come to terms with the reality that I may never see you again. I may never hold you again. How do I live with that, Brie? How do I live without you?

Taking the scene slow and not rushing through it, I can see the nuances he tries to inject into Griffin, the creases between Finn's eyes betray Griffin's conflict as he stares into the assistant's eyes. *Believable,* I write in my notebook. *I think he'd settle into the role nicely.*

Move on? There is disbelief in his voice. *You and I both know that is not what either of us want. I know the last thing you want is for me to forget you. Ever. And you know that, Briela.*

His hand moves from the assistant's chin to her hair. I hold my breath as his hand slowly moves down her shoulder-length hair until just the blunt-cut tips are between his fingers. My throat hitches when he runs the same thumb that caressed her chin over the bristley ends of her hair, a paintbrush fanning as he adds more depth of color to the character. I had seen Griff do the same thing in my head, but had never written it into the book. And now the Griffin Chase look-a-like was stealing the move. *Mannerisms on point,* I jot down, so fixated on how he had handled her hair, that I never actually heard the next few lines because they were drowned out by the voices in my head.

I will do everything in my power to get you back across this border. Have someone get word to me and I will come get you.

Shaking his head, he listens to the assistant's lines.

No. He's emphatic. *The only risk to me is losing you forever. There are no other risks.*

As the scene nears wrap-up, his hands slide from the assistant's hair down to her shoulders and down her arms until her hands are lost in his. Softly, he pulls her into his arms and then wraps them around her tightly. He begins to rock and she goes along with his lead. With his cheek pressed against her head, he whispers, *Be safe, Gabriela. Stay safe until you're back in my arms again.* He buries his face in her hair.

There is silence in the room, the energy of the performance leaving us all spellbound. Looking down the table, Marlena catches my eye and mouths, "Oh my God!"

Finn releases the assistant from his embrace and thanks her before turning to us. Slowly, he exhales as if he's been holding his breath with the rest of us.

"We'll be in touch with your agent, Finn," Richard informs him.

"Thank you for letting me read for this." He approaches the table to shake everyone's hand.

Taking mine, I once again enjoy his fresh scent, "Thank you for letting me read for Griffin. I really loved the book."

"Thank you." I can't take my eyes off him, and our eyes stay locked one moment too long.

Finn

I never expected to get so emotional.

I think it was good that I did. I should know for sure in a few days if I'll be getting a call back. If I don't, then I can assume it wasn't a good thing. Or I'm just not what they're looking for. Or maybe somebody with a bigger name wants this role and that will get them more at the box office.

Turning the car's A/C on full blast, I know I need to decompress from what happened in the audition before I actually drive. I was immersed. I got totally lost in that character. It's been a long time since I've played a part where it feels like someone else takes over and my body is just their vessel. And I did not expect it to happen with a romantic film like *Fleeing an August Moon*.

The book actually got better as I read on last night. I'm just so not used to reading romance, that it was initially hard to wrap my head around. But now, at about halfway through, I'm actually enjoying it, and it's easy to understand why this became such a huge smash hit. The author's very detailed prose paints an extraordinarily clear picture in my head, and I feel like I'm watching a movie screen as I read each page.

Griffin Chase. Well, he would certainly pluck Finn Parker out of obscurity and make me a household name.

I hope I came across gruff enough. And emotional enough.

This character's traits are a contradiction trapped in one body. Complex. I'm hoping the rest of the book gives me more insight, so that if I make it further in the process and read again, my performance exudes the primal essence of this character.

And now, I need to know more about him. Putting the car into reverse, I finally pull out of the spot and head off the studio lot and down Melrose toward La Brea and then down to Venice Blvd., which gives me a straight shot home.

Hitting the Bluetooth button on my steering wheel, I'm finally centered enough to talk to another human being, and who better than the person who sent me to the audition.

Picking up before the first ring is completed, he barks at me, "Sebastian Cho," even though I know my name came up on his phone.

"Hey, Sebastian." I can see him clearly in my head, wearing a well-tailored, fine gray-and-black weave suit, impeccable white shirt, which sets off a deep cranberry-colored silk tie. All this atop some expensive, hipster pointy-toed shoes. The man really is an impeccable dresser.

"How'd you do? Who'd you meet? Did they give you feedback?"

"I think I did okay. I met the Director, Executive Producer, Head of Casting, the book's author, and one other person. And no feedback."

"Was it Sherri Pinsker from casting?" A Koreatown native with two parents who worked at studios, his mother in sets and his father in accounting, there was no way this guy's life was not going to be in the business.

"Yeah. Yeah, it was," I confirm, hoping he didn't hear the growl in my stomach, which oddly sounded a lot like tires screeching.

"Excellent. I've been talking to Sherri about you for a while. You said the author was there, right?"

"Yeah, I met her, too."

"Her agent inked the sweetest deal. But I guess when a book sells one-hundred-million copies worldwide, you get to call the shots. She is the final say for casting on every role in the damn film."

"Yeah, I'd heard that." And it wasn't something I'd heard very often in my fourteen years out here working as an actor.

"What was she like?"

I thought for a moment, and my mind came up blank. I had been so focused and in the zone that I didn't take detailed note of anyone.

"Nice, I guess, I just said hello and goodbye."

"She's pretty hot, I've seen her on some of the talk shows. She's a blonde, so not your type. No wonder you didn't notice." He speeds through his sentences as if he's hawking a product on late-night television. "I'll call Sherri at the end of the day and see what they're thinking. If I've got anything, I'll get back to you."

Hitting end, I look at the time on my dashboard, it's only about 1:00 p.m. and my stomach rumbles at the thought. Auditioning on an empty stomach is one of my superstition things, I can never eat before a reading, and now I am paying the price. The acid churned up by nerves and focus infiltrates my gut with a nasty sting. One o'clock still gives me plenty of time to get to Rose Café while they are still serving breakfast. Now, if only I can score an outdoor table and hang out there to read while I enjoy their amazing egg white and veggie omelet, and the best avocado toast in Venice Beach.

The lunch crowd is now gone and there are only a few of us left at the tables in the covered area outside, making it the perfect spot to crack open the book.

"Can I get you anything else?" the waitress asks, as she refills my water glass.

Looking up from my book, I smile and nod. "Yeah, I'd love a latte with oat milk and an extra shot."

"That should give you some energy." She smiles down at me.

I need it. Auditioning always causes an adrenaline burst for me, and afterward, I am depleted and running on empty.

Returning a few minutes later with a steaming mug, I smell the latte coming my way before it even gets here. "Thank you, I really need this," I admit as she sets it in front of me.

"What are you reading?"

Holding up the paperback so that she can see the cover, simultaneously we say, *"Fleeing an August Moon."*

Her hand immediately flies to her chest, covering her heart. "I love that book. Griff and Briela. I had such a book hangover after I read it. I couldn't pick up another book, so I just read it again," pausing, "and again."

How many times did she read this book? Is that normal?

"I've never heard of a book hangover," I admit. This appears to be a crazy world about which I know nothing.

"It's when a book just blows you away and you can't even begin to think about picking up another book because you're just not ready to say goodbye to the characters from the hangover book."

Tilting the paperback, I ask her quizzically, "And this book did that to you?" I can hear the disbelief in my own voice.

"Yes, aren't you loving it?" She's now looking at me like I'm the crazy one, her eyes wide and questioning.

"I still have a ways to go." Holding up the book, I show her that I'm less than fifty percent into it.

"It's amazing. You are going to be blown away. I made my boyfriend read it. And he loved it. I think everyone in this country should read it. With everything that has gone on and is going on with families being torn apart, I think reading this book makes it so much less of a charged, political issue and it becomes the story of people. And of love and honor. I heard they're making it into a movie. My boyfriend already knows that we are going to see this movie the day it comes out."

"This book definitely resonated with you. But why?"

"Do you have an hour?" She laughs and gives my shoulder a squeeze as she walks off, leaving me with a latte and Griffin Chase.

"You did good. I just got off the phone with Sherri. She described you as one of the best auditions of the day." Sebastian pulls me out of a dream with his ebullient delivery. I must have fallen asleep on the couch while reading.

Trying to exorcise the cobwebs from my voice, I attempt to quietly clear my throat. "That is great freaking news. Do you think I've got a shot at this?"

"I don't know. We'll see. She also told me that Mav Dailey really wants the role."

And just like that, my shimmering bubble from merely a nanosecond before, bursts, dissipating as rapidly as it had appeared.

My reaction is a guttural groan.

"It's really going to come down to the author. The characters need to match her vision. I've only seen this a few times, where the source writer has so much control."

"I'm reading the book right now to get a better take on the character."

"Did you read any of it before your audition?"

"Yeah, I was probably a little under halfway through."

"Mmm."

I can tell that is a disappointed, "Mmm." A *why weren't you better prepared* Mmm. And he's right, I should have started the book a week ago when I found out I'd be reading for the male lead.

"Well, Sherri really liked you. She said if not this one, now that she's seen you, she'll keep you in mind for future roles."

"So, does that mean I am out of the running for this one?" My mind immediately veers down the path of negativity, a place I have made a comfortable home out of for the past few years. Hollywood will do that to you, no matter how tough you'd like to think you are, the rejection always kicks you squarely in the balls, and it's a punch of searing pain every single time.

"No. No. Not at all. She thought you did very well today. She even said that the author really liked you a lot."

"Francesca Simonelli said that?" Her eyes, when I thanked her for letting me read, it was as if she were searching mine, but I'm not sure for what. I wonder if she saw Griffin Chase when she looked into my eyes, or maybe she was searching for him within me?

"Apparently." Pausing for a moment and then adding, as if it's an afterthought, but I know that it isn't, "Yeah, I understand she's staying not too far from you. She's at the Casa del Mar in Santa Monica."

"Really. Interesting that she's staying out at the beach and not something closer to the studio."

I know it's not a money thing, the studio can certainly afford to keep her in the lap of luxury. Heck, what she made on the book sales and screen rights, she could afford to rent a mansion for the duration of the film's production, or just buy one outright. So, why the Casa del Mar in Santa Monica? Maybe, like me, she needs the ocean close by to feel right. I wonder if that's what gives her a recharge or feeds her creative energy.

"How did Mav's reading go? Does he even have to read?" I wonder if Sebastian knows.

"Funny you bring that up. Sherri was saying that they were having dinner with him tonight and that the author was not happy that he hadn't auditioned. She wants to see him read." He lets out an audible, annoyed sigh. "Giving an author this much control in the process is like having a first-class cabin filled with screaming toddlers who have yet to be potty-trained." Sebastian was a huge proponent of separating families from business travelers by putting them on totally separate flights.

"Really? She wants to make Maverick Dailey audition for the part?" I'm sure that went over well with him.

"I know, crazy, isn't it? They shouldn't let outsiders on the lot. I'll call you when I hear something." He quickly ends the call, a Sebastian Cho trademark.

Picking up the book off the couch where it had fallen out of my grasp when I dozed, I stare at the words on the page as my brain replays Sebastian's words. *One of the best reads of the day. The author liked you a lot.*

Her eyes. I was so focused on the way she was looking at me, the intensity, the unasked questions she silently demanded answers to, that it didn't even really register just how beautiful her eyes were. A blue-green hazel, her pupils rimmed in yellow flames giving the appearance of a sunflower.

What was it she was trying to ask me?

Reading on, I'm again surprised at how topical this book is, and that if I look past the surface of romance, there's a whole lot of other stuff going on. How is this ex-Marine turned junior congressman going to deal with immigrants passing through the borders illegally? Is his allegiance going to be to his country and the oath of his office, or to the woman he loves and the people with whom he grew up? Will he assist her in crossing over the border again knowing she's walking right into the lair of a drug cartel? This guy is about honor and commitment to his oath of office, but he also knows what has been put in place by the government is destroying families and hurting good, law-abiding citizens in his district. People who have never known another home, ripped away from their lives, their children, their aging parents. I can feel his conflict. It feels different when you look at it as individuals' stories.

Rising from the couch, I pace my living room, internalizing Griff Chase's struggle, as I stalk from corner to corner. He's always been Briela's protector, from the time they were kids. She's part of the fabric of his being, and like a thread catching on a jagged edge, the pull leaves a hole, that while others might not take notice, you know irreparable damage has been done.

Shit, this story that I initially thought sucked, that I wrote off as commercial trash is emotionally stabbing at my gut. I want to get lost in this guy. I want to be the Griffin Chase everyone saw in their head when reading the story. I want this.

Sinking back down into the worn leather couch, I pick up the paperback and stare at the cover for a long moment and think about the reissue they'll do of it for the film. I need my face to be on that cover.

I need to be Griffin Chase.

But the things I need to do above all else is finish this book, learn more about this character, and see where this story goes, since, yes, I admit, I'm totally hooked and I need to figure out how to make sure Francesca Simonelli sees me as her one and only Griffin Chase.

I want to be Griffin Chase.

Lord knows, I need to be Griffin Chase.

Frankie

I'm sitting across the table from Maverick Dailey. Let that sink in for a moment. I am seated in a crimson leather banquette at Dan Tana's in Hollywood engaged in conversation with Mav Dailey. Uh-huh, yup, you heard that right.

Under any other circumstance, I'd be fangirling and batting my barely mascaraed pale lashes at him. But tonight, I am doing neither. I'm being polite, I know better than to go into diva-bitch mode with a bonafide, superstar sex-symbol. But I really want to. I want to tell him he's not Griffin Chase and he needs to audition for the part like everyone else. I'm not an idiot, I know this *let's make nice to the author because final casting approval is in her contract* charade is just that. It's a charade.

"I get to the Houston area quite often." He smiles and tips his head, his eye contact with me impeccable. "You'll have to show me the best B.B.Q joints when I'm there." It's impossible not to notice the way his eyes crinkle when he smiles. Or the single dimple.

He's trying to bond with me.

As I open my mouth to answer, he cuts me off. I have yet to jet off my first syllable. Not good, dude.

"And I'll bet the guacamole is fabulous."

"What is it with you people and avocado?" I'm still jetlagged, and I'm tired and cranky and we're talking avocados. Again.

Thank God my hotel is a straight shot down Santa Monica Blvd. Boots off. Jeans off. Bra off. Balcony overlooking the ocean. And a chance to look over all my notes from today. That's all I want.

I give him a wide-eyed look and he laughs.

"Point taken, don't show up in the mornings on set with avocado toast and a latte for you."

His smile is slow and mocking, the kind that makes you want to scream, "Screw you," at him and hurl your blow dryer at his head. And then follow up the outburst with a headboard banging, back-scratching, triple-orgasm fuck.

Looking down at the menu, I notice they have an appetizer of garlic toast, a welcome reprieve from the avocado toast on every other menu.

"Garlic toast," I say aloud, first smiling to myself and then at Sherri. "Finally, toast that my people like."

Mav nods to a nearby waiter standing at attention, and tells him to bring me garlic toast.

"Sure thing, Mr. Dailey."

"So, garlic toast is more in your wheelhouse," he chuckles. "Is your family northern Italian?"

I know he's assuming that based on my blonde hair and light eyes and a classic Italian last name. I nod. "Yes, my grandparents were from Trento, but I've got a lot of Sicilian blood in me, too." *Don't judge a book by its cover.*

"Yet, another point taken." His laugh is hearty. And it's sincere. That, I can tell. "I know better than to piss off a woman with Sicilian blood coursing through her veins." Leaning across the table toward me, he lowers his voice and smiles, "I'm particularly fond of my *cojones*."

"I'm sure you've been very good to them."

His smile is dazzling me. Another truly sincere smile. This man knows exactly how to measure and manage his charisma. I know some of it is learned and honed and becomes as natural as eating avocado in this town. But it's the inherent piece that is what makes most of the women on the planet feel an electric sizzle snake through their bodies at just the sight of him. *And he's working overtime to try and bond with me. I'm reading that as he really wants this role.*

"Can you stay for a few minutes and have an after-dinner drink with me?" he asks later on when the bill arrives.

Nodding, I note from the corner of my eye, Sherri and Maverick's agent, Evan Katz, give one another a look and a smile. I know we will see a hasty departure from them, and when they both rise to leave a minute later, I'm just shocked at how quickly that happened.

He really is the king here, isn't he? I can feel Mav's eyes on me as I say goodbye to Sherri and Evan.

"See you in the morning," I bid Sherri goodnight before turning my attention back to Maverick. I'm annoyed. I know I shouldn't be, but I have the feeling that a very smooth operator is going to railroad me before I even know I'm in the train yard.

This is my book. He needs to sell me. And right now, I feel like I'm not in the market for his brand.

"Limoncello?" he asks, giving me the deep stare into the eyes. "Perfect way to end a meal of Italian food."

"Only if you'll split a piece of cheesecake with me," I counter, garnering yet another robust and unexpected laugh from him. "Seriously." He now has me smiling with his laugh.

"I will absolutely share a piece of cheesecake with you." He shakes his head, looking surprised, as he calls the waiter over to place the order.

At attention for the star, the staff has the two apéritif glasses and the cheesecake with two forks to the table almost immediately.

Picking up his glass, Mav toasts, "Salut," to which I return the sentiment, before sipping the pungent liquor and reaching for a fork.

The cheesecake melts in my mouth and I close my eyes to focus on the explosion raining down on my taste buds. When I open my eyes, Maverick is staring at me like I'm a new breed at the zoo.

"What?" I start to laugh.

"Do that again."

"Do what again?" I'm genuinely confused.

"Take another bite."

What an odd request, but I go with it and sink the side of my fork in, surgically slicing my next bite from the creamy triangle. "Don't tempt me, I'll eat the whole thing." Bringing the fork to my mouth, I again let the cheesecake melt along my tongue.

"I said another bite, not my portion of it." Smiling, he whittles a piece from the other end of the cake and now it is my turn to watch his reaction as the flavor explodes in his mouth.

As I go in for my third bite, he surprises me again. "This is like a perverse thrill for me to watch you eat cheesecake."

The forks tines are in my mouth, with the fork upside down and I'm afraid to pull it out to speak. But I do, slowly, and watch Mav lick his lips. My intent was not for it to be sensual, but I know that is exactly what it was.

"You've lost me," I admit.

"I don't think I've seen a woman eat cheesecake in the past fifteen years."

Covering my mouth with the red cloth napkin so I don't spew the dessert as I laugh, all I can think is he only sees women eating avocado toast.

"Maybe someone needs to perfect a recipe for avocado cheesecake for the women of Southern California," I suggest. "I'm sure there's some hotsy-totsy chef who can create it and win a James Beard award for launching the next hottest trend."

Smiling, he plows another bite into his mouth, leaving the final bite on the plate. With a gleam in his eye, he slowly pushes the plate across the table toward me.

"You don't have to ask twice," I inform him and scoop up the remainder of the cheesecake.

Maverick pulls the plate back, and using the side of his fork scrapes any last bits off the dish. He appears to be a master of bonding and now I'm just waiting for him to go into his pitch as to why he is the perfect Griffin Chase.

He does not disappoint.

Taking a sip of his Limoncello, he begins, "How has it been for you being thrust into the international spotlight the way you have?"

"An adjustment, to say the least. Do you have tips for me?"

"Don't read reviews and follow your gut instinct."

"I don't think you get a lot of bad reviews." The man is a beloved superstar. Paul Newman. Tom Hanks. Sir Laurence Olivier. I can't think of many actors who are so loved and respected for their talent, and like

Paul Newman, Mav has the added esteem of being a sex symbol. Gazing into his deep blue eyes, I can easily understand why.

Laughing, he treats me to his single dimple again. "Trust me, I have my share of critics."

Pulling out my phone, I pull up Amazon's page for *Fleeing an August Moon* and click to sort one-star reviews before handing my cell to Maverick. "We may want to order another round of drinks for this," I advise and catch the waiter's attention. "Another round of Limoncello, please."

It's amusing to watch his face as he begins to read the scathing reviews. "Damn, these people are harsh."

"I definitely have had my share of skewering."

He begins to read aloud, a sardonic smile on his face, "I haven't read this book." He stops and looks up at me. "People really leave shitty reviews on books they haven't even read?"

"All the time."

He continues, "But I already know that I would hate this hero. A congressman who breaks the law helping people cross a border illegally is not a hero, he's a criminal, and I would not give this author a dime of my money to glamorize the support of criminals." Shaking his head, he comments, "This person has no idea what this book is even about and yet they leave a shitty review." He actually appears offended.

"There are hundreds just like it."

"Well, I've read it three times already, and if this person had actually read it, I doubt she would have written that review." A deep crevasse forms between his brows as he scrolls down the page and reads on. "Wow, people are brutal. I'm on my third read and I disagree. The book looks at all aspects of the reality that affects people. It's about conscience and consequence, not judgment. "

"Third read?" I'm surprised and nearly choke on my Limoncello.

"The first time I read it was just a straight read-thru for story. Everyone was talking about it and the woman I was involved with kept telling me that I needed to read the book and that she thought it would make a great movie."

I know he's talking about Hayley Hicks, his actress ex-girlfriend.

"The second time," he continues, "was to pick up the subtleties I knew I didn't pick up the first time around, and with this third reading, it's to really get inside Griffin's head, and internalize him so that I can understand his mindset and motivation. That's the roadmap to the nuances for me."

"Do you see different things each time you read it?

"Yeah, absolutely." Smiling at me he adds, "And what I also see are some of the threads and fibers you have woven throughout to create the story's fabric, that I definitely missed in the first reading, and to some extent, the second time, too. You lead us on an incredible journey."

"Thank you," I acknowledge the compliment. "I appreciate your kind words."

"I mean them, Francesca."

He knows I'm questioning his motive for the lavish flattery.

"Please, call me Frankie."

Lifting his glass, the corners of his mouth rise slightly, never quite engaging a full-smile, but enough for that one dimple to tease me with a flash. "I prefer Francesca."

"And I prefer Frankie."

He regards me for a moment, then shakes his head. "It might be hard. I've been thinking of you for months as Francesca."

I level him a look saying, *"Really?"*

"It's true. I've thought about this conversation since the first time I read *Fleeing an August Moon*." He leans into the table as he speaks, as if he's sharing something intimate with me, and I wonder if that is for the benefit of everyone in the dimly lit restaurant who are all watching us out of the corners of their eyes.

I can just see it now, tomorrow's *Hollywood Hotline* headline, "Maverick Dailey and Francesca Simonelli share an intimate moment discussing Mav's role as Griffin Chase in the upcoming adaptation of *Fleeing an August Moon*." More likely, he's thought about this conversation ever since he learned I had final say on all casting.

"I would be honored to bring Griffin Chase to the big screen."

There. He said it.

"I am really flattered, Mav. More than you can imagine. It's a dream to have a star of your magnitude want to take on the role of this character that I created." I smile and pause for a moment prior to launching the Scud missile. "But, to be very frank with you, you are not at all how I envisioned the character of Griffin Chase, and I am having a devil of a time coming to terms with that." I continue quickly so that he doesn't cut me off before I say what's truly been on my mind. "I know your ability to masterfully bring life to all your roles and I know that you would do that with this role, too. But I'm just not seeing you as Griff."

Sitting back in his seat, he digests my words. I am sure no one has said anything like that to him, at least not since the earliest days of his career.

"How can I change your mind?"

"Audition for the part and let me see your interpretation."

"You want me to audition?" There's no dimple in this smile.

I can't tell if he's insulted, angry, or amused by what I'm sure he considers my naiveté.

"Yes. But I don't want you to read at this juncture. I'd like to cast Briela first, and then have you read with whomever my choice is." I intentionally use the word *my* to reiterate that this project is mine and will not be hijacked by his star power.

"Why would you not want to cast the male lead first, and then find a heroine with whom he has incendiary chemistry?" he counters.

I shrug. "Would you prefer to read before we cast the female lead?"

"I would prefer the female lead is cast around me." I can see him walking the tightrope in his mind. "And the read is to ensure she is the right fit, not am I the right fit."

"I understand. But I'm still going to need to see you audition for the role." Texas girls in cowboy boots do not back down.

"Well, then, I welcome that opportunity." He twirls the stem of the apéritif glass.

I laugh. "You look like you want to toss your drink at me."

"Never." He takes a sip. "Obviously, I'm not used to being in a position like this. But I do respect that you want the right person in this role. Though I can tell you right now, that person is me. I am Griffin Chase."

His confidence is more than a little hot. Who knows, maybe he'll soon have me believing he is Griffin Chase. Stranger things have happened.

Including sitting across the table from an actor who is a household name and international superstar.

Finn

I *should have gone for a run on the beach.*

Looking up at the TV screen mounted on the wall as I pound out my grueling seventh mile on the gym's treadmill, I see her on *Hollywood Hotline,* the number-one television and streaming entertainment news channel. My reaction is immediate. I can't wipe the smile off my face. It's like I'm seeing an old friend, even though we've only met briefly, once. But reading her book, I feel like I'm inside her head with a window to her soul so crystal clear that I can reach inside and grasp it. I know how she creates, and I get that. As an actor, I totally get that. And it makes me feel this connection — which I know is ridiculous. How many millions of people have read this book?

I was so focused on nailing the audition that I didn't really *see* her. How did I not notice how cute she is? Girl-next-door cute. Your best friend's little sister cute. The one who grows up and the little tomboy who bugged the crap out of you now has a great rack and perfect ass and the same sass that used to drive you crazy. This is one you want to bang, even though you know you're strolling, eyes open, right into the danger zone. She was the little brat whom you wouldn't let tag along with you and now you want to cut off the legs of the guy she's leaving with. *Motherfucker.*

And the guy, *that motherfucker,* is Maverick fucking Dailey. Insert groan.

Leave her alone. You can have anyone. You can have any part.

As I pound the treadmill deck, the taut pull on my stomach muscles initiates that sick feeling as I read the closed-caption type on the TV screen.

Last night Hollywood Hotline *ran into Mav Dailey and* Fleeing an August Moon *author, Francesca Simonelli, as they were leaving Dan Tana's.*

"Mav, are you going to play Griffin Chase?" a paparazzi calls out as camera flashes illuminate the couple.

"Do you think I'd make a good Griffin?" he smiles back at the reporters.

"You'd be great," someone yells.

Mav slings an arm around Francesca's shoulder, pulling her into him and he mouths the word, *"See"* to her. His action is both very intimate and possessive.

See *what,* you smug douche? See that the paparazzi kiss your ass?

Her smile appears pained. It doesn't look anything like the smile I shared with her. Did I share a smile with her? Or is that just the way I want to remember our interaction?

Mav Dailey.

How the fuck do I compete with that?

I don't.

I feel as if I've been slammed over the head with a pane of glass. And it's shattering and splintering all around me, piercing my skin. Stinging everywhere. Disappointment burns. Kind of like the way my stomach does right now and my calves, too, from pounding this treadmill with an angry intensity.

Did I jinx myself initially thinking the book sucked?

Because I was wrong. Dead wrong.

I admit it. I was totally off-base.

I confused an easy-to-read style with the book being light fluff. *I was wrong.* And the characters, not a single one of them, are one-dimensional. Their complexity is rich, they're conflicted, and like real life, the struggles are both internal and external. The story is not only personal, it's topical, people's struggle for freedom from repression, a global, if not universal, battle. I can see them all in my head, walking the dusty streets and back alleys, feel the sweat soaking my brow in the squalid border town, the stench of desperation and death unrelenting and as unescapable as the heat blaring from the southwestern sun itself.

Griffin Chase would not be a cakewalk, pretty boy character, like I've played throughout my career, I know that. And that complexity is what is drawing me to him. I want to get lost in this guy. Feel his pain, experience his heartbreak. Revel in his love for Gabriela. Charge forward with his convictions and challenge myself, as he battles the injustices of the world. Griff is a freedom fighter harnessing a global war into a personal skirmish. But the true battle royale plays out within himself and how he comes to terms with the conflict, while retaining his integrity and following his moral compass in a world where morality is viewed as weakness.

I get him. I am him.

Hollywood is just a glitzier version of a town where dreams are futile for most of us, but we still cling to them in hopes of landing that next role. The one that is always just a day away. *Just one more day.* And that's the role that will finally be the breakthrough, allowing the trade of keys to our small, shithole apartments for a grand home on the hill overlooking the kingdom.

I want this freaking role.

I need this freaking role.

Fuck you, Maverick Dailey. And get your goddamn rich, manicured hands off her.

Reaching for the towel, I mop the sweat stinging my eyes, and when I refocus on the TV, the show has moved on to the catfight between a model and her ex's new starlet girlfriend who has been openly piling on the shade.

Get these losers off the screen. I need to see Francesca again. If I were home, I'd be tracking back to watch that clip a few more times and see if I could pick up anything else, some clue as to how serious she is about casting Dailey.

Standing under a hot-as-I-can-handle spray from the gym's showerhead, I roughly rub my skin, needing to wash away the feeling of not being good enough that has trailed me from the treadmill. I can see the redness rising on my chest where I've scrubbed too hard without even realizing it, while obsessing over her dinner with Maverick.

Dan Tana's, how fucking Hollywood predictable.

Where would I take her?

Manchego.

I would take her to Manchego and share a cheese board and tapas with her. We'd slowly pick at our shared food, engrossed in conversation about Griffin and Gabriela, digging into things that aren't on the pages of *Fleeing an August Moon*, but rather ensconced in Francesca's brain. I would listen intently, internalizing all his feelings until they were my own.

Drying off, the crimson stripes across my chest stare back at me in the mirror. I look like I've been attacked by a feral beast. And maybe I have. Have I lost my humanity living in this town? Have I turned into just another animal trying to claw my way out of this tarnished, shimmering squalor we've convinced ourselves is paradise?

Paradise by the sea — but only a select few are permitted on the beach. And I feel like I am on the sidewalk bordering the sand — I can see the swells, hear the waves crashing, smell the salt on the breeze, even feel the scratching sand on my bare soles that has blown onto the sidewalk. But I'm still not permitted on the beach. I've been allowed as a guest for short stints, but have never secured permanent entry on my own.

I want my own keycard.

Packing up my gym bag, I know I need to get out of here and go someplace to sit down and finish reading the book. I need to know what happens. Will Briela find her way back to Griffin again? Can he get her back into this country? Does it deviate from the screenplay?

"Finn."

Turning to see who's calling me, I'm being waved over by Henry, one of the club's top brass. The guy he's with looks very familiar, but I can't place him. Probably an actor I've seen in something. Everyone looks familiar in this town.

"Doesn't he look like he could be your much younger brother?" Henry questions the other man.

"So, what are you telling me, you think all us blond-haired, blue-eyed guys look alike?" he responds, appearing quite amused.

"I think you look like you could be related. I've always wanted to introduce you two. Finn, this is Schooner Moore, the owner here at L9."

As we shake hands, I realize, of course, that's who this is. He's not an actor. This guy owns one of the largest health club conglomerates in the country. No wonder why he looked so familiar.

"Pleasure meeting you." I shake his hand. He really does look like he could be related to me.

"You were certainly pounding that treadmill," Henry comments.

"Yeah, thinking about this role I auditioned for. Just stressing out about it."

"Good role?" Schooner asks, and I'm kind of amazed at how truly genuine his interest appears to be.

"It could change my life," I admit, and just verbalizing those words makes it all seem crystal clear. This role *would* change my life forever. I am on a precipice, and either the parachute is going to open and I will be sailing smoothly, catapulted by changing winds, or it's not going to open and yes, I will pick myself up, dust the disappointment off, treat my scraped-up ego, probably spend more than a few inebriated, self-loathing nights fucking women whose faces will be a blur within twenty-four to forty-eight hours. And somehow, I'll try to regain my self-worth and dignity by having to dig my way back up from my unseemly pity party.

Giving my arm a friendly tap, Schooner smiles a smile that makes me wonder why this guy isn't in movies. "I hope you get it, man. Bring us back some good news."

"Thanks." As I leave, I say to myself, *I hope I get it, too.*

Finishing the chapter, I allow myself to pick up my phone again to check the time. Twenty-seven minutes have passed since I last checked at the end of the prior chapter. I'm trying hard not to obsess about my phone not ringing...and I'm failing miserably.

Why does my apartment seem smaller than usual today? And seedier. The price of living right near the ocean. Seven-hundred square feet of old, no matter how you slice it. The only thing saving it from feeling like a cell is the view. Facing north and west, I can open the blinds and crank open the ancient jalousie windows and let the sea breeze in. From the living room, I look right out onto Venice Beach across the street, and from my bed, the northwest view is of the famous curve of Malibu. Not too shabby.

Where the hell is Sebastian?

I wonder if he saw the *Hollywood Hotline* segment with Mav Dailey and Francesca Simonelli. With a TV in his office always tuned to all the gossip, all the time, I'm going to go with he's seen it and watched that schmuck Dailey say "See" to her. Would that prompt him to call Sherri for some inside info? He's gotta give me something.

I look at the phone one more time. *Ring already.*

Focus on the book. Keep reading. Just keep reading. I turn the page.

Another half hour passes before Sebastian's name appears on my ringing phone.

"Sebastian," I greet him.

"Boychick, I got your messages."

Shaking my head, I will never get used to hearing the word *boychick* come out of this thirty-something, Korean-Angelenos mouth. I always picture a sixty-year-old, bald Jewish guy named Morty puffing on a stogie.

"Did you see *Hollywood Hotline*?" It's out of my mouth in a nanosecond.

"I did."

"Does Maverick Dailey already have the role? Is this a done deal?" I'm about to spit out another question when he stops me.

"No reason to panic. I just got off the phone with Sherri, this thing is far from a done deal."

"Seriously? What did she say?" I need to chill. Even I can hear the desperation in my own voice. How did I get from thinking the book is a piece of shit to feeling like my life depends on this part? It's like that girl you don't think you like until your buddy asks her out and you want to cut his dick off before he sticks it in her.

Sebastian starts to laugh. "She said our boy, Maverick, is kind of in uncharted territory and he's not handling it very well."

"What does that mean?" I'm confused.

"Well, you know the author has final decision on all roles. It appears she came right out and told Mav that he needs to audition for the part."

"Holy shit." I swear my dick just twitched. I think I'm in love.

"Yeah. Well, as you can imagine, he's not too pleased."

"He's probably thinking they shouldn't let non-industry people into this town."

I can hear Sebastian laugh on the other end of the line. "You know that's exactly what he's thinking. So, it appears she told him that she'd give him the star treatment and that she wouldn't have him read until the female lead was cast so that she could see if their chemistry was right, and if she saw him in the role at that point."

"That's odd, the hero is contingent on the heroine. It's usually the opposite."

"I know," Sebastian commiserates, "but this time around, it's whatever way Francesca Simonelli wants to do it. When you blow up the charts all over the world and sell a gazillion books, you get to call the shots, as unorthodox as they might be. Her agent did a brilliant job negotiating this deal."

"So, it appears." My mind is racing. "Okay, so it sounds like I might not be hearing anything for a while."

"I wouldn't say that. Sherri mentioned that when they've narrowed down the female lead to a few, she'll probably have you and two or three other guys come back to read with them. And, of course, Mav. So, if there are a few actresses they like in the next few weeks, you might be brought back multiple times to audition with them. Which gives you an opportunity to have quite a bit more face time with the team." His pause is dramatic, to make a point, "And with the author."

"I'll come back as many times as they want me to." I can feel the adrenaline snaking its path through my veins, elevating me from the valley I'd tumbled down into earlier in the day when I first saw the *Hollywood Hotline* segment. For the first time in hours, the muscles in my stomach stop feeling like stretched rubber bands on the verge of snapping.

"I told Sherri it wouldn't be an issue, and that you were seriously interested in the role." Pausing, I know he's remembered something when he begins his next sentence with, "Oh, oh, oh, Sherri mentioned that Mav told Francesca that in addition to reading the script, he's read the book three times so he could understand the nuances of the character, and of course, being the author, she totally loved hearing that. She was impressed and it made her take him a lot more seriously."

Three times. Of course, he did. The guy is a pro. *The fucker.*

"I did mention that she's taken a suite at the Casa del Mar in Santa Monica, right?" he tells me again as if he's relaying a secret encrypted message.

"Yeah, you mentioned it."

What the hell does he want me to do? Go stalk the woman?

"From what I understand, she's taken the suite long-term and is going to be staying there for the duration of the project, until they start filming on location."

"Okay." I'm not quite sure how to answer him.

"Seems she's a beach lover like you."

"Well, I've got a load of reading to do if I'm going to catch up to Maverick."

"Good man. I'll let you know when I hear something."

"Okay, I'll wait to hear from you. Until then, I'll keep reading."

"It's a good book." Sebastian surprises me with that statement.

"You read it?"

"Of course, I did. Everyone's read it. And like most properties, the book is probably better than the script."

"Yeah, I'm actually kind of surprised at how much I'm enjoying it."

"Keep reading, boychick. They liked you. You just need to convince Francesca Simonelli that you are Griffin Chase."

"That's the goal, boss."

Frankie

I'm not an early bird. Rather the opposite. My biorhythms are a bit out of sync with most people's and it's only late at night, when the world around me has long since retired, that my brain and my energy finally lock step with one another, consigning me to both the roles of night owl and night writer. Cranky as all hell in the morning doesn't even begin to describe me. My mind is scattered when I wake, as if slumber is a stealth, nocturnal thief, trying to make a getaway with all the files stored in my brain, but trips in the dark and gloriously bungles the job. By the next evening I have all the files picked up again, sorted through, and begin to organize all the focused thoughts that have successfully eluded me throughout the entire day.

So, the question I ask myself is this, *why the heck am I awake, wide awake, at 7:00 a.m. after writing until well past 2:00 a.m.?*

Time zone difference? Maybe.

Not my bed and pillows? It's possible.

The new book I'm writing? Could be.

Sitting down at the desk, it's impossible not to immediately fixate on the water's edge and the waves spooning the sand in a conciliatory dance. Mindlessly thumbing through my notebook, the pictures I've stapled onto the pages draw my eye until I begin scanning my notes on the actors and actresses who have read for me. With each page that I turn, I try and remember the sound of the voices that match their headshots. Some of them I can hear clearly, others I try to jog my memory with my somewhat cryptic page scrawls. Sitting back and letting out a long sigh, I realize making final decisions is going to be harder than I ever could have imagined.

"Only allow three potential candidates for the role on your list at any time." Was Sherri's advice to me. "The fourth one gets knocked out. And never look back. Remember, three is your limit for each role. From there, it will make whittling it down much easier."

I know this is solid advice that she's given me. I do, I know that. But even with three, the decisions will be painful. So many of these actors and actresses are amazingly talented, and each one brings something so unique to the table.

And then, of course, there's Maverick.

Ugh. I can't even think about this. How do you say no to a huge box-office leading man? Do I even want to? Maverick Dailey as Griffin Chase is just cash in the bank, any way you slice it. He is clearly the first choice of every investor in this film.

And that's true whether or not he's a good match for the role.

The man is box-office gold.

That thought makes me take notice of the early morning golden sidelight illuminating the day's first runners and walkers. Fully awake now, there's not a chance in the world that I'm going to be falling back to sleep with the sun's luscious, warm rays calling to me. Quickly changing into shorts and running shoes, I grab my earbuds and my small running waist-pack, shoving in my phone, room-keycard, ID, and some money for coffee, which is actually my ulterior motive for this run. A huge iced coffee can fuel a full morning's worth of writing, especially if I throw an extra shot in it, I muse, struggling with the zipper on the little pack and then sticking it inside my shirt.

Emerging from the hotel, I savor that first blast of salt air, breathing in deeply through my nose until my lungs are fully expanded. Stretching out my calves and quads, it is impossible to resist the allure of the Golden State and I'm ready to explore in the relative quiet of early morning.

The sidewalk or the sand?

That is my big question as I gaze into the early morning mist partially obscuring Malibu to the north.

It takes less than a second for sand to emerge as the clear winner for my run. Making my way toward the water's edge, I begin a slow warm-up jog, settling into the beat of PJ Harvey's version of "The Mess We're In." Breathing in the heavy salt air, I focus on the dulcet tones of her voice as my breathing steadies itself and my pace increases until I fall into my natural rhythm.

I'm running north toward Malibu. Let that settle in.

This is my life. *This is my life.*

Two years ago, I spent Saturday mornings at my little desk, the one with worn, wobbly drawers. I had written my earliest stories at that desk, from the time I was seven years old, and it was still, to this day, my favorite place to write. Tucked into a corner of my cramped studio apartment, I had spent every free moment writing a story inspired by my friend, Josh.

Truly believing he was being noble, Josh helped a grad school friend's uncle and aunt find safety from the horrors they and their three young daughters were facing in a town in Mexico, not far over the Texas border. Riddled by drug trade and teeming with criminals, the family knew the only way they could ensure their children's safety was to get them across the border.

As he loaded the family of five into his Jeep Cherokee and drove them on a desolate ranch road into the dark Texas night, he had no understanding of the enormity of the consequences of being apprehended. There was not a thought in his mind that this one night could alter the course of his life, ultimately severing the dreams of this brilliant biochemistry grad student. He was denied job after job after having to disclose to all potential employers, his status as a felon. What was done with good intention had a devastating and lasting impact on my sweet friend.

The family he was aiding and abetting's fate was even more tragic. Deported, they settled temporarily in a border town with the hope of earning enough money to legally return and support themselves. It wasn't until a few years later that we learned that their thirteen-year-

45

old had been raped repeatedly by drug dealers and took her own life by the time she was fifteen. She was four months pregnant at the time.

Wiping tears, I'm not really sure if they were nudged from my eyes by the sting of the cool, salty air or the memory that proved to be the inspiration for me to sit down and write *Fleeing an August Moon,* a book I had never planned on writing. But once I began, it poured out of me faster than any other book I'd written. Creating the story had been cathartic, as I processed the horrors of what had happened to this family and watched my friend's future irrevocably altered by one mistake. And although I had never really had strong political feelings one way or another about immigration, because it really didn't affect me personally, I truly began to wonder if what my friend, Josh, had done was a mistake, a wrongdoing, or if it was a humanitarian act attempting to save his friend's relatives from fate that was certain to catch up to them. And ultimately did.

At that point, it was no longer about policy for me. It was people. Real people and their stories. People who were destroyed wanting a better life. How could that ever be so wrong? Could loving your children so deeply that you wanted to give them the best, be a crime? I grappled with this. More deeply than I was conscious of at the time.

And somewhere from that sadness, anger, frustration, and a feeling of helplessness in not being able to give people their lives back, Griffin and Gabriela were born. The story was personal for me, and surprisingly, through my words, it became a love story people could understand. The issue of faceless, shoeless people crossing the border took on faces. Human faces. People trying to shield their families from drug cartels and criminals, people who would lay down their lives to protect the ones they deeply loved.

Griffin Chase was such a man.

Maybe the timing was right. Maybe the world just needed a love story at that time with a hero who was a man of honor, a man battling for both his country and his heart, and finding himself torn between honor and loyalty — but to whom?

Smiling, I realize just how much I miss my desk and that although the desk in my hotel suite is much newer and grander, perfectly positioned for a full view of the ocean, it just isn't my comfort place to create. And I wonder if I'll ever feel that energy that flowed through me as Griff and Briela's story poured out of me.

"Francesca." My name is being called from behind.

Did I just imagine that? Who knows me out here? Am I hearing this over my earbuds?

Slowing down, I turn my head to surprisingly see Finn Parker, the Griffin Chase look-alike who auditioned for the role. He had obviously just run past me and I'd been so caught up in my own head, that I'd jogged right past him.

Stopping short, my hands immediately go to my thighs to take a breath before I straighten up and start to walk toward him. "It's Finn, right?" I confirm.

"You have a good memory." He smiles a smile that is described to a T in the pages of my book. *To a T.*

"So do you. You recognized me. Do you live near here?" I'm nervous. This guy is beyond handsome and I'm feeling sweaty and very far from California girl perfect.

"A little bit to the south, but this is my beach run route. Do you live here?"

"No, I live in Houston. I'm staying here in Santa Monica through casting and I'm not sure where I'll be during shooting. I know they're scouting locations now." *Should I be talking to him about this?* I'm rambling, words tumbling out of my mouth, but the only thought running through my head is that his eyes are a perfect match to the clear morning sky.

He's nodding, and it appears as if he's grappling with his next thought. "I don't want to interrupt your run."

For some reason my heart is sinking, like I've just reached the last page of the last chapter and I'm not ready to say goodbye to the characters yet.

"But I'd love to take you for coffee," he continues quickly, and it feels like he is feeling the same thing.

Should we be talking to one another?

I don't want it to end with us running in opposite directions. "Now you're talking my language." I'm smiling on the outside, internally feeling a sense of relief. *I want to know about him. Who is he? Is he Griff?*

"You okay with heading back down south? There's a great local place not too far."

"Sure. Do they have food?" My stomach is starting to growl.

"Yeah. Actually, one of their locations has got a good breakfast menu. We can go there."

Putting my earbuds back in, I nod, and we take off down the beach, the sun now warming the left side of my face as we head south. I know he's slowed down his pace to accommodate me, because his muscular legs are significantly longer than mine, and he's holding back every time he gets ahead of me. It's impossible not to notice his calves. Shapely and well-defined, they look like gladiator calves, or the way I picture a gladiator's calves based on ancient Roman marble statues. I don't mind falling behind a little because his butt, tight thighs, and broad shoulders are the stuff of romance novels. That thought makes me smile and not just in my head.

He's turned around at just the moment I'm smiling and looks at me questioningly.

I can't tell him what's on my mind or he'll be joining the Hollywood #MeToo movement as a victim of sexual harassment. *I love your ass and I'd like to feel your thighs between my legs* would definitely not be appropriate. And probably not appreciated. I know I can't hold a candle to these California women and Hollywood starlets.

Turning off the beach and heading east, he removes his earbuds and I do the same.

"Where are you staying?"

"The Casa del Mar."

"You're really close to here," he comments. "Why not stay closer to the studio?"

"This exact reason. I get to run on the beach. I get to look at the ocean and enjoy glorious sunsets. And I can just remove myself from the whole movie craziness and come back here and try to write."

Stopping in front of an institutional eggshell-colored building that looks more like a stucco box than a coffee house, Finn smiles down at me. Damn, he's tall.

"We're here."

Taking a deep breath, I close my eyes and smile, the air outside TerraTravail Coffee Co. hangs heavy with the scent of fresh roasted coffee, which I think might be what heaven smells like.

"This smells heavenly," I verbalize my inner thought.

"Their coffee is amazing, and their breakfasts are really good, too. Great omelets and tacos."

"They have tacos," I say over my shoulder exuberantly as he holds the door open for me. *Good manners. Definitely a Griff Chase trait.* I jot that down in the notebook in my mind, fully aware that I am not so secretly hoping I can tick off a lot more of Griffin's characteristics by the time I reach the bottom of my coffee mug.

"You're a breakfast taco person?" he asks, then chuckles before answering his own question. "Of course, you are. You're a Texan."

Surveying the menu up on the wall, I approach the counter as I'm greeted by a young, male barista sporting a very happy smile for so early in the morning. "What can I get started for you?"

"I'll have an order of breakfast tacos minus the avocados and a large iced Americano with milk."

"You don't like avocados?" There's a hint of confusion in Finn's voice.

"Ugh, no. I hate 'em." I shake my head.

"I'll take her avocados," he instructs the barista, "along with a California omelet and that iced Americano sounds good. I'll take one of those, too."

As I reach to unzip my runner's pouch, he gently puts a hand on my arm, "No, no. I've got this."

Opening my mouth to protest, he shakes his head. His hand still on my arm, his touch soft and warm.

"No, I asked you, and you know I want something from you." His sly look is accompanied by a matching crooked smile that makes my breath catch in my throat.

"Well, thank you, I'll go grab us a table." My mouth has already gone dry as I voice those words, making me sound as if I'm about to go into a coughing fit. He wants to talk about the role and I feel inexplicably nervous.

As soon as Finn places my breakfast in front of me, I immediately remove from my plate the ribbed ceramic ramekin containing the offending avocado and slide it across the table toward him.

"Thanks."

As he picks up his butter knife, I start screaming in my head, *Don't do it. Please, don't do it. Oh God, don't do it.*

My taco is halfway to my mouth, suspended, as I watch him smear the avocado chunks onto his gazillion-seed, hemp, gluten-free, whole grain, reduced-carb, cardboard-looking toast. The first bite is already in his mouth before he realizes I'm staring.

"What?" He looks alarmed. "Is there something wrong with my face?"

No. The problem is everything is perfect about your face. Everything.

I can't help but smile as I gesture toward the toast in his hand. "It's the avocado toast. Everybody out here eats that shit." The cuss is out of my mouth before I can stop it.

Choking on the toast as he begins to laugh, Finn takes a sip of his iced Americano to recover from coughing. "You're right, we do. It's the new bottled water." Laughing again, he explains, "I thought maybe I had some squished bug on my face from running or some large unsightly pimple had popped out." And then, as an afterthought, he adds, "You know us actors, we're all so insecure."

I shake my head as I finish my first taco. "I don't really know any actors. I know a lot of authors, but no actors." I pick up the second taco on my plate. They're actually pretty good — for a non-Texas taco, that is, although the tortillas are not quite thick enough.

It's weird sitting across from him and having breakfast. This is Finn Parker. It's not Griffin Chase. But it is so easy to let that blur. I've scripted his life and everything that came out of his mouth for a long time now, and I don't know what this person sitting across from me is going to say. And it's kind of weirding me out.

"So, Francesca." He puts down the offensive green and cardboard concoction.

"Call me Frankie."

There's that smile again. I'm going to need a cold shower when I get back to my hotel room. Men only look like this in my head... or on movie screens.

"Frankie. I like that. It fits you."

Thank God he's not another one who insists on calling me Francesca. It always makes me feel like I'm going to get in trouble with nuns. I don't know why Maverick insisted on calling me Francesca. A control thing, maybe?

Why do I feel guilty that Mav is crossing my mind while I'm sitting here with Finn? Like I'm cheating. But not quite sure on who.

"Is your real name Finn Parker?" I'm expecting Brian Smith.

"Yes." And there's that sly look from earlier. "And no." When I remain silent, he continues. "My name is actually Parker Finn. Parker Jameson Finn. My dad, grandparents, siblings, and family friends call me PJ. My friends always called me Finn, so it was an easy transition for me."

"What would you like me to call you."

"Finn. PJ feels like a person I knew a long time ago or like it was in another life. And Parker feels like I'm about to get into trouble with the nuns."

"I was just thinking that very same thing about Francesca." Okay, so something in common.

Looking up from his plate, his eyes lock onto mine as if he's sizing me up. "So, Frankie," he begins slowly. "I saw the *Hollywood Hotline* clip last week. Is this a done deal with Maverick Dailey or do I actually have a shot?"

"This is not a done deal."

"I'm sure the investors would like to sign him on." He's very matter-of-fact in his delivery, yet almost world-weary, it seems. Like he's expecting to lose. I can't even imagine the resilience it takes to survive in this town.

"The investors don't have the final say."

"I'd heard that. That's pretty rare."

I can't help but laugh. "That's what I hear." Good fortune doesn't even begin to describe the past two years of my life. Me and my wobbly desk in a studio apartment feels like it was yesterday. But as Finn referred to it just before, it feels like another lifetime.

"I really liked the book."

"You read it?"

"Yeah. I did. I really wanted to understand what was in your head and what you saw in the character's heads. Helps me digest the character and understand where they are coming from."

"And did it do that for you?"

"Yeah, but then it raised more questions, mostly about things that weren't on the pages, pieces of their lives that weren't covered in the book. Let me get this out of your way." He snatches up my empty plate and brings it back to the front counter. "Sorry. Once a waiter, always a waiter." He shrugs, his smile disarming, but as soon as he sits down it's easy to see the intensity grip him again. I suddenly have the feeling this is a hard guy to get to know.

"So, Frankie, I don't want to make you uncomfortable or waste your time here if you don't feel I'm in contention for the role."

"Finn, this is all really new to me and I am totally in uncharted territory." I don't quite know why I'm confessing to this man except for the fact that he looks like the hero in my book, which makes me feel like I know him, like we're old friends. But in reality, I don't know squat about this guy beyond the fact that he is one really hot, handsome guy who flipped his name around. Is he a good guy? I don't know. Is he an asshole? I don't know that either. "You did really well when you read for the part."

"But..."

I can tell he's waiting for the other shoe to drop. And again, I'm sensing it's the conditioning of being in this town and not being a box-office darling by the time you're twenty-six.

"There are no buts. You were one of the standout performances for Griffin."

"Do you see me as Griffin? You created the character, so clearly you know him better than anyone."

"Physically, absolutely. You look very much like the character I envisioned." I'm not telling him that I never, ever saw Griff's face clearly until the first time I saw him.

"I want this role, Frankie. I hope you're seriously considering me because I think," he closes his eyes and takes a deep breath, "I think I could really bring Griffin to life. And I just want to pick your brain about this guy. I hope you don't mind."

"No, not at all. I love talking about my characters and I want this to be cast right, Finn. I want my readers to walk out of the theatre with the same feeling they had when they reached the last page of the book."

"Yes." He's nodding at me. "That's exactly why I have to know him better."

Finn

Don't fuck this up. This is the chance of a lifetime. She just confirmed *that the rumors are true and she is the final decision-maker on casting. Who knew she'd be an early riser and a runner. Yeah, Sebastian told me that's where she was staying, but I didn't think I'd run into her. Divine providence, maybe? So glad I asked her where she was staying, now I don't have to worry about that slipping out and her wondering how the hell I knew that little piece of information.*

C'mon, dude, convince her you are Griffin Chase. This is your chance.

"Anything you want to know? If I can answer it, I will." She smiles at me and seems very sincere in her offer.

There's a messy lock of hair that's slipped out of her loose ponytail and it's distracting the hell out of me, seriously interfering with my brain's ability to come up with coherent questions, questions that will impress a writer. I have the urge to reach across the table and tuck the errant, loose blonde spiral behind her ear. But I'm kind of digging the sexiness of how real she looks with it all messy. This woman has never seen a plastic surgeon in her life and everything that is imperfect is actually refreshing. And beautiful. And I don't usually have a thing for blondes. But this one, she's really cute.

"But hold that thought." She smiles, abruptly getting up and going to the counter at the front of the shop.

It's impossible not to admire her tight bottom, muscular legs, and the natural sway of her hips. *Damn, that is sexy.* I wonder if she even knows she's sexy.

Returning with a plate covered by two large cookies, she shrugs, giving me an impish grin. "They were called cowboy cookies. How could I not?"

I can smell the dark chocolate and butter as she sets them down. "What exactly are they?"

"Oatmeal with chocolate chip." She breaks off a piece of the one closest to her.

"Raisins are overrated anyway," I assess with my first bite as the dark chocolate bathes my taste buds. Like everything else this place serves, the cookies are delicious.

"I figure we've already run off these calories." Washing her cookie down with iced Americano, she locks eyes with me and asks, "Okay, I'm ready. So, what questions can I answer for you?"

Taking a deep breath, I tell myself not to overthink this. *Just let it flow.* "Okay, so they met as kids, Griffin and Gabriela, but I didn't necessarily sense the love story then. Was it a love story at that point? Did I miss it?"

"No, it wasn't a love story. He was seven years older than her and when you're kids, that's a big age difference. When he was leaving for college, she was still in elementary school. I think he thought of her as a cute little girl, more like a friend's little sister, although she was the daughter of the domestic help who worked for his best friend's family."

"Right." I'm slowly savoring my cookie. This might be the unhealthiest thing I've put in my mouth in months. Well, that's if you don't count Eva Armeni. Definitely unhealthy for me and nowhere near as sweet. "Coming from a well-to-do background, I was surprised that he enlisted after college."

"He came from a family where public service was pretty much expected and his father had political aspirations for him from the time he was in the womb. In some ways, his military career was an expected part of his resume, but even with that said, it was his choice. I think what we saw in Griff was a deeply patriotic man with a sense of duty that had been instilled in him from the time he was young."

"Griff," I chuckle at the intimacy of the nickname, as I mindlessly roll a straw wrapper between my fingers and consider my next question. "So, when he comes home after having been away at college and then being overseas, he was late twenties?"

"Yeah, because he runs for office at twenty-nine and he's about two years into his term when they cross paths again."

"Has she always loved him?"

"I think when she was young it was more of a crush. From the time she was little, though, she was definitely in awe of him. He's this big, tall, handsome blond guy and she's maybe eight when she dubs him *Captain America*."

"Oh, yeah, that's right." Remembering that scene has me smiling. "When he sees her again, he's already in Congress, and it felt like he knew immediately from that very first moment he saw her, what was missing in his life."

"Yeah, well there's that immediate kinship you have with people you've known your entire life, that shared experience and memory that is uniquely yours. Are you on Facebook?"

Why the heck does she want to know that? Her question puts me on high alert. *Have I posted anything questionable lately? Like I'm reading the book a movie script was adapted from and it sucks.* "Uh, yeah. I am."

"Okay, so have you reconnected with people from childhood whom you had no contact with for decades?"

I nod, internally letting out a sigh of relief. I see where she's going.

"And the memories you share with these people bring back good feelings, because it's experiences that belong exclusively to you. It's the story of your life. Even if you couldn't stand the other person way back when, right?"

"It's true." I laugh, thinking of some of those douches I said I'd never speak to again and now meet for drinks every so often.

"So, there's that bond between them, that shared history. And at twenty-four, standing before him is a woman, not that cute fourteen-year-old from the summer he graduated from college, who, by that point, had a huge crush on him. This is a very direct woman with a Masters in Journalism from Columbia and she's calling him out on his policies."

"I don't think either of them expected that spark. Well, at least, that's how I read it."

"Especially him. His memory was of a little girl whom he had always found bright and engaging, and if anything, had brotherly feelings toward her. Like he's an older kid from the neighborhood kind of thing, so he'd protect her if someone were beating up on her or picking on her or something."

"Even though she was clearly the child of his friend's housekeeper and not really a neighborhood kid. There's always that class distinction," I'm thinking out loud.

"Yes, to some extent. But when the kids are out on a hot, summer night playing tag, they're all just kids and they are part of one another's worlds without the socio-economic distinctions instilled in them by adults."

Nodding, I take the last bite of my cowboy cookie. "Yes. But now they are the adults."

Frankie pushes the plate toward me, half her cookie still uneaten. "Kill it." She smiles.

"You don't have to ask twice." Without a moment's hesitation, I pop it in my mouth.

This woman has me eating processed sugar. What the hell? Am I such a Hollywood whore that I'll do anything for the part?

"And yes, they are now the adults, and the day when they first reunite at his press conference, she gets under his skin immediately. Calling him on the carpet, and all of a sudden, his policy decisions take on a very personal tilt. The things he has enacted have adversely affected people who were very good to him while he was growing up and that is an eye-opener for him, something he doesn't take lightly and something he had not previously considered."

"She really does become his touchstone to the past and the future." God, I hope what I'm saying is right.

"Yeah, that's a good way of putting it."

There's that smile again. Her teeth are not capped, I note, and not perfectly aligned. Only someone in this town would notice those details.

"I'm going to steal that from you," she adds.

"Only if you give me the part," I quip back, wanting to slap myself down the minute those desperate words are out of my mouth.

Oh Frankie, Frankie, Frankie, if you only knew how much I need this part for so many damn reasons.

"If you're the right actor to play the role, you'll get the part."

I can tell that I've made her feel uncomfortable.

"I appreciate that. And I really appreciate you taking the time this morning. I really hope you'll take the chance on me."

"I promise you'll get a fair shot, Finn."

"That's all I can ask." *I hope I haven't blown this.* "Well, there is one other thing I can ask." I smile at her. "Would you share an email address with me, so if I have questions, I can shoot you a note." What I really want to do is ask for her phone number, so that I can text her, but my fear is that will be crossing a line she doesn't want me stepping over.

At least, not yet.

Staring at my laptop screen, I delete the email for the fifth time.

Frankie-

Great running into you today and thanks for taking the time to share your thoughts with me about the characters. Obviously, it was invaluable, so again, thank you. Oh, and thanks for the cookie and a half.

Finn

Hey, if you want to go running, let me know.

I started my second reading of the book when I got home. I'm seeing how much I missed the first time around now that I know how the story ends.

Send.

Frankie

Writers are great researchers. What some might term stalking, we squarely consider to be research.

Finn Parker. PJ Finn. Parker Finn. Parker J. Finn.

After spending over two hours in his company, I really can't say that I know any more about this guy than I did when he walked out of the audition.

Who are you?

Let's start with IMDB and then check if there's a Wiki page on him — see if they've got more than the basic information on the bio I got with his headshot.

Those eyes. The moment the IMDB webpage opens, my breath actually catches when I see his eyes. Geez. *My breath catches.* Ha-ha, that's like something I would write. But damn, it really happened. Robin's egg blue. Yes, that's what shade they are. Robin's egg blue. I shudder to think how many women have fallen into his bed with just one look into those eyes. And they are even more striking up close and personal. The man should be illegal.

Thirty-four years old, almost thirty-five, originally from Las Vegas. Hmm, interesting place to grow up, I'd think. No wonder why he loves being near the ocean. Looks like a lot of small roles, mostly TV, a few films, and then the streaming series for three seasons, which appears to have been his steadiest gig and the one for which he is best known.

Can you make a living doing this? Pay the bills? Afford to live on the beach? He probably did pretty well when he was doing the series, though. That would have put some money in the bank, I guess.

Lord, I totally get that. Or, at least I did before *Fleeing an August Moon.* I was living from book to book. Enough from each release to self-publish and do the marketing for the next title, attend a few signings that were close enough for me to drive to, and pay the rent on my studio.

What a difference one break can make. I truly do know that better than anyone.

Okay, Google Image time now.

Lots of promo shots, posters from shows and movies, a bunch in front of steps and repeats at award shows and premières. In those photos, there's a beautiful woman on his arm, always. Well, that's not a surprise. The man is hot.

Long, straight dark hair appears to be his thing. I have to look closely to discern if these are actually different women. And they are. One. Two. Three. Four. Five different women. They could be freaking quintuplets. Boy, does this guy have a type or what? Tall, thin, tan, and dark, with straight noses (wondering if these chicks all use the same plastic surgeon?) and big, button brown eyes adorned with lots of smoky eyeshadow and serious sets of false eyelashes.

They ALL look like avocado toast eaters, minus the toast part. Every single one of them.

He looks good with them, though, his fair coloring a contrast to the women's. I must look like a ghost to him.

Reading on, I'm not getting a whole lot on the Internet. Same promo stuff. But nothing that doesn't seem like it's been put out by an agent or PR firm. There's nothing here that's not pre-packaged.

Who is this guy?

What makes him tick? Does he have the depth for this role? He's really easy to look at, but I certainly didn't get much in the way of insight into him. Was there vacancy behind his eyes? Or is there a deep well? I can't figure out why I couldn't figure that out.

Staring at the images on my screen, I wonder what it is I'm hoping to find. Griffin Chase? Because this man is not Griffin Chase. He's an actor. He's Finn. Or Parker. Or PJ. Or maybe that's the problem as to why I couldn't quite get a handle on him. Maybe he doesn't know who he is.

Or maybe he knows exactly who he is.

And it's just me who is confused.

He's not Griff. So, don't go all loony, crazy psycho here, letting lines blur between who is just in your head and who's actually here.

I want him to be Griffin. And he's Finn. And I wish he would be like Griffin. I don't know why I feel that way. Who really cares who he is in real life, as long as he's believable in the role and that translates onto the big screen. So, why is this such a huge concern to me? Why do I have this expectation that he needs to be a real-life superhero? It doesn't take a rocket scientist to know that I'm setting him, and myself, up for failure.

And lookie-here, just when I feel like he's all wrong, he goes and sends me this nice email. Maybe I'm just totally overthinking this guy and I need to stop. I definitely need to stop.

Frankie-

Great running into you today and thanks for taking the time to share your thoughts with me about the characters. Obviously, it was invaluable, so again, thank you. Oh, and thanks for the cookie and a half.

Finn

Hey, if you want to go running, let me know.

I started my second reading of the book when I got home. I'm seeing how much I missed the first time around now that I know how the story ends.

He's picking up the nuances in my writing. Excellent. He's seeing the journey I've created for the reader. I like that. Who am I kidding, I like him. This man is just so hot.

God, I feel shallow.

Going back to Google Images, I look through the photos again. I can guarantee those dark-haired chicks aren't sharing cookies with him.

As almost an afterthought, walking through the stylized, grand lobby of my hotel, sweaty and disheveled from an early morning run, I stop at the concierge's desk to ask, "Can you recommend someone for hair and make-up that I can go to locally?" I'm kicking myself for not asking anyone at the studio before I left on Friday.

"Golden Globes?" he inquires.

"Yes!" I know I sound astonished, like *how did he know?*

"It's Los Angeles." He raises his brows to my unasked questions. "I bet the *Fleeing an August Moon* movie will be up for an award next year, Miss Simonelli."

"Well, I don't know about that." I laugh. Everybody is so up on everything in this town.

"Have you chosen an actor for Griffin yet?" He laughs when he sees the surprised look on my face. "Of course, I've read it. Griffin is my new book boyfriend," he informs me and then adds, "I was so excited when I learned you were staying with us."

"Well, thank you." My newfound fame is still somewhat of a shock to me. I've always felt like this invisible observer of life going on around me, not necessarily to me, and that has always granted me the ability to weave in and out, unnoticed, as I gather and tuck away new threads for the tales I will someday weave.

"I can certainly arrange to have a hair and make-up artist come up to your room tomorrow afternoon, if you'd like."

"Yes, I would love that."

"Will you be needing a car to bring you to the Beverly Hilton?" He's obviously well-versed in this, and that is not a surprise as the hotel really is Hollywood's version of an opulent beach club, and I imagine I'm just one of many guests who will be attending Sunday night's awards ceremony.

"No, thank you. That's already been arranged for me."

From what I understand, I'll be sitting at one of the studio's tables along with Sherri and two of the film's producers, as well as other people associated with the studio. I'm looking forward to my first red carpet event, ready to fan-girl all over Hollywood's A-list. Everyone's been telling me that this is the fun awards ceremony, with the champagne and other alcoholic beverages freely flowing.

"Do you have cocktail or evening attire with you?" my agent, Caryn Crane, inquired in a phone conversation a few days ago.

"I do." I know my response is a surprise to her. "It's beaded and sparkly and very fitted through the bodice with a handkerchief hemline."

I can hear her relieved sigh three-thousand miles away. A New York lady, with true Manhattan-style sense, I know she just shakes her head when she sees me in jeans and cowboy boots. She can barely hide her longing to drag me to a make-up counter.

"I'll be out in two weeks after I get back from London. You should have the lion's share of your cast together by then."

"One can only hope," I comment, as I scroll through my emails.

"Why? Are you not seeing good candidates?" There's alarm in her voice.

"No. That's not it at all. I think it will be just the opposite. Too many good people. I really thought it would be cut and dry. That I'd see someone read and boom, I'd know that they were *the* person to play Griff or Briela. That it would be one person who was *the one*. And it's just not that way."

"Has Maverick read yet?"

"No. Not yet." Ugh. I knew it, here comes the pressure pitch.

"Keep an open mind, Frankie. He's a brilliant, versatile actor."

"I know he is, Caryn. He's just not the vision of what was in my head when I wrote this character, and so it's very difficult for me to see him as Griff. And if I feel that way, so will my readers, and I don't want to disappoint them."

"Your readers will love whatever you put out. They're already sold, they love the story. It's about everyone else. It's about expanding your audience and what that will do for your brand and future book sales."

"Let's be honest here, this has nothing to do with me or my brand. This has to do with everyone's bottom line."

"Of course, it does, Frankie. This is business. No one is in this for artistic measure."

"Almost no one," I mutter. It is very clear that I will not have the support of my own agent on the Mav Dailey issue. Caryn is a brilliant negotiator and I owe much of my success to her, but I can already feel that she's not going to be in my corner on this one if I don't pick Mav for Griffin's role.

"Be smart here and keep an open mind."

I don't answer. I'm seething. It feels like the bullying has already begun.

"Are you still there?" she asks.

"For now." My message is loud and clear. I can walk my next manuscript to another agent after giving thirty days' notice. And as much as it would pain me to leave and how difficult it might be to start with someone new, I know that if Caryn's and my interests are no longer aligned, then I need to find someone who is more in sync with me and my vision.

Ugh. I hate change.

After hanging up, I look out the window at the ocean and up toward the Ferris wheel on the Santa Monica pier just north of me. I have the overwhelming feeling I'm in one of the tubs and it's descending too rapidly from the ride's apex. If I do this wrong, I'm going to come crashing down, and I highly doubt that Hollywood is a forgiving place.

On the desk behind me, my cell dings alerting me of a new email and snapping me out of my emotional freefall.

Finn. How apropos.

Frankie –

How did I not pick up all these things on the first read? Griffin has come to terms with his internal struggle by the time he hatches his plan, right? He knows what he might have once thought was wrong is actually right, and what he has stood by as the right thing to do, uphold the law, is actually the crime. Am I reading that right? But him getting to that point took his guts being ripped out before he goes all commando. Is there any part of him that is still questioning himself? I feel like that struggle would be engrained so deeply that he'd still have doubts that he's doing the right thing. But this all is bigger than him, and seeing the big picture vs. just how it affects him (and Gabriela) makes everything not so cut and dry. There is a war raging here and it's not out on the streets – it's internal. It's Griffin's war. Am I on track here with what is going on inside him?

I've got to know!

Finn

Btw, I've never read a book twice before. I need to do this more often. I didn't realize how much I'd missed. (Either that, or I have comprehension problems. Which could be the case.)

Leaning against the window frame, staring at my phone, my heart hurts. Yes. He's dead on. He's reading all the words I didn't put on the page, interpreting the actions and interactions and understanding the motivations as well as the reservations.

"Yes," I say to my phone screen. "Exactly."

You are not making this easy for me, Finn Parker. Why do I feel this one casting decision is going to be the lynchpin of my entire career? Caryn's thinking long-game, I know that. But right now, I'm her cash cow. And this heifer is not going to take any bull.

"Looking fine." The concierge gives me a wink of approval as I walk through the lobby to meet my limo. My hair is in an updo with sparkly clips and bobbie pins that match my boots and my make-up is camera ready. I just have to remember not to rub my eyes, a bad habit of mine, or I'll smear it all.

Hey, isn't that raccoon-looking chick the one who wrote that book?

Hollywood stresses me out.

"Ms. Simonelli?" the dark-suited driver asks. He returns my nod and opens the back of the stretch limo for me.

Lifting my dress to climb in and not catch it in the heels of my boots, I fall backward onto my seat at the surprising sound of a voice.

"Boy, do you ever clean up nice." Maverick Dailey, looking illegally handsome in a dark suit, holds out a tulip-shaped flute of champagne, his fingers grazing mine as I take it.

"You're looking rather handsome yourself." Good recovery. I'm proud of myself. Smiling, I flirt right back, successfully hiding my shock at not being the only one in the back of the limo.

"Swarovski?" He points to my crystal-encrusted cowboy boots.

"Yes, I'm impressed." The rush of the chilled champagne snakes through my bloodstream like Valium injected into an IV PICC line, the effects immediate, the high soothing, and all of a sudden, Maverick Dailey's smile and single dimple are mesmerizing and I'm wondering why I have such an attitude toward this guy. He likes my book. He likes the lead character. Why have I not been over-the-moon thrilled that one of the biggest male stars in Hollywood wants to be in *Fleeing an August Moon?*

"Well, you are dressed appropriately." Taking a sip of his champagne, his eyes are smiling at me over the flute's rim.

What an odd comment to make.

He continues, "We're going to be making a stop before we head over to the Beverley Hilton. I hope you don't mind."

"Are we picking up someone else?" This limo is quickly becoming an upscale Super Shuttle.

"No. No. Nothing like that. I just need to head up into Malibu Springs and check on some horses." He points to my boots. "That's why you are dressed appropriately."

"Are they your horses?"

"Some are and some I'm just taking care of for several people in the area. They were displaced in the recent fires and I'm fostering them for the time being until their owners rebuild and can take them back."

"That is so nice of you." Holding my glass out, he refills it.

"I have the space, so I'm happy to help. These fires robbed so many people of so much. After getting family members to safety, everyone worries about their pets and animals."

"You are a nice man, Maverick Dailey."

"Don't tell anyone." And there's that smile again.

"Ruin your rep?" I'm enjoying our banter.

"I haven't been a bad boy since the '90s." He laughs at the thought.

"Only with the women." The champagne has hit third gear and my inhibitions and ability to hold my tongue are waning, rapidly.

"I'm not even a bad boy with women anymore."

I can't think of any actresses I've seen him associated with recently.

Briefly, he glances at his watch. "Don't worry, we have plenty of time. We'll be on time for the awards and late enough to make an entrance on the red carpet."

"I'm sure you make an entrance no matter what time you arrive."

"That's very true. Is this your first red carpet event?"

Nodding, "Yes. It is. And I'm both scared and excited. Am I really dressed okay?" My champagne bravado takes a sharp dive off a turn on the curvy road as we ascend into the hills.

"You look lovely. Your hair is fabulous up. It really brings out your eyes."

"I am so not Hollywood, and I know my agent was freaking out that tonight I would embarrass myself, and by extension, her."

"You look beautiful, Francesca. And the boots are amazing. And different."

"Hmm, different. That might not be so good. I don't want to get a worst-dressed-on-the-red-carpet moniker."

"Walking the red carpet with me, no one is going to say any bad shit about you."

"I'm going to walk the red carpet with you?"

"Well, we are arriving together, and I'd be honored if you would."

"Well, thank you. This is going to be quite the debut for me, and arriving with Hollywood royalty, no less."

I know everyone is going to assume that Mav is going to be playing Griffin when they see us on the red carpet together. *Why else would we be together?* And I'm sure that is exactly what he wants the Hollywood columnists to think.

Driving through the hills, I am struck by the wide-open spaces just minutes from the city's congested sprawl. The roadway is lined with cacti, succulents, and rocks. Lots of rocks.

"This kind of reminds me a little bit of some of the trails at Big Bend National Park, down on the Mexican border. In Texas," I qualify, assuming it's a national park with which he might not be familiar.

"I can see why you think that. With the addition of the ocean view, of course." As if timed perfectly, we round a bend and are treated to a sweet expanse of the sea stretching before us for a moment before the road takes another sharp twist and obscures the view.

Making a right turn off the main road through an open gate, we continue to climb, now on a dusty, unpaved drive.

"Almost there," Mav informs me, his face relaxed and happy and I have the feeling from his energy that something spectacular awaits me.

Up ahead, I now see large paddocks with horses grazing on the sparse vegetation, seemingly oblivious to the long limo's engine and cloud of dust it has kicked up on what now appears to have been a very long, private driveway. A red barn and a group of smaller buildings are beyond another set of smaller paddocks. Several horses in the pen closest to the barn gather at a bale of hay. They, too, appear to be oblivious to our car's approach.

Stopping near one of the paddocks, the driver comes around to open the door for us, extending a hand to help me out of the vehicle, which I do with unsuccessful grace, nearly catching my pointed boot toe on my sparkly hemline.

"Come this way." Mav directs me to the post and rail fence.

Lifting my dress a slight bit as I walk, I follow him, and there is just something so surreal about being in this surrounding dressed the way we are. A prissy part of me is concerned with the dust from the dirt road all over my crystal-encrusted boots and I immediately hate myself for the shallow thought and consciously tell myself to get over it. When did I ever give a crap about dusty boots? Umm, never.

Maverick puts two fingers in his mouth and lets out a whistle, then yells, "Jua."

Immediately, a pale golden Palomino, with a light blonde tail and mane lifts her head from the bale, ears perking at the sound of his voice. Turning her face toward us, she lets out a loud whinny, breaking into a canter as she heads straight to Mav, nuzzling him with her muzzle, all the while making soft whinnying and nickering sounds, speaking to him eloquent words of love in a language universally understood. I can feel my eyes fill with tears, the connection between this magnificent animal and equally as magnificent man is so evident. And surprising. My heart is bursting watching this scene.

"How's my beautiful girl?" She nuzzles him more as a response. "Yes, I've missed you, too. Let me see how you're doing." She turns, as if understanding his every word, readying herself as he begins to inspect her flanks. I can now see her right side for the first time, marred with large, raised, hairless leathery ridges. I wince just seeing the scars, immediately realizing this horse was a victim of fire and the tears I'd felt well up a moment ago now have a mind of their own. In my head,

I can hear the make-up artist screaming at me, "You are ruining my masterpiece." The guy would have needed to have been Michelangelo to make a masterpiece out of me.

"You are looking good. So much better, Jua." He slowly pets the injured area and she lets out a soft whinny, scraping the dirt with her left front hoof.

As the horse turns to let Mav inspect her injuries, I swear she gives me the stink-eye and I instinctually know she's thinking, *Who are you, bitch?*

Taking a step closer, I slowly reach out, holding my upward palm flat, to let her come to me and get my scent. Fully expecting her to check out my hand, she takes her muzzle and forcefully pushes it away. I did not imagine the stink-eye, not one bit. This is one very possessive animal.

"Jua, be nice to our guest. Francesca is a friend of mine," Mav reprimands the horse and reaches out to tickle her softly under her chin groove. The mare looks like she is in heaven.

"What an interesting name," I comment, as I watch the two of them together in what is clearly a mutual love fest.

Mav smiles. "It's Swahili for sunshine."

With her coloring, that's certainly appropriate. "Is she yours?"

"She is now. I adopted her shortly after the fire. Her burns were extensive. Her original owners wanted to put her down and the vet, who's a good friend of mine, told me about her. He said this girl wants to live, she's got plenty of fight in her," Mav recounts, as he tenderly strokes her mane. "At first, I thought maybe the owners didn't have the means to care for her, so I anonymously offered assistance. But they were ready to let her go. They wanted to put her down. She was being treated at the veterinary school over at UC Davis. My buddy called and asked if I could come down, and from the moment I saw her, I could see that this girl wanted to live. My friend contacted the owners and asked them if they'd be willing to adopt her out, and they were. And the rest is history." Smiling at me, he grasps my right shoulder. "I didn't mean to make you cry. This is a happy story."

"You are a really nice man, Maverick Dailey."

I need to be more openminded. This man might definitely be Griffin. Look at the things he does. He certainly has the depth and compassion.

If I don't get the picture of the physical character I wrote out of my head, then I might be missing out on a casting gem, letting Griffin's soul be truly captured on the big screen, slip away.

"Come on." He guides me with an arm loosely around my shoulders. "Let's get you to your first LA red carpet."

Finn

No doubt about it, Eva Armeni makes excellent arm candy and she probably thinks the same thing about me. We were an item, once. Then my series got canceled and she moved on. That's the way of this town. Everyone loves you when you're winning. Otherwise, it's a cold, cold place. And lately, I feel like I've been stuck in Siberia and the trek back to warm sunshine is seriously wearing me out.

It does, however, feel damn good to be walking the red carpet again. The photographer's flashes, the reporters, smiling wide, as they slide the mic over to you and more flashes momentarily blinding you. Damn good.

"Finn, what's next for you?"

"I'm in discussions on a few projects now," I lie. "Hopefully, I'll be able to announce them soon." I flash my best smile and hope I'm not edited out for a commercial break.

"Anything you can give us a hint about?" the reporter presses.

"Not yet." I smile directly into the camera, hoping that at next year's Golden Globes everyone is talking about my portrayal of Griffin Chase. It might be a long shot. But hope is the only thing we sometimes have in this town and you've just got to hold onto it for dear life.

As we make our way toward the entrance, we're stopped multiple times, giving the media outlets and the viewers exactly what they want.

Eva's asked about her skin- tone sequined dress, informing each of the reporters that it's Monique Lhuillier, as she poses for the camera, hand on left hip, knee bent, eyes looking up past her dipped shoulder.

There's a rush in doing this that never gets old. It makes me remember what I love about Hollywood, why I needed to be an actor. For as bad as I might be feeling about myself or my career, to make it to the red carpet is the first big accomplishment and only happens for a small percentage of actors. Then, there's being sought out to stop and give a comment and pose for a photo. An even smaller percentage walking the carpet are in this category. And when I look at it from that perspective, I feel like one lucky bastard, doing what I love and yeah, that next role, is only a phone call away. It just takes that one role to change the course of your life. My phone just needs to ring. The thought makes me touch the inner breast pocket of my white tux jacket, as if just thinking it is going to make my phone mystically start vibrating.

"What table are we at?" Eva asks, as we enter the Beverly Hilton.

Placement is everything in this town, it's how you're judged and definitely affects self-worth for weeks. If I give the wrong answer here, I know Eva, she'll pout all night and make snide comments while smiling at me as if she's telling me she loves me.

The people in the pit, up front at tables 1-20, are the A++ list of Hollywood elite and nominees. The biggest stars. The hottest agents. Studio heads. Coveted directors. If your table is #45 or under, you're in the front third of the room, on the first tier, and your ability to mingle before, during, and after commercial breaks is greatly enhanced. It is definitely prime placement and where everyone in Hollywood aspires to be.

"We're at table 28," my delivery is nonchalant, but I know her teeny, tiny silk thong just got very wet. Possibly she was expecting second tier, and would have been happy with that, but first tier, right behind the pit, is a serious badge of honor, kind of like a backstage pass at a sold-out concert.

"Nice," she confirms, slipping her arm through mine and giving my biceps a squeeze.

"Sebastian's had a good year. Amy Fielding is a really hot property right now and she'll be at our table." Amy is one of Sebastian's clients who got her big break this past year when she landed the starring role in a superhero movie.

"Her movie is up for three awards," Eva's eyes are now sparkling, "And I've never met her."

And just like that, I have very quickly morphed into the best ex on the planet. Anymore excitement, and she'll be all over me by the end of the evening.

"Boychick!" Sebastian draws me in for a back-slapping hug. "And Eva, great to see you again." Dressed in a greyish-silver sharkskin tux, Sebastian Cho is one of the only people I have ever met who can pull this off without looking like a slimy lounge lizard.

We're introduced around the table, greeting some people we've known for years and a few we've never met before. Surveying the room, my height is an advantage. The A++ list is upfront near the stage, all mingling, champagne coupes in hand sparkling under the crystal chandelier dotted ceiling.

Eva touches my arm. "Look, Finn, my agent's table is way back on the third tier. Serves him right for not inviting me."

"Wave at him," I urge her, and catching his attention, she does.

"Oh, that felt good." She smiles up at me.

Looking at my watch, I know they'll start flashing the lights in about five minutes for everyone to take their seats and get ready for the live broadcast. The buzz in the room is palpable. This is Hollywood's fun awards night, due mostly to the constant flow of alcohol. Tonight is the night we will not only get a glimpse of what the Oscar wins will most likely be, but we'll also have the best gossip come out of tonight because an inebriated Hollywood always puts on a most-amusing and newsworthy show, much of it away from the camera's glaring lens.

As I'm about to take my seat a few minutes later, the lights flash with the first warning. You can feel the energy in the room elevate to a fevered pitch as everyone takes their seat.

"I see Maverick Dailey is making a fashionably late entrance." Eva whispers in my ear, her eyes focused on the front of the room. "I'm sure he's stopped with every step he takes on the red carpet."

Turning in the direction she's gazing, I see him making his way to a front table, clasping his peers' hands along the way, while swiftly moving past them. Clasping the hand of a woman, he leads her through the maze of tables, until they get to Table 3. As he lets go of her hand, I watch as he pulls out a chair, his hand skimming her back as it moves down her pale blue-sequined dress. It's impossible not to notice the curve of her backside, and for that I'm hating the guy even a little bit more.

As soon as his palm falls on her lower back, she turns to him and I'm too far away to read her expression, but close enough to recognize her.

"Who's the blonde with Maverick?" Eva's checking her out in the way only beautiful women can check out other beautiful women.

"Frankie Simonelli." My eyes have not left her, and I watch as she takes her seat, only to have my view blocked by her date a second later.

"Who?" she asks. And it annoys me.

"Francesca Simonelli, the author."

Clasping my shoulder, she whispers in my ear, "The author of *Fleeing an August Moon?*"

I nod, my gaze now trained on Maverick. *Move, you motherfucker.* I want to see Frankie. I can't believe I didn't recognize her when they were walking in. She looked hot with her hair swept up — and that dress. The last time I saw her, we were both sweaty messes. Even still, I took notice of her fine behind.

"I bet this means he got the Griffin Chase role," she speculates, excitement in her voice, as if she's just solved the Daily Double on *Jeopardy.*

Her words make my stomach knot. Okay, so now this is the second time I know of that they've seen one another. There's probably quite a few more that I don't know about, I assume. *Move out of the way, douche, I want to see her.* I hate that she's with him. *Have I been a fool thinking I was in the running? If I wasn't, why would she continue to respond to my emails, answering questions about Griff's motivation?*

"You read the book?" I instantly regret the surprise in my tone as I turn to Eva.

"Of course." Those two words come accompanied by an annoyed look.

She knows nothing. It's bad Hollywood juju to talk about a part you've auditioned for before hearing something back on it. She has no clue that I auditioned for the part of Griffin Chase.

Shit, I hope Sebastian doesn't mention anything tonight.

"I'd love to audition for the part of Gabriela." I barely hear her say, as the lights go down and the first strains of the theme music fill the immense facility.

Wouldn't that be a kick in the gut, Eva playing Briela opposite Maverick Dailey's Griff. Yeah, that would be par for the course, the cherry bomb perched atop the shit sundae known as my life for the past two years.

Ladies and gentlemen, welcome to the Golden Globes.

It's impossible to watch anything happening on the stage with Frankie sitting there next to that cocksure ass. I can see him laughing, slinging his arm across the back of her chair, and dipping his head to whisper in her ear. The man is attempting to play her like a fiddle. An appearance as public as this is sure to have all the entertainment media outlets speculating that he is the unannounced lead in *Fleeing an August Moon,* and the actual announcement would only serve as confirmation.

"You look tense, boychick." Sebastian's brow is furrowed as he turns to me at the start of a commercial break.

"Mav Dailey is here with Frankie Simonelli. I guess I can assume he's a lock for the part."

Why does losing this part feel so monumental? I haven't landed any other major part I've been up for in the past two years. Why does this one feel so gut wrenching? So personal?

"I wouldn't take it as anything. The studio knows they can generate buzz and rumors, and as far as I know, they haven't seen him read yet."

"You've certainly got a good source."

"A great source." He looks confident. "Us Angelenos have each other's backs."

With my eyes trained on her table, my muscles jolt when I see her rise. She's on the move. Probably in search of the ladies' room and Mav's not with her.

"Excuse me for a moment," I say to Sebastian, as I bolt. I know, he knows, exactly where I'm headed.

I am off to do battle. Time to fight for what I want. I might not be the A++-lister that Dailey is, but I know Frankie saw something in my performance, something that hasn't made her say to me, *I don't think you're right for the part.* Which her people would actually say to my people, so she probably wouldn't exactly be the one sharing that news.

Heading out the door closest to my section, I hang a left, hoping it puts me directly in Frankie's path. Scanning the crowd, I wonder how stalkerish it is to wait near the ladies' room. I shake my head at just how desperate I've become, overwhelmed by the feeling I'm sinking and I know that's not a pretty sight. Especially not here, not now. Not ever.

It's not helping that I'm in a sea of contrived perfection.

Look at them.

Hell, look at me.

Hollywood's brightest glitter sparkles under the light of crystal chandeliers. The evening an ongoing spotlight, and in its glare, I'm sinking deeper into darkness with every sequined glint that catches my eye.

Where is she?

Again, my height becomes my greatest asset, my vantage point allowing me to easily survey the mass of glitterati milling here in the lobby and among all the statuesque beauties in flowing gowns...there she is, walking in my direction. And yeah, my stomach is doing a flip-flop, tossing around tonight's Chilean sea bass, as a tsunami of emotion tows me under. I neither expected that, nor did I anticipate the darkness dissipating at just the sight of her.

As I get near, I call out, "Frankie." Her head snaps in my direction. She mouths my name, and as she walks toward me, her pace quickens as her smile widens with each step. How can I do anything but smile back? She looks amazing, her face bright, long hair styled in an intricate updo.

And the woman is wearing cowboy boots. Cowboy boots with bling. Damn, she's fine.

"Finn!"

Throwing her arms around me, she catches me totally off guard. As the initial surprise dissipates, I hug her back. And it feels... right. And natural. The scent of lemon in her hair is calming and the noise in the crowded foyer slips away. *I don't want to let go.* But I do.

"Finn, I didn't know you were going to be here." Smiling up at me, she adds, "It is so good to see a familiar face. So good." And I can see that sentiment in her eyes.

"I didn't know you were going to be here either, but I'm glad you are." And I am. More than I had imagined. Yeah, I want the role, but damn it is good to see her smiling at me.

"It's kind of overwhelming," she admits, her eyes darting around the crowd.

"Are you here with the studio?" I need her to tell me what is going on.

"Well, I thought I was." She looks genuinely confused. "But my executive producer, director, and casting director are at the next table." Gazing down at her crystal-encrusted cowboy boots, she takes in a deep breath before looking up, her eyes meeting mine directly. "And I'm seated with Mav Dailey."

My Chilean sea bass fights to swim up my esophagus as I try hard to control my facial expression, but clearly by her reaction, I have a tell.

"Finn." She reaches out and touches my arm.

Immediately, I lower the veil on my eyes, a trick I learned at a very young age. I can't let her in to see the pain of yet another defeat.

"Finn..." she begins, before her eyes widen and suddenly shift to my right.

"There you are. I've been looking everywhere for you." Eva is suddenly by my side, sliding her arm through mine, the same arm Frankie's hand is on.

I recognize the veil that comes down over Frankie's eyes, it appears she's no stranger to that trick, too. As her hand abruptly drops, our connection severs, and I plummet back into my darkness.

"Hi, I'm Eva Armeni." She extends a hand.

"Francesca Simonelli."

Immediately, I am struck that Frankie introduced herself as Francesca. It's easy to see how she distances herself.

"I am totally having a fangirl moment here," Eva announces. "I loved, loved, loved *Fleeing an August Moon.*"

"Thank you."

Frankie's smile looks forced to me and I wonder why such a cool reception for Eva, who is clearly a fan of her work.

"Have you cast Briela yet? Oh my God, I would love to audition for that role."

Damn, woman, you just met her and you're already asking for something. Welcome to Hollywood, Frankie.

Again, Frankie's smile is forced. "Well, have your..." And once more she is interrupted before finishing her sentence.

This time I'm glad she wasn't able to complete her thought, until he pulls up beside her, casually putting an arm around her shoulders.

He should have peed on my leg. It would have been just as effective, delivering the exact same message.

I have seen Frankie Simonelli at her most relaxed, scarfing down a cowboy cookie, sweaty and spent, and this is clearly far from her comfort zone.

"Francesca, I was wondering where you disappeared to." Maverick hits her with one of his multi-million-dollar smiles.

Francesca? What an ass.

Eva is the first one to introduce herself. "Eva Armeni. We've met before. You probably don't remember." She extends her hand to him.

"It was at The Polo Lounge, was it not?" He still hasn't let go of her hand.

"You have a very good memory."

From her stare, she's giving him her *I'm available* look. I don't know whether to be pissed or not. She's here with me and it feels like I keep losing to this guy. But maybe she can distract him from Frankie. And for *that*, I would thank her, and most gladly hand my date over to him, giftwrapped.

"You are an unforgettable woman, Eva."

Oh, please.

As my eyes shift to Frankie, she doesn't look upset. She actually looks like she's about to bust out laughing, and that lifts me out of this dark space. Obviously, she is not emotionally attached in any way to Dailey, and for some reason, that makes me incredibly happy.

God, I'm actually feeling possessive of this woman.

I can see that she catches my smile and I feel like we're co-conspirators. Her eyes are laughing. I can read them and it's making my heart smile.

What a weird thought.

Sounds like a line from her book.

I guess I really want the role.

And, if I'm being real, she's really damn fine to look at. Grubby from running or all dolled up for a red carpet, she is fine, with her totally non-Hollywood way. For God's sake, in a sea of Manolo Blahnik's, the woman is wearing cowboy boots.

"Excuse me," Frankie says, motioning to the ladies' room.

"I'll join you." Eva steps away with her and I hope the groan I heard was only in my head.

Why don't I want her talking to Frankie?

"She'd make a great Briela." I'm not sure if Dailey is talking to me or to himself.

That's exactly why I don't want her talking to Frankie.

Frankie

Thank the Lord this ladies' room is huge. You could get lost in here, which happens to be perfect for me at the moment. Each toilet area is a floor-to-ceiling private enclosure with a door. I need private right now, very private, as I lean up against the wall of this not-so-little cubicle. Maybe I can stay in here until Finn's girlfriend is gone.

I wonder if she is his girlfriend?

Why should I care?

But maybe she's not because that was quite a flirtation between her and Maverick. Finn looked amused, not at all like a jealous boyfriend. And then that look he gave me. It was like can we just ditch these two? *At least, I think it was.* But maybe this is just the way they do business in Hollywood.

I guess Eva could possibly make a good Briela, if her glam was way toned down. Under it all, I think she is definitely a natural beauty. She's just so... Hollywood.

And Maverick absolutely was trying to make Finn think he was my date tonight. That was weird. *Why?* God, he's a confusing man. Seeing him with Jua today showed me a side that is anything but Hollywood glitz. It was all heart. And selfless. That horse loved him. And animals know. They know the souls of humans.

But all these people want something from me. Maverick does. Finn does. And now Finn's girlfriend, or whatever she is, does. They all want to be cast in this film.

Finn and Eva as Griffin and Gabriela. My body involuntarily shudders.

Well, they'd probably have great on-screen chemistry together. *But could I watch that?* Ugh, I don't know. Though, that is something I shouldn't have a problem with. So, what's my story here? *Why the jealousy?* He's not Griffin, you dumb-dumb. He's Finn.

Separate your shit out, Frankie. You're not feeling anything for this man. You don't know this man. Although, tonight it felt like I knew everything in his head. But I don't.

This is so weird.

Would I have problems if Mav was starring opposite Eva in the role?

No.

If I'm totally honest. No. Although I just don't see him as Griff.

I need to separate my love of writing a character from feelings for this man, because that is some cray-cray shit. *Even I know that, after three glasses of champagne.*

I really liked being with Finn, though. Yes, he's pretty to look at. But he's kind of raw and real and I sense a sadness. How can a man that good looking be sad? When I saw him tonight, standing there in his white tux jacket and skinny black pants, he looked—perfect. Every dirty blond hair on his head was perfect. The day-old scruff was perfect. His strong chin was perfect. Women were doing double-takes.

And, I was so happy to see him standing there. I can't believe I hugged him. Oh God, what a goof I am. I didn't think about it, if I had, I probably would have known that I shouldn't. But I wasn't thinking, I was just... I don't know, it just felt like the right thing to do. And then he hugged me back.

If I'm really being honest about it, I didn't want him to stop.

But that moment was gone in a nanosecond when I upset him by telling him I was here with Mav. I could see the distance in his eyes. He didn't have to say a word, and yet, I watched him retreat and God, I didn't want him to go.

But get real, Frankie, he was upset because he assumed Mav was a lock for the role and he was no longer a contender. It has nothing to do with Mav being here with me as a date. Which he isn't, anyway. But Finn doesn't know the story. He just keeps seeing me with Maverick in very public places.

Okay, I think enough time has passed and I'm safe to emerge from the sanctuary of my lovely toilet stall. Eva is probably long gone, and Finn, too. And maybe Mav won't be waiting for me, either. That would actually be okay. Even though he's been nothing but kind to me, I know being seen together makes everyone think him getting the role of Griffin Chase is a fait accompli.

Opening the door, I step out into the glare, immediately catching my reflection in the long mirror lining the wall across from me. The vanity is loaded with products and beautiful women are all lined up, fixing imaginary imperfections in their unnatural perfection.

I stick out like a sore thumb. Even with all the help I got today from the hair and make-up artist, I look like an alien. One of my front teeth slightly overlaps the other. My nose doesn't have the perfect lines of everyone's I'm seeing in the mirror. And I'm wearing cowboy boots, not skyscraper, strappy sandals.

What was I thinking?

Caryn would be shuddering at the sight of me.

As I finish washing my hands, Eva appears at the sink next to me. She's still here. Just when I thought the coast was clear. *What is she still doing here?*

"I am so excited that I got to meet you tonight." She smiles at me in the mirror.

Okay, maybe I'm just being a bitch. Maybe she's really nice.

"Are you working on another book now?"

"Yes. I'm about two-thirds of the way through." I smile back.

"I cannot wait to read it." She picks up a can of Redken Quick Dry spray and gives her hair a once over. "And I'm not kidding, if it hasn't been cast yet, I would love the opportunity to audition for the part of Gabriela."

Holding my breath so that I don't start coughing from the spray, I tell her to have her agent call, and pull my lipstick from my bag.

"So, are you and Maverick a thing?" she asks, before I even pull off the cap.

"No." I shake my head.

"Finn and I aren't either," she offers unsolicited. "I guess you could say we're exes with benefits."

TMI. I do not want to know he's fucking you. I really don't want to know that.

I guess she sees the surprised look on my face, because she quickly follows up with, "I just wanted you to know we were exes. I saw that look pass between the two of you. I know that look." An abbreviated laugh escapes. "I know that look very well. You are totally not Finn's usual type. I don't think I've ever seen him with a blonde, but you're an A-Lister and Finn likes to attach himself to A-Listers." The last sentence, delivered over her shoulder with a toss of her hair as she turns to walk out, has the definite tone of a warning.

Bitch, I am the hand that feeds you. You're not auditioning for shit, lady.

They are all still there.

Shit.

Go back to your tables, people.

Eva is engaged in a conversation with Maverick, and from the subtleties of their body language, I'd say Eva might get lucky tonight. Finn, maybe not so much. There are a few people milling about Mav, trying their hardest to get the star's attention, but he seems oblivious to everyone but Eva.

As I walk toward them, with Mav and Eva deep in conversation, Finn appears to be solidly in his own head. Or maybe bored, I can't really tell. Standing there, just staring out over the crowd, with hands shoved deep into the pockets of his dark dress pants, I can't help but think he looks like an Armani ad or something. I suppose there are a lot of them in this town — men who get better with age, but this one, he sure looks fine and he looks like Griffin Chase. And he can act.

And... I am so drawn to him.

Yes, I know that sounds shallow. But every time my computer dings and it's an email from him, asking me about Griffin's intentions in a certain scene, I get butterflies. And I really can't tell if it's because I can't separate fiction from the flesh and blood man who sent me the message. Or do I really like *this* particular man?

And his messages...

Hi, Frankie,

Quick question. You don't cover it in the book, but do you see Griff making amends with his father? Or do they stay estranged?

Hope you've had a great day and enjoyed the rare rain here.
Thanks,
Finn

Hey, Finn,
I think it could go either way. Griffin has grown so much as a character that I think he might try and make amends with his father. But on the other hand, because of that growth, I think he would be comfortable on his own and breaking away from an ideology in which he no longer believes.
Loving the rain. I think it helps me hunker down to write.
Frankie

You know what I was thinking. I was thinking he makes amends with the old man, and then walks away. He's no longer going to let himself be dragged down by his past, and once he comes to terms with it, by making peace with his father, he's able to finally walk away to a very different destiny than what had been planned for him.
Finn

I love that, Finn! Don't make me write a sequel!

Hmm, that might mean the possibility of repeat employment. Don't let me keep you from your writing.

Just thinking about our email interactions lightens my mood, but unfortunately, their tone feels polar opposite of the vibe I left him with when our conversation was interrupted, and how checked out he looks now.

Maverick sees me approaching and bestows the million-dollar smile upon me. "There you are."

I'm finding it hard to smile through gritted teeth. I can see Eva's eyes shift to Finn to see his reaction to my arrival and I hope he gives none, so as not to feed into her liking A-Lister's theory.

"I think Eva and I should read together for Griffin and Gabriela," Mav announces. "I think we'd have good chemistry together on the screen, don't you?" He winks at her and I can see the fanning of her peacock feathers.

The energy to my left feels heavy and I'm not sure if I'm imagining it, but without even a glance in his direction, I can feel Finn seething. I can't look at him, but I imagine this is as uncomfortable for him as it is for me, and I feel like I have some role in hurting him, even though that is not the case.

I *need to escape this. I'm not good at Hollywood.*

"I'm going to go sit down. Good seeing you," I say to Finn and Eva without really looking at either one of them. I can't look Finn in the eye. Eva and Mav reading together for those two parts. I can't even fathom what emotions are running through him.

And although not my fault, I feel guilty. And just as shitty as he probably does.

The after-party is loud and crowded and I'm just done. Put a fork in me.

Now that I have experienced a real live Hollywood after-party, I want to be back in my hotel room. Alone. Boots off. Hair down. Make-up washed down the drain. I need to get lost in my new manuscript because it's a great place to hide when I'm overwhelmed.

And I am definitely overwhelmed.

I need to leave. But I have not been successful accomplishing that as I keep getting introduced to familiar and unfamiliar faces. I'm surprised by how many of these people are fans of the book, but it's hard to get drawn into conversations with the noise level, so I sip my champagne and observe. A lot of air-kissing, ruckus laughter, and roving eyes. Everyone appears to be working the room. This is not fun for them, clearly not fun. It's business. All business. And it's a lot of work. Inside all the heads tossed back in laughter, there are lengthy agendas.

And yes, I wonder if I have one, too, when I find myself searching for Finn. I feel like I need to apologize to him, and I'm not quite sure for what, but running into him here was weird and not pleasant. I know he felt it, too. Well, I don't actually know that, and maybe it's just me again thinking I know him better than I actually do.

After a requisite thirty minutes and two more glasses of champagne, I excuse myself and walk past the restrooms toward the main lobby.

"Do you need a ride, ma'am," one of the young men working the door asks.

Ma'am? It's definitely time to get out of here.

"I was just going to call an Uber."

"We have Town Cars waiting if you'd like one," he offers, gesturing to a long line of vehicles across from us.

"I would love one." This is the best thing I've heard all evening.

As we drive west on Wilshire Blvd, I ponder texting Mav or Judith or someone to let them know I've left, but I'm too tired to do even that.

Tonight was an energy zapper. I think the people out here are used to it and feed off it, but this is so not my deal.

I am just not Hollywood.

Even pulling off my blingy cowboy boots in the back of the Town Car is exhausting. As I lie my head back into the plush leather seat, I can't help but wonder if Eva and Finn will be exercising their benefits tonight.

What's he doing with her? She's a bitch.

And not a very bright one at that.

Do I want to watch her and Mav read together? No. Not really. But if forced to sit through that, I could.

Do I want to watch her and Finn read together? No freaking way. No, with a capital N.

The thought of Eva and Finn reading together is not sitting well with me. Being *Exes with Benefits,* they'd probably burn up the screen together and could capture the passion of Griff and Briela, which is what makes a movie great.

Maybe I just need to be more open-minded. And professional.

This is business and it's these people's livelihoods. So, I need to take all my crazy crap out of this, and look at it as what are the correct business decisions to make the best screen adaptation not only a success, but something of which I can be very, very proud.

With boots in hand, I stroll through the lobby barefoot, the cold tile refreshing my tired feet.

All those women in heels tonight, how do they do it?

Glancing over at the concierge desk, my friend isn't there, and I'm glad, or I'd feel obligated to stop and chat. Getting to my room is my only mission. I need to be alone in a quiet space. My quiet space.

My first awards show, I later muse. I should have stayed in and ordered room service.

Flipping open my laptop, I'm more than ready to get lost in a world of my own creation.

The sun is now up, but the exhaustion that slayed me last night when I crawled between the sheets has not yet released me from its clutches. I'm revived neither physically nor emotionally. The Finn-Eva-Mav encounter from last night definitely did a number on my head, spawning weird dreams about Eva taking over production of the movie.

As I tie the laces on my running shoes, I wonder if I should shoot Finn an email to tell him I'm sorry we didn't get to finish our conversation last night, but my gut is telling me to leave it alone, as I tie the lace on my right shoe.

Down on the street, I grasp a lamppost as I stretch out my hamstrings and quads, before heading south along the beach toward Venice, the opposite direction of my usual northerly run toward Malibu, but closer to where Finn lives.

What am I doing?

Finn

The walls are mocking me.

You're as empty as we are. Just another soulless casualty of the Hollywood glitterati.

And you know what, I believe them. I believe the walls.

I would probably sell my soul at this point to land a decent role, to break this two-year drought that is wreaking havoc on my savings, not to mention ripping apart my psyche. Look at the shit I did, jogging up near Frankie's hotel in hopes of running into her. Literally.

And when I did, that day was the first time in many months that it felt like my luck was turning,

But then last night, it seemed I was just kidding myself. Freaking Maverick Dailey. The dude was giving me a message loud and clear. Fuck him. And fuck Eva, too. Telling me she wanted to stay at the after-party and would find her own way home. My guess is she found her way to Mav's home, unless Frankie was his plan for the night.

For some reason, I don't like that thought. It makes me uneasy. Not sure if it's because that would give him a lock on the part or because I just don't want him touching her. Testosterone makes us men very territorial. And I'm feeling very territorial about her. Which is freaking ridiculous since we're only acquaintances.

But that hug when she first saw me. What was that about?

That was real. It was her gut reaction. It might very well have been the only real response of anyone in that building the entire night. She threw her arms around me as if she'd just run into her oldest friend.

Or lost great love.

Hmm, well, I don't know about that since I am neither.

Hitting the beach for a run, my decision not to run north toward Santa Monica, not to run toward Frankie, is a conscious one. Chances are I wouldn't run into her anyway, and that's okay. I just need to try and let go of last night, put it out of my mind, so that damn scene stops gnawing at me. But if there is one thing I know, a good run on the beach can exorcise even the most steadfast of ghosts.

Guess I could sell the BMW, move away from the beach, if I don't get the part.

Or get my ass out there and start networking as hard as I did in my twenties. Stop being a morose shit, lamenting breaks not going my way. Seriously too early to call defeat, especially with all the new streaming series that are no longer the low-budget, or no-budget, red-haired stepchildren of the acting world. Big, big stars have made the transition to these well-written, envelope-pushing shows. Yeah, time to put a plan together for a comeback. I'm ready. Note to self: Call Sebastian when you get home and see what day he can meet for lunch. It's time to blow off this gray cloud I've been hiding under for way too long now.

What the fuck?

The grasp to my biceps as my arm swings back naturally with my stride is alarming, immediately yanking me out of my thoughts and thrusting me into fight or flight mode with a jarring burst of power-injected adrenaline.

Am I being mugged? Shit!

Without turning, I swing my arm back hard. Over the sound of Moby playing loud from my headphones, I hear and feel the striking of my arm against flesh and turn as the body sprawls backward onto the hard-packed, wet sand, landing with a sickening thud.

Two long, blonde braids cascade like silk ropes in the breeze as I see Frankie's head hit the sand, her face already smeared with blood from where my arm has made contact with her nose.

"Frankie, holy shit!" Stopping dead in my tracks, confused by the scene sprawled on the sand in front of me, I go running back to her, dropping to my knees at her side. "Don't move," I warn her, as she tries to lift her head.

"My leg." Her voice is no more than a hoarse whisper.

I can see the pain in her eyes and glance down, immediately noting the odd angle of her left foot.

Oh crap. This does not look good.

"I called your name, but you didn't hear me, so I was trying to catch up." As she speaks, blood drips onto her lips. Swiping it away with the back of her hand, she regards the red smear as it takes a moment for her to fully realize it is hers.

"I didn't hear you. Oh God, I am sorry. Your neck and your head, do they feel okay? You went down pretty hard."

"I think so." Lifting her head slightly, she nods.

Looking toward Ocean Front Walk, I quickly assess where we are. "I'm going to pick you up, okay. My gym is really close to here. I'm going to get you over there. I know that they at least have first-aid stuff on premises, and we can either call for an ambulance or I can get my car and get you over to an emergency room."

"Finn, I don't..." she begins to protest.

"Yeah, Frankie, you do." I can see the pain in her eyes, even though she's trying to be so tough. Pulling my t-shirt off over my head, I place it under her nose, careful not to do any more damage than I've already done. "I'm going to put an arm around your upper back and one under your knees. I want you to put your arms around my neck, okay, until I get you up, and then try to put slight pressure on your nose with my shirt. Maybe we can get the bleeding to stop."

As she reaches up and wraps her arms around me, I hoist her up, and straighten to my feet, careful to jostle her as little as possible.

"I'm going to try and get you there as quickly as possible, but let me know if the motion is too much, and I can stop."

"Okay," the word is muffled by my shirt.

"Frankie, I am so sorry. I didn't know it was you there when I swung back. I am so sorry."

"I'm sorry, Finn. I was trying to catch up to you to tell you I was sorry."

"For what?" What could she possibly be sorry about?

"Last night. It was so uncomfortable. I wanted to apologize for that."

Glancing down at the pain-filled eyes gazing up at me over the now blood-soaked, yellow shirt, I tell her, "Frankie, you have nothing to apologize for. You didn't do or say anything wrong. It was weird, for sure, but my being uncomfortable was really based on Eva's behavior."

"And Mav's."

"Yes, and Mav's"

"I'm sorry about that, Finn."

"Frankie, you are not responsible for other people. The only one here who needs to be sorry is me."

"For what?"

"For this." I can feel my eyes widen.

"This was an unfortunate accident."

"I'm so sorry, Frankie." Taking a deep sigh, mostly for strength, I yank open the front door to L9, my health club.

The receptionist looks up, "Finn," she greets me, before processing the scene and the injured woman in my arms.

"I'm going to need some help."

Out of nowhere, Henry Clark, the guy who runs the show, appears. "Follow me." He directs me and quickly orders the receptionist, "Page Carlos, he's an EMT and tell him to come to my office immediately."

Following Henry through a door and down a hallway into an area of the facility I didn't even know existed, he leads me to his office and points to a black leather couch, where I lie Frankie down as gently as possible.

Behind me someone enters the office. "What's up, boss?" The man's voice is slightly accented.

With a slight movement of his head, Henry motions to where Frankie is lying.

"Hey there, what happened to you?" The man approaches the couch, crouching down next to Frankie.

"I hit her," I mumble, before she can respond. "Her head hit pretty hard. And her foot." I point to her left leg, aware all eyes are now on me with that admission.

"Let me look in your eyes," Carlos's voice is soft. "Your pupils look good. That's a good sign, but it doesn't necessarily mean you don't have a concussion." He nods and smiles at her. "I'm going to ask you a couple of questions, okay," he says, as he moves the bloody t-shirt from her nose.

It appears the bleeding has stopped on its own, and I'm glad for at least that.

"Can you tell me your name?"

"Francesca."

"Hi, Francesca, I'm Carlos."

"What's your last name, Francesca?"

"Simonelli."

I hear muttering from a few people standing behind me near the door to Henry's office. *Oh, Christ. They all know who she is.*

"Where do you live, Francesca?"

"Houston."

"Wow, you are far from home. What are you doing out here?"

"Making a movie."

Carlos laughs. "This is LA. I should have guessed that."

"Can you tell me what day it is?"

"Monday."

"Good. Now, can you describe to me what happened?"

My stomach knots.

"I was running on the beach and I saw Finn. But he couldn't hear me with his headphones on. I was behind him and I grabbed his arm to get his attention and his arm swung back and hit me in the face, then I went backwards."

Standing with my arms crossed over my blood-stained, bare chest, I internally take a relieved sigh upon hearing her explanation. It doesn't sound as bad as it feels in my own head.

"I'll bet that foot is hurting pretty badly, huh?"

Her eyes speak volumes as she wordlessly nods her head.

"I'm going to take a quick look, okay, and I'll try my best not to hurt you anymore than you are already hurting."

As Carlos focuses on Frankie's left ankle, her eyes focus on me.

"You're going to be okay," I mouth the words, trying to reassure her and feeling like shit. *I freaking did this to her.*

"I got you all bloody," she says, looking at my bare chest.

"Lara, go bring Finn a wet towel and a club t-shirt," Henry instructs one of the girls standing by the door.

"Do I get a club t-shirt?" Frankie attempts to smile at Henry, but I can see the pain she's trying hard to hide.

"Sweetheart, you get a free lifetime membership. It's not every day a gorgeous woman in distress gets carried into my office."

As Lara returns with the t-shirt, she hands it to me, and smiles at Frankie. "Maybe that will make it into your next book." She is clearly fangirling.

"You're a writer?" Henry smiles at her.

"Henry, this is Francesca Simonelli." The girl is aghast that her boss doesn't recognize the woman on his black leather couch, who, with her hair in braids, looks more like a college student than a famous author.

Henry just shrugs and smiles at Frankie, clueless as to who she is.

Turning to me, Lara gasps slightly and puts her hand over her mouth. "Oh my God, you're going to be Griffin Chase." She looks from me to Frankie and then back to me again. "And you carried her in here." The girl is going into swoon mode.

"No, no, no. I'm not Griffin. Frankie and I are friends."

"You are Griffin. You look like Griffin. Actually, just like I pictured Griffin."

"Really, I'm not."

"He's not." Another female voice from near the door, interrupts. "Maverick Dailey is going to be Griffin Chase."

My eyes momentarily lock with Frankie's, and I'm trying as hard as I can not to show anything. This doesn't hurt. Nope. I'm okay with it, because it is inevitably going to happen. No matter how perfectly I nail this role, the studio is going to want him, and they will pressure her until she acquiesces.

I see a new kind of pain on Frankie's face and it's not from the mishap on the beach. She feels like *she's* hurting *me*. I can tell. I can see it in her eyes. This woman does not belong in this town. She is way too decent for all this. By the time the film releases, she'll either be destroyed or so hardened that this Frankie, the one I'm seeing now, will be hidden by a rock-solid shell.

I'm not sure which is worse.

"The role hasn't been cast yet," she quietly corrects everyone.

"It should be this guy." Lara points to me.

Yeah, Frankie, listen to her. She's a reader and she sees me as Griffin.

"Would you like us to call an ambulance for you? You really need to get to the ER and have that leg and your head looked at." Henry's manner is soothing, but I feel like he's picked up on the tension in the room that spiked from the previous exchange.

Frankie's eyes immediately dart to me. I can see her anxiety rise at just the mention of an ambulance, and interject, "How about if I go get my car. I can be back here in about ten minutes?"

She nods, and I swear I can feel her relief. An ambulance to an unknown hospital in a city that is not home has got to feel stressful, and I can't let that happen.

"Where are you going to take her?" Carlos inquires.

"Cedars-Sinai in Marina Del Rey is closest, but I'm thinking UCLA would be the best place to go for orthopedics. The Lakers and Rams team doctors are on staff there.

"I think you're right," Carlos concurs. "That's where I would want to go for an injury like this."

I knocked the woman to the ground and broke her leg, the least I can do is make sure she gets to the medical facility with the best orthopedic surgeons in the city. Because she is going to need surgery, of that I have no doubt.

"I'll be right back," I tell Frankie, giving her a long look, hoping that I'm conveying that she's going to be okay. "Take care of my girl," is my instruction to the L9 staff as I leave Henry's office.

"Take care of my girl," Lara repeats, as I walk out the door. "I'm sorry, but that man is definitely Griffin Chase."

Frankie

Take care of my girl...
Yeah, that felt damn good, like I almost let out an *mmm* sound, good.

Maybe it's just the way he talks, but hearing those words come out of his mouth was like being on the receiving end of a swoony moment that wasn't written in my head. I guess that hasn't happened too often lately, but boy, doe5s it ever feel good. It made me momentarily forget the searing pain in my very swollen, purple ankle or the fact that I can't breathe out of my nose and have the headache from Hell.

"What does Level 9 mean?" I ask about fifteen minutes later, as we turn out of L9's parking lot, and I notice that the club's logo says Level 9 with an L9 stamped over it, and Finn and the staff had referred to it as L9. "Is it like some Zen levels or something? Get to level nine of workout nirvana?"

Shaking his head, Finn smiles, "I have no clue."

"They are very nice in there," I comment. "So, how long does it take to get to the hospital from here?" I'm hoping I like his answer.

"This time of day. On a week day." He pauses, thinking. "We should be able to make it in about a half hour."

I nod and close my eyes for a second. I'm nauseous and not sure if it's from the intense pain, or because I haven't eaten anything. My fear is that in the next thirty minutes I will lose it all over his beautiful BMW.

"I'm not sure if I'm nauseous from the pain or just hungry," I say as we pass a Del Taco and think about their hot, salty crinkle fries.

"We could do drive-thru, but if you need surgery, they are going to want you to be on an empty stomach."

Ugh. This dude is practical and detail-oriented. Which I should have guessed from the many questions he's asked me in a multitude of emails.

"You're right." I focus my sight back out the window for two reasons, but both have the same purpose: distraction. I'm trying to distract myself from the pain and from staring at Finn's profile. The man is so damn handsome. His features possibly too perfect, but in a very masculine way.

The warmth of his hand as he gives mine a squeeze and gently runs his thumb back and forth, catches me by surprise. "Would listening to some music help take your mind off the pain?"

"It might."

"Okay, what do you like to listen to?" He removes his hand from mine to find a radio station.

"Country."

"Of course, you do." He laughs. "Country music is my avocado toast, you know." And there's that smile he bowled me over with the morning we had breakfast.

"Channel 56. The Highway," I tell him, seeing he's tuned to satellite and not local LA stations.

"Thanks."

I'm again caught off guard when his hand finds mine again after he's tuned the radio. This time I squeeze his back, looking at my hand lost in his and liking it, a part of my heart wishes it was for other reasons.

"Frankie, I am so sorry about all this. I am really sorry I did this to you."

"Finn, it was an unfortunate accident. I never should have grabbed you from behind."

"So, you were really coming to find me?" He has a half-smirk on his face and I'm not sure how to read it.

"What's that look?"

"It's surprise, Frankie. Surprise that you would care enough about my feelings that you actually came looking, hoping to find me."

Squeezing his hand a little tighter, I nod. "Last night, it felt like people's words and actions were robbing you of hope. I didn't want to be part of that, and I wanted you to know that wasn't how I felt. No matter what it might have looked like, that wasn't how I felt."

"Well, I appreciate that, and I appreciate you coming to look for me. I was trying hard last night not to let it knock me down, but you lose your soul in this town, and I've been fearing for quite some time now that mine is lost."

"Well, then, how do you expect to play the role of a man who is all soul?" The question comes out harsher than I intended, and immediately I regret my words challenging him.

Staring straight ahead as he drives, I can see his jaw muscles twitch and nostrils flare slightly. I'm not sure if he's grappling with how to word something or fighting with himself about something he really wants to say.

"Don't you see," he pauses, "that is why I want to step into him. I need to go there."

Is he telling me that playing Griffin is going to bring his soul back to him?

"A character role is not going to do that for you, Finn," my tone is much more conciliatory this time.

"Yeah, it will," he sounds certain, "because if I can feel that. If I can feel those emotions. Then there's hope, Frankie. There's hope."

As he turns to me, I can see the desperation in his eyes, and it's not about a role, it's about his self-worth and humanity. It's about taking back whatever it is that this man has lost. And whatever it is, it feels substantial.

"Hope is at the core of the storyline." I tighten my grip on his hand.

"I know." He nods, again looking straight ahead.

"What if you can't get there?" *Can he be Griffin if he's lost his soul?*

"That's not an option." His tone is resolute, and with the set of his strong jaw, I believe him.

I believe him.

I feel something in my hair. Maybe a fly. I'm not sure. It's moving from the top of my head down toward the side of my face. And now it's up by my forehead and its movement is tickling me. I go to swat at it, but my arm is somehow restrained. I want to open my eyes, but my lids aren't listening and I'm so tired. Maybe it will just fly away.

"Hey there."

I hear a voice very close to me. Then the fly comes back. It keeps starting up by my forehead and moving down toward my cheek. It's relentless and I'm going to get it this time. Again, I jerk my arm toward the offensive insect only to feel a stab at the back of my hand stopping me from getting to it.

"Hey." It's the voice again.

And now the fly is not wandering as delicately as it was earlier. A tanned forearm with golden hair is sweeping past my eyes just as I force my lids open. *That's my fly.* My fly is a hand smoothing down my hair.

"You're awake." His voice is welcoming, as is his smile. That smile. "They put your ankle back together. The doctor said you should heal nicely."

"My throat hurts," I croak.

"Let's find out if you can have some water." He presses the nurse's button and is told I can have sips. Bringing the cup with a bent straw to my lips, "Slowly," he instructs, letting me have a short sip before taking the cup away.

"What did the doctor say?"

"He put in two screws and casted your foot. He said it should take about six weeks to heal, and at that point you should do physical therapy. Once it is strengthened you can run again, as long as you take it slowly. He wants to see you in his office in about two weeks."

"I have a cast?" As soon as he says the words, I'm aware of the cast's weight on my left leg. "I couldn't just do a boot?"

Finn shakes his head. "But the good news is, no concussion and I didn't break your nose."

"Can I go home?" I motion to him for more water and he brings the Styrofoam cup back to my lips, allowing me to take a quick sip before pulling it away. I'm not sure why he's keeping it so far away from me. I'm beginning to think he's some kind of control freak.

"The doctor wants to keep you overnight for observation, but said he would be willing to release you if you could be watched. He doesn't want you alone for the next forty-eight hours."

"I don't need to be watched. I can go back to my hotel and order room service. I can call the concierge if I need anything."

He's shaking his head. "I don't think so."

I must have an *are you kidding me* look on my face because it elicits a laugh from him.

"What do you mean, you don't think so?"

"You either stay here tonight or you come home with me." He lays out the options, neither of which are acceptable.

"No."

"No to what?" he asks, sitting back in the green leather and wood arm chair and crossing his arms over his chest.

"No. I'm not coming home with you."

"Okay, that's fine. You can spend the night here and have them wake you up every few hours. Your choice." His delivery is smug.

"I just want to go back to my hotel, Finn," I plead.

"Is there someone who can watch you there?"

I can see that tension in his jaw, the one I noticed when we were driving to the hospital, and I just know he's bracing himself to hear Maverick's name come out of my mouth. But the truth is, I have no one.

Shaking my head, I can feel my eyes fill, and my embarrassment at falling apart charges in right behind, forcing the first tears to cascade from my eyes. I can't turn my head away from him fast enough.

Control yourself, Francesca. You are a Texan. Now, buck up. You've been through so much worse than this.

"Hey, hey."

Out of his chair and at my bedside, I feel Finn slip my hand in his, but I still can't turn back to look at him.

"If you don't feel comfortable staying with me, seeing that you don't know me very well, I won't be offended. So, let's add a third choice if it makes you more comfortable. I take you back to your hotel, but I stay. Does your hotel room have a couch?"

I nod. Still not looking at him as I try and make the tears quit the crap they are pulling.

"The reason I thought my apartment was the best option is because I have everything there. Kitchen, stocked fridge, and the ability to get you anything you need. I even have a pull-out couch that has never been used. I just think you'd be more comfortable there."

His other hand is now stroking my hair again and I lean my head into it, momentarily closing my eyes. I feel tired and emotional and I want to be alone, but that doesn't seem like it's in the cards for me.

"Okay."

"Okay, you'll come back to my place?"

"Yes. I just really hate to put you out." Turning to face him, the first thing I notice is how tired he looks.

"Frankie, you are here right now because of me. I put you here."

"Finn, an accident put me here," I tell him yet again, giving his hand a playful tug. "Shit happens. Now, how do we get me out of here."

"That's my girl." Smiling, he presses the button for the nurse.

My girl. There it is again. Those words. Why do I feel those words in my heart when he says them? It's apparently just a phrase he uses.

"I was just coming in to check on you." An attractive, dark-haired nurse enters the room. "How are you feeling? I hear you've had some water."

I nod.

"Any nausea."

"No."

"That's good. Let me get your vitals."

Sitting back down in the chair, Finn gives us space. And in that moment, it feels very weird to have this almost stranger with me while I'm being checked.

As soon as the nurse sticks the thermometer in my mouth, she asks, "You don't happen to be the Francesca Simonelli who wrote *Fleeing an August Moon,* are you?"

I nod, thermometer still under my tongue.

"Oh my God, I loved the book. You're making the movie, right?"

I nod again, and the damn thing finally beeps.

"I am so excited. I loved the book. Griff and Briela." She sighs, clutching her chest dramatically.

Out of the corner of my eye I can see Finn's half-smirk. Is he still here because he wants the part? He's got to be feeling as strange about this as I am. And I just told him I'd come back to his apartment. Is this a huge mistake — on so many levels?

"Are you feeling up to leaving?" she asks.

"Yes, I definitely am."

"And you'll have someone with you?"

I nod and look over at Finn.

"Well, you certainly look capable." She smiles at him, really taking him in for the first time.

"I promise to take good care of her." He smiles back and I can see she is charmed.

"We'll let the doctor know. After he's seen you and signed off, we can start the paperwork," she advises, talking to Finn and not to me. Those blue eyes of his have her spellbound. I can see that even from my hospital bed.

"How long do you think that will take?" Finn asks.

"Realistically, a couple of hours," she tells us, before leaving the room, turning back one more time to make eye contact with my ridiculously handsome companion.

"Here's a thought, to get you into bed as quickly as possible," he pauses and smiles at his unintentional double entendre, "well, you know what I mean. Do you want me to run over to your hotel now and pick up some stuff for you and then come back and get you? This way you don't have to spend too much time in the car and we can go directly back to my place."

Talk about uncomfortable. A handsome man whom I don't know well going through my stuff. But he's right, having him do that will be so much easier, because all I really want to do is sleep.

"Will you hand me my running pouch?" I see the small pink pack on the counter near the sink. Inside are three things I put in there what now seems like a lifetime ago: my room keycard, along with my running trifecta: my driver's license, my health insurance card, and a credit card. No phone, I realize. I must have left it in the hotel this morning.

"Do you have shorts or skirts or something? I don't think you'll be able to do jeans with the cast."

It's at that moment that I have the horrifying realization that this very handsome, near stranger is going to be bringing me clean underwear.

"Maybe we should wait, and I'll go with you."

Shaking his head, he laughs, clearly understanding my hesitation. "Frankie, I've seen women's personal, umm, stuff before."

"Eva's?" Why that came out of my mouth I do not know, but I want to slap the crap out of myself.

"Yes, Eva's. And maybe a few others." His smile tells me he's totally enjoying my discomfort, but then takes pity on me and pivots, "Okay, so what do you need for the next few days?"

"Few days?"

"The doctor said forty-eight hours."

"That's a couple, not a few," I correct him.

Sighing, he has a look on his face that says *what have I gotten myself into here.* "Semantics. And maybe you won't want to leave."

I don't know how to answer that. *What if I don't?*

"So, tell me what you need." Another adept pivot on his part.

You would probably not be the right answer, so I start giving him my list.

"Got it. I'll be back as soon as I can."

As he approaches the door, I call out to him, "Finn."

Turning, he cocks his head, looking at me questioningly.

"Thank you."

Nodding his head, his voice is emotional when he responds, "Not necessary."

The nurse is just entering as he walks out and does nothing to hide her double-take. "I can see who was your muse for Griffin," she comments.

I nod and smile, but don't correct her.

13

Finn

Nice *freaking digs.*

Flipping on the light in Frankie's suite, I'm immediately struck by the posh, yet comfortable space. And the view. Holy shit, the view. Two walls of arched windows, one facing due west toward the ocean, the other northwest with a spectacular view of the coastline and Malibu. Maybe we should have stayed here. My apartment looks like a dump compared to this.

Nice to see how the other half lives.

If I get the part, I'll be looking at real estate. A condo on the beach would work.

Moving to the bedroom, again I'm taken by the wall of arched windows set above custom moldings. These, too, face the ocean. A king-sized, four-poster bed does little to fill the large room. Quickly, I go through the drawers and start gathering up what I think will be comfortable for her for the next few days. Before pulling open the top drawer, I pause. This is very personal and I'm a little uncomfortable doing it. But, at the same time...

I'm met by an assortment of lace and silk bikinis in mostly pale pastels and a few pairs in black. I grab a handful and put them into the Costco bag from my trunk that I've put the rest of her clothes in. Before I close the drawer, the one garment in bright red catches my eye. Pulling it out, I hold it up. *Damn, woman!* How is a guy supposed to react when he's holding a red lace bodysuit with a very plunging neckline? I know what my reaction is just holding the garment, and I'm starting to feel like a creeper. I want to see Frankie Simonelli in this lace deal and nothing else because I am not going to be able to get the picture out of my mind if I don't.

I shove the bodysuit into the Costco bag knowing she's going to be mortified when she sees that I've found it. And packed it. I am messing with this girl. Or maybe it's her who is messing with me. I'm not really sure.

In the bathroom, I just gather everything on the marble counter next to the sink because if I pick and choose what I think she needs, it will be totally wrong. And rule number one, known by every man who has ever been in at least a semi-long-term relationship, you don't mess with a woman's toiletries. That much I know, and I sweep it all into the Costco bag. As I turn, out of the corner of my eye, I see, perched atop a stack of neatly folded bath towels, a little yellow rubber duck holding a blue surfboard. Laughing out loud, I snatch him up. *He'll keep Frankie company.*

Back in the living room, I head over to the desk in the corner with its western and northern views of the ocean. I know she wanted her laptop and her phone and her notebook, and luckily for me, they are all sitting right next to one another, so I don't have to search them out. Touching the computer's keyboard wakes the screen, and I can see from the dialogue on the page that this is something she is working on, so I hit save before closing the computer and packing it up.

Picking up her phone, the screen illuminates when I touch it. I shouldn't be looking at her phone. But I do.

A call and voicemail from Caryn, three calls and two voicemails from Maverick Dailey.

And a text from Maverick.

I hope you're okay. I've left you a few messages today, but haven't heard back. Hope you are not upset with me for any reason. When did you leave last night? I looked all over for you, but you were nowhere to be

found. No goodnight? Should I be offended? Call or text when you get this. Doesn't matter how late.

I want to throw the freaking phone against one of the arched windows, but I've already broken enough in Frankie's life for one day.

This guy is every goddamn place I turn. Frankie. Eva. This part. He is up my ass with everything, and the joke of that is he has no clue, because I am a nothing to him. He doesn't know I've auditioned for the part. The man has no clue how much I want it. How much I need it.

For so many freaking reasons.

And what Mr. Superstar really doesn't know is how it sticks in my gut every time I see him near Frankie. The production company is never going to let her choose me for the role over him. On some level, I know that. Basic economics and all. But I also know, if it's me she sees as Griffin Chase, she will fight like hell for me. The girl is tough as nails. She certainly proved that today.

And while I'm at it, the other thing about him that bugs the shit out of me is the way he pretentiously calls her Francesca and uses her as a photo op to make everyone think he's a lock for the role. So, what is he going to do if by some against-all-odds reason he isn't chosen? Is he going to say it was a scheduling conflict with other work? Or does he know something that maybe even Frankie doesn't know yet — the role is his.

But last night, the dude was threatened by me. He made damn sure I knew she was with him. So, maybe, just maybe, he knows there's a chance he might not get what he wants. And in this case, I think his aspirations are two-fold; he wants the role and he wants Frankie in his bed. She is like a ray of sunshine out in this filler-injected, soulless, smog-encased gutter. The new girl in town. The one who reminds us all of who we used to be before we were engulfed in this jaundiced vision of success. She is who we wanted to be, before we all lost our way.

And the fucked-up part is — I think I want the exact same things he does. I already know I want the role. Tonight, she'll be in my bed, but the joke's on me, she'll be drugged and passed out, and I'll be tossing and turning on the pullout couch thinking about slowly taking that red lace thing off her hot, little body.

As I grab the worn, leather-bound notebook with her initials embossed in the lower right corner, it splays open to the page where the ribbon bookmark is placed. Stapled to the page is the headshot of a dark-haired actor I've seen before, but he's not someone I know personally. I'm pretty sure he's done cop roles, playing the tough guy. The rest of the page is filled in with handwritten notes, clearly scrawled quickly as she was watching his performance. On the page facing that, are neatly written notes that she must have added afterwards.

Scott Burke
Wow! Unexpected. Seriously powerful. I would never have thought of him for GC's role, but he is so believable and commanding.
I want to see more.
Physically can he pull off hero? He's not the "look" readers are expecting for GC. That's going to be a hurdle. But I think after 30 minutes he'll win them over – if they give him a chance. Glad I gave him the chance.
Definitely want to see him read again!!! Boy, was he good. Nice surprise and goes to show you, don't judge a book by its cover.

Three pages later, there I am, my page, with my headshot stapled to the upper right corner, with nearly illegible notes under it. Again, on the facing page are clear notes, neatly laid out.

Finn Parker
Yes! He can act. Yes!
Physically this is GC. But does he possess the essence of GC? The soul? Not sure. He'd be an easy sell to the readers because he's probably pretty close to what is in their heads –very close to what was in my head!
Does he have the heart to be Griffin? A good actor can pull anything off, but will he be believable? Not sure.
Definite for a read again. I'd like to see more, see how far his range expands. I like this guy.

Do I have a heart or a soul she wants to know? Good question, Frankie. Good question.

Leafing through a few other pages, most say things like Not a top contender, He didn't make me believe, Pass. Might be worth another look.

I know I shouldn't be doing this. She's trusted me to come into her hotel room and gather her stuff, and here I am violating her privacy, not to mention having thoughts about violating her.

Shit. I should stop this. But I just have to see if he's got a page.

Maverick Dailey

The page is blank. No picture attached. No handwritten notes. I'm not sure if that's a good thing or a bad thing. Or if it is a thing at all.

Placing the leather notebook into the Costco bag, I turn off the lights and leave Frankie's hotel suite. I feel like I have violated this poor woman in every way possible today.

And now I'm taking her back to my apartment.

"Tell me about you," she asks, and I can't help but feel she wants me talking to keep her mind off the pain. I can see in her eyes how uncomfortable her leg is even with the front seat pushed back all the way.

"Umm, let's see." *What's there to tell?* I'm a loser. A few years ago, it felt like I had it all, and now I'm questioning every life decision I've ever made and feeling like each and every one was a fool's folly. And I'm the fool. *I am the fool.* "Well, I'm originally from Vegas."

"Yeah, I know that." Her smile is a bit loopy, and I assume that is from the drugs.

"How do you know that?" We're at a red light and I turn to look at her, surprised by her admission.

"I've totally stalked you online," she admits, grinning. Then adds, "I shouldn't have told you that."

She's clearly pretty high from the pain killers and probably the remnants of the anesthesia in her system. Oddly, I'm not weirded out. I just want to know more.

"What else did you discover about me?"

"Actually, not too much. Just the basic press release kind of stuff." Lying her head back on the padded, cream-colored headrest, I can see the smile playing at the corners of her mouth, teasing, and then receding. "And I noticed you have a type."

"A type?" I choke on my own saliva and begin to cough. "What type is that?"

"Eva," her voice is soft. "Eva is your type."

"Ah, you mean brunettes," I clarify. She really did check me out online.

Nodding, she then asks, "Has that always been your type?"

"Since my first girlfriend." It's impossible not to smile at the memory, a wave of that feeling of untethered possibility momentarily washes over me as I steer onto the 405's on-ramp.

"Was that in Vegas?"

I nod, as we merge into traffic and veer over a few lanes. Out of the corner of my eye, I watch Frankie's face. She appears to be gathering the pieces as if putting together a puzzle. Lucky for her, I'm one with only a few large pieces and a simple image and not an intricate one with a thousand tiny pieces and an abstract design.

"What happened to her?" The line of questioning continues.

"The captain of the football team." I laugh, then add, "Who wasn't me...I ran track."

"Where is she now?"

"Still in Vegas. Still married to him. Two kids and he's a drunk."

"She picked the wrong guy." Frankie is quick to respond.

I can't help but notice the irony of that statement. *Will you pick the wrong guy, too, Frankie? Will you pick the wrong guy, too?*

"So, you and Eva?"

"What about me and Eva?" My tone is too sharp, and I immediately regret it. Reaching out, I find her hand in her lap, giving it a squeeze. "It's been over for more than two years. It ended when my series got cancelled."

"Coincidence?" she asks.

It's hard not to chuckle at her naiveté at the inner-workings of LA. "No. Those aren't coincidences in this town," I explain, suddenly feeling more world-weary than usual.

"I'm sorry." She now is the one to give my hand a squeeze. It's reassuring.

"Don't be. Did she lead you to believe that we were still something?"

Frankie's response is a nod and I can feel my anger sparking.

WTF, Eva?

"Really, wow. What did she tell you?"

"Nothing bad. Just that you were exes with benefits." Adding quickly, "Which is cool."

"Why would she tell you that?" I don't like what Frankie is telling me, but I can't take my eyes off the stop-start traffic to look at her face. "I mean, what context did it come up in?"

"She asked me if Mav and I were an item."

Now I turn to look at her, momentarily taking my eyes off the bumper-to-bumper freeway to catch a quick glimpse of her expression. *Is she going to tell me what I don't want to know?* Immediately loosening my grip on her hand without even thinking, I'm shocked when her grip tightens in response. She's not going to let that connection sever. *Is that the answer?*

"I told her no and that's when she told me that."

"But why?"

"She said she saw a look pass between us, a look that she knew well, and umm," pausing, I can see from the corner of my eye that she is nervously licking her lips, "that I wasn't your type, except for the fact that I'm an A-Lister and that you like to attach yourself to A-Listers."

Feeling Frankie's grip slacken, I tighten my hand around hers. Too angry to speak, all I can do is vigorously shake my head as we ride along in silence.

"She was leading you to believe we were something and making a play for Maverick Dailey. That is just classic and shows me that not having her in my life is no loss. No loss at all."

Driving along, the silence is excruciating. I can feel her million-and-one questions hanging in the air, questions she feels she has no place asking.

"There are no benefits," I finally offer. "I mean, the only benefit is an attractive plus one. I know that must sound really shallow to you." Staring straight ahead, I know I can't look at her. "And as far as the

A-Lister thing, I don't even know how to respond to that, Frankie. I really don't. I have enjoyed every conversation we've had, every email we've exchanged. Reading for this part is yeah, something I take very seriously, and having access to your insights has made the process very different for me, and I'll admit, exciting. I get to really internalize your vision and hopefully make this character very three-dimensional and alive. I don't think I've ever gone into the auditioning process feeling so connected to a character, understanding him so deeply." I stop talking when she doesn't respond, wondering if I'm just making myself sound less sincere. *Fucking Eva.* She's jealous of Frankie. That's what this is all about. That, and she thinks Maverick is getting Griffin's part, and wants him to advocate for her to get to at least read for Gabriela.

Still no response from Frankie. *Fuck you, Eva, for putting that A-Lister shit in her head.*

Gazing to my right, I find myself smiling. Well, I was dead wrong.

She didn't respond not because of what I said. Her silence is because it has all caught up with her and she is fast asleep. Finally.

Leaving her asleep in my bed, I quickly pick up the empty water bottles and food wrappers off my coffee table. Luckily, she was totally passed out when I carried her in. Regrettably, I didn't get a chance to change my sheets, which is most unfortunate for her.

Moving onto the kitchen, I place all the dishes in the sink into the dishwasher and wipe down the counters. It's been a while since anyone else has been in my apartment, and now I'm looking at it with the eyes of a guest, and it could look a whole lot better than this.

The refrigerator looks anemic. *What did she eat when we were together?* Tacos and a cookie. *What did she drink?* Iced Americano with milk. There is nothing in my fridge that resembles any of those things. I know she's not going to eat these avocados, and I'm thinking protein powder might not be her jam. Immediately, I start making a list in my head, eggs, tortillas, milk, maybe some stuff if her stomach hurts from the painkillers. And cookies. I need to get her cookies.

Grabbing the Costco bag, I dig through, momentarily distracted by the red lace bodysuit. Pulling it from the bag, it ends up in my face.

Imagine that. I don't know what I'm hoping to smell on it, perfume maybe, but I don't pick up any scent at all. No trace of Frankie, so I decide it's never been worn. For some reason, I like that. No one has seen her tight little ass in this hot number.

Reaching back into the bag, I root around until I find her little friend and her phone, leaving her buddy on the pillow next to her and her phone on the nightstand with a note.

Frankie – Just ran out to the store to pick up some stuff for us. I'll be back in a few. If you wake up and need anything, call me at (323) 555-1525. Finn

Frankie

The little rubber duckie with the blue surfboard is next to me on my pillow when I open my eyes, but I can't put it all together. This is not my suite at the Casa del Mar. I'm in a very non-descript place and I'm confused.

But the bathtub duck is here?

On the nightstand I see my phone and there's a note from Finn. I'm at Finn's, and the moment I go to move my leg, I am met by searing pain and the weight of the cast. I remember everything. Or at least, I think it's everything.

Pulling the smooth, white comforter toward my face, I can smell his scent on the blanket, and I snuggle deeper into it. Bringing a pillow to my nose, I breathe in deeply, again catching his scent. It's a less sweaty version of what filled my nose when he carried me off the beach. It seems like a zillion hours ago that happened. But it was today. Earlier today. Another lifetime ago.

The sun has maybe another twenty minutes before the ocean gobbles it whole. It's hard to believe it's still light out. This has been one long-ass day. Picking up Finn's note, I read it again, hoping he brings home food. My stomach has that feeling where it's hard to figure out if it hurts because I'm hungry or because all the pain meds have raunched it out. And I'm not sure which one it actually is. Across from the bed is a TV, and through an open door I can see the bathroom. I really need to go, but I'm not sure if I can walk there.

How long could Finn possibly take?

There's not much else in the room. No art on the walls. Nothing on the dresser top or nightstand, except lamps and what he left for me. Hotel rooms have more decoration than this place. There's literally nothing personal in the entire space. I'm in the Kansas portion of the *Wizard of Oz.*

It kind of fits. I remember feeling I didn't know him any better after having breakfast with him. There was something very elusive about him, and now his apartment is giving me the same impression.

A blank impression.

There is nothing personal in here. Monks have more belongings than this.

I've been in this man's arms and he still feels like a total enigma to me, so it's not that odd that his living space is also devoid of clues. White comforter and latte-colored sheets and pillowcases. My bright yellow and blue duckie is the only splash of color in the room.

As someone who paints my surroundings with words, Finn Parker is leaving me with a blank page, and as a writer, I detest blank pages. They freak me out.

He is certainly a handsome man, but is there more than that? He has been pleasant and kind. And I've felt comfortable with him. But is that only because he looks like my vision of Griffin? Am I giving this stranger too much credit?

And I'm in his bed, alone in his apartment, a space that boldly flashes vacancy, and I wonder if that is what is going on beyond those hypnotic, sky-blue eyes of his.

Picking up my phone, I punch in the number he left on the note and send a text.

Frankie: Bring ice cream.

It only takes a moment before my phone dings with his response.

Finn: Already did that. On my way back. C U in a few.

Within minutes, I hear the door open, followed by the sound of bags rustling, in what I'm assuming is the kitchen. Sitting up, I want to get out of the bed. His bed. I don't want to be lying down in it when he walks in. Scooching my butt along the sheets, I get to the edge and attempt to swing my legs over to the floor. Unaccustomed to the new spatial orientation of being in a cast, I ram my plaster prison into my uncasted right ankle.

"Ow," I moan.

"You okay?" Finn rushes to the bedroom door. "Hey, what are you doing getting out of bed?"

"I..." And I point to the bathroom.

"Where are your...? Oh crap, I left your crutches in the trunk of the car." He points to the door, as if asking if he should go now.

Shaking my head, I point to the bathroom, and try not to laugh at the look on his face. "If you could just help me across the room."

With his arm around me, I lean into him and hop.

"I'll go get them," he stutters, depositing me in the bathroom and closing the door.

I'm surprised by the first burst of color I see in Finn's oddly monochromatic world. Immediately catching my eye is his shower curtain sporting a bright array of thick paintbrush strokes in primary colors. The bold lines raise my spirits. I've just entered the technicolor portion of this movie. The bathroom is Oz!

"Let me know if you need help," he calls into me a few minutes later. "Your crutches are right outside the door."

"Okay, thanks." Taking a few deep breaths as I wash my hands, I prod myself to calm my little ass down. This man gets me nervous. I feel slightly intimidated by him and I'm not sure why. He's a big guy, over six feet and clearly a gym rat, but usually size doesn't intimidate me. It's his looks. The pale eyes and thick head of wavy, dirty blond hair, and that asymmetrical smile. It kills me. No one should look that good and I should be able to respond to it better. But damn, I could easily and happily fall prey, which would be a huge mistake, especially before the Griffin role has been cast.

Inspecting my face in the soft bathroom light, I can see that my nose looks a little wide at the bridge and there's faint purple under my eyes. It's not dark circles from exhaustion. I'm bruised, and in a day or two, I'm going to look really bad.

In the small kitchen, I find him putting food into the refrigerator and cabinets.

"Hey, what can I get you to drink?" he asks over his shoulder as I sit at the table with my leg straight out, shifting around to try and find a comfortable spot. "Let me get you a pillow and we'll pull a chair over to put your leg up." It only takes a few seconds for him to return with a tan suede throw pillow from his couch to prop my leg up on a chair.

Handing me a cold bottle of water, he moves away from the table back to the counter. *Great, now I get to obsess over his back and shoulders and his truly fine butt.*

"Do you like bread?" he asks.

I nod, now talking to his back. "I'm totally a bread person."

"Good. I stopped at Lodge Bread and picked up a few loaves. Have you had it?"

"I don't think so."

Turning from the counter, where his body is blocking what he is doing, he gives me a smile that says he's got quite the surprise in store for me, before turning back to what he was doing. "I've been thinking," he begins, still turned away from me. "You could probably use one of those scooter things that you rest your leg on to move about. I bet it will be much more comfortable than crutches." Turning back to the table, he's carrying a big, wooden cutting board with a boule of crusty bread, several hunks of cheese, a tub of Irish butter, and an avocado.

Placing it on the table, he turns away again, this time back to the cupboards for dishes and silverware. Watching him move is interesting. The man owns his space. He fills it well and that is how I imagined Griffin in his world, a presence, even when performing the most mundane of tasks.

"Where would I even buy one of those things?" I know the scooter thing he's talking about. A friend cruised around on one after painful bunion surgery.

"I think we can get it online."

His use of the word *we* sticks out to me, although it doesn't seem to faze him at all. He's still moving around. Now looking through the cabinets for something else.

"Frankie, do you need anything? Are you in pain? Do you need meds?" He shoots out the questions in rapid succession.

"I need you to sit down so that I can eat. My stomach hurts and I'm not sure if it's from the meds on an empty stomach or if I'm hungry. Either way, I need to eat. Sit," I order him.

My command elicits a sexy smile, and I get the feeling he likes it when I'm a bit lippy with him.

"Start eating, please." Finally sitting down, he cuts a few pieces of bread, handing them to me on a plate. Help yourself."

Immediately, I go for the butter. The bread is tough-crusted, crispy, with a porous interior that smells heavenly. "Bread is like porn for me," I admit, slathering a slice with the butter.

"Here." He hands me a little dish with coarse pink salt.

"I like a man who knows how to eat bread." He has really thought of everything.

"Wait until you taste this." He sits back, clearly planning on enjoying my reaction to the first bite.

I don't disappoint. This bread is delicious, and I am starving. I forget he's in the room as I focus my attention on this simple piece of buttered bread.

"Hey, you forgot something." Smiling, he rolls the avocado over to me.

"Where's your garbage?" I kid, before rolling the offensive fruit back to him. "This is really delicious, Finn." Bread nirvana.

"Yeah, I'm a great host, feeding my injured houseguest bread and water." He cuts a piece of cheese and puts it on my plate before slicing one for himself. Pulling out his phone, he starts looking at something and then slides the cell over to me. "So, we can get this thing delivered tomorrow."

I look at the picture of a little red scooter. "I'll go online and order it in a little bit."

"Too late, just got it."

"Finn, I would have…"

He shakes his head. "Frankie, please, let me do this. I'm responsible."

"Did you send it to my hotel?"

"No, here. It'll be here tomorrow. It's going to need some assembly. It's the least I can do."

I'm feeling bad that he feels so responsible for what was an accident. "Finn," I begin my protest.

Shaking his head, a smile begins at the corners of his mouth, immediately teasing my heart. "Resistance is futile and will result in the force-feeding of avocado." He holds up the green grenade to make his point.

Reaching behind my back, I can't contain my own smile, "Just thinking my bra is the only thing I have to wave as a white flag."

"Feel free to remove it anytime, and if you need any help..."

"I still have two working arms."

"Guess I didn't do my job. If I'd taken out one of those, too, you'd need help with your bra." Looking down with a full-fledged smile, he slices another piece of bread. As he hands it to me, we lock eyes and he adds, "White, huh? I would've taken you more for a red girl."

What?

"Umm, I don't wear a whole lot of red."

"I was thinking more of a whole little red." He appears surprised by his own comment, his face reddening slightly.

"Can I ask you a question?" I desperately need to change the topic. Under different circumstances, I'd have given him a run for his money with the banter, but tonight, I need to move away, far away, from anything with sexual connotations. Surprisingly, I've just learned, Finn and I can escalate at warp speed. I'm surprised, but I'm not surprised.

"Ask away." He looks up from the offensive avocado that he's busied himself cutting open after his face-reddening comment.

"How long have you been living here? In this apartment?"

"A little over six years."

"So, why is there nothing of you here? There's no art on the walls, no pictures anywhere."

Putting down the knife and avocado, he sits back in his chair, and holds my gaze. I'm surprised to note his eyes narrow slightly. It's almost imperceptible, but it's there. And in that moment, the energy shift is palpable, accentuated by the throb of that muscle above his jaw.

I feel my last bite of bread stick in my now-dry mouth, the crust scraping on its way down my constricted throat. I've clearly hit on something with him.

"I really hadn't noticed," his affect is flat.

Tilting my head to the side, I remain silent, my gaze holding his, daring him to let go, in more ways than one. Something in my gut tells me I'm either going to find out who Finn Parker is, right here and now, or if this moment passes without a reveal, I will never know...and it would be a waste of time to continue trying.

"I guess I haven't done it consciously. And oddly, no one has ever pointed it out to me before." His gaze softens. "You're very observant, Frankie. Which is, I guess, what makes you a great writer."

Reaching for my water bottle, I take a swig, partly to dislodge the bread stuck in my parched throat, but mostly as a prop to remain silent and to let him continue. I want him to continue. I don't know why, but I just need to know why I can't get a handle on this man. What, if anything, is below that beautiful surface? There has to be more. *There has to be.*

Or maybe not.

The expression on his face is dynamic, a panoply of emotion appearing as a struggle. "My mother was an art therapist. And an artist. A really talented one, actually. She filled our world with color and beautiful images. She dragged me and my brother and sister to art museums in every city we visited on family vacations." Letting out a nervous laugh, he takes a moment, then continues. "She hated wall space. I mean, really hated it. If there were a few empty inches anywhere, she found something wonderful to fill it. And she had a knack for finding just the right thing."

In my mind, I'm picturing the walls of his childhood home as a canvas, brightly colored with images to make the imagination soar.

"She was diagnosed with ovarian cancer when I was twelve, and gone before I turned sixteen." The emotion I see on his face now colors his tone.

My water bottle slides from my hand, luckily landing upright on the table. "I'm so sorry, Finn."

Silently, he nods and begins to smear a thick chunk of avocado onto his bread. I restrain myself from making any stupid avocado toast comments.

"My dad's a drunk. I haven't talked to him in about eight years. He never *got* my acting thing and we just never saw eye to eye. On anything. Leaving Las Vegas was more of an escape than anything else."

"I'm sorry," I repeat. "I'm sure it was very difficult for him, for all of you. Grieving and still having to raise children has got to be rough."

His eyes once again lock with mine. "He didn't raise us. He spent more time in local bars than he did with his own kids."

"I didn't mean to imply that it was rougher on him than it was on you. I can't even imagine what you went through." I again find myself apologizing. "So, is the lack of art because it reminds you too much of your mom?" I'm trying hard to understand why he's purposely stripped from his life something that obviously brought him joy.

"I don't know." He appears lost as he shakes his head. "Honestly, it never occurred to me until you just brought it up."

"It was the first thing I noticed when I woke up." My heart is starting to hurt. There was a reason I could not get a handle on Finn Parker. All that glitters is not gold, and in this beautiful golden boy's private space, there is little that appears to shine.

"So, that's my story. The stuff that doesn't appear on Wikipedia or IMDB."

"Do women try to fix you?" I ask. It's a personal question and it's out of my mouth before I can reel it back in.

This elicits a hearty laugh. "I'm that broken, huh?"

I just nod, smiling slightly.

"I think more in the past than now. Women out here aren't generally interested in anything that doesn't further their careers." He takes a swig of water, washing down his last bite of avocado toast. "Case in point, Eva last night. She was all over Maverick Dailey like a fly on shit. I ended up leaving her there last night."

I feel like it's important to him to make sure I know that he left without her.

"Do you think she hooked up with Mav?"

"If she got what she wanted."

"He's actually a nice man," I add, offering my opinion. Meeting Jua, and knowing what he has done to nurse her back to health told me a lot about him, about his spirit.

"I'm sure he is, *Francesca*," baits Finn, making no attempt to hide his snark.

"You don't like him, do you? Is it because of Eva?" Maybe he's jealous and wants his ex- back. Men always want you when another man shows interest.

"Eva? No." He appears to find that amusing.

"Have you had bad experiences with him in the past?" There must be some reason why he doesn't like the guy. Everyone loves Maverick Dailey. He's one star who has never had the reputation of being an asshole.

"No, actually, last night was the first time I've ever met him."

"I'm an outsider, so I just kind of assumed everybody knows everybody else in this town."

Shaking his head at my comment, he doesn't volunteer a reason for disliking Mav.

"So, why don't you like him?" I press, as I cut a piece of cheese.

"Why don't I like him?" He repeats my question. He pauses before adding, "You. I don't like him because of you." Sitting back, he crosses his arms defensively, still holding a water bottle in one hand.

"Because of me?" Like him, I am now repeating the question. "Because he's interested in the role, right?" They're going for the same job, that makes sense.

He takes a swig from his bottle, not answering me. I'm sure that's his reason, although a part of me wants it to be more than that.

"And there's something between the two of you."

I'm actually surprised when I hear those words coming from him. Trying not to get ahead of myself, I need to know exactly what he means. And I need to tamper any momentary excitement sparked by his last statement.

This time I remain silent, pushing for an elaboration from him, and he doesn't disappoint.

"I don't like seeing you with him, okay," he confesses. His eyes are pinning me to my chair.

"Okay," I respond, looking back to the cheeseboard and cutting another slice from a block of smoky cheddar.

"Just okay? Nothing else?" Now it's Finn who is pressing the point.

I measure my words carefully. "I think this is kind of a confused situation for both of us, and I don't think either of us is doing a very good job at separating *Fleeing an August Moon* from other dynamics happening between us." The moment those words are out of my mouth, I begin to count. *One beat. Please let him not have to correct me and tell me nothing is going on. Two beats. Did I just make a huge, desperate fool of myself with a really handsome man? Three beats. I'm going to be sick.*

A small, closed-mouth smile curves the corners of his lips. "It's pretty dynamic alright."

Understatement.

"Yeah. It is."

He's having a hard time repressing a smile. "I really like you, Frankie."

"I like you, too, Finn."

"But?"

"You know the but. This is a funky situation. I have a decision to make that will impact your life. And mine, too. This would be easy to get mixed up."

"And?"

I shrug and shake my head. "And what?" I'm not sure where he's going with this.

"And are you questioning my intentions?"

"I don't want to," I admit. "But probably on some level I do. If I'm being totally honest with you, I have to also question my own." How do I tell him that I fear mixing him up emotionally with Griffin? That sounds positively insane. *Do I like you, the man, or is it just because I'm attracted to you because you look like my character?* That is crazy. Batshit, crazy. And I'm just imagining confessing that and him thinking I'm some kind of loser lunatic.

And maybe I am.

"And this is exactly why I like you, Frankie. I can't imagine any woman I've met in the last eight years being this honest with me. I agree, this is a, what did you call it, funky situation. Yes, I want to be Griffin Chase. I don't think I've ever hidden that from you. But I really like you, I like the time we've spent together. Our conversations and emails have been fun. I really enjoy being with you."

"Even though I'm not your type." I raise my eyebrows trying to lighten the moment.

"Beachy blonde waves can definitely become my type." Tilting his head, he regards me. "Last night, you saw me, and your response was so real, it was from your gut. And what I felt at that moment, when you wrapped your arms around me, was very real, too. It was like I'd been looking for someone in the crowd whom I didn't even know I was searching for, until you were in my arms. And I hated Eva and Dailey for stealing that feeling away. I was a miserable fuck the rest of the night."

I hated them, too. I hated them, too.

"Look, Frankie, I've been in this town long enough to know how things go down. They are all playing nice with you now, because ultimately you do have control, but get ready for the pressure. Everyone with a financial stake in the film wants Maverick Dailey in that role. He is box-office gold and as much as we might like to think this is about art and entertainment, it's about business and money. By the time they are done with you, he's going to be your only choice."

"What do you mean *done with me*?" All of a sudden, I am feeling quite naïve and also trying to keep a filter in place for Finn's agenda. He's got an agenda here and we both know that.

"There will be people who put subtle pressure on you and others who will do it more directly. They will all make their case and they will all *steer* you toward Dailey. By the time you make your decision..." He stops short.

"You think the decision will no longer be mine."

"No. It will be yours."

"Or I'll think it's mine."

He nods. "Or you'll think it's yours."

"I don't want to mess with you, Finn."

"And I don't want to mess with you, Frankie. That's not why I'm telling you this. I want you to understand how this town works. Protect yourself, okay, because I have the feeling some of this might eat up your insides. And I don't want that to happen. And I certainly don't want to add to it."

"Maybe I should go back to my hotel."

He shakes his head and I can see from the look on his face that he's having none of that. "No. But maybe you should get some sleep. You've had a hell of a day and there's all kinds of anesthesia still in your system. Let's get you to bed."

Using the table as leverage, I'm able to hoist myself into a standing position.

"Okay, Hopalong, lean on me."

"I've been doing a lot of that today." My arm goes around his waist.

The minute I'm back in his bed, I feel the exhaustion slam me.

He turns on the TV. "*House Hunters International.* Do you like this show?"

Nodding, I smile at him. "I do. It's one of my favorites. Can I ask you for one more favor?"

"Anything." He's standing next to the bed, looking unsure as to what to do in his own bedroom.

"Can you get me ice cream?"

"Yeah, sure." Looking relieved, his grin becomes positively dangerous and I'm still smiling from the sight of it when he leaves the room.

Returning with a pint and a spoon, he sits down on the edge of the bed. Digging the spoon into pale yellow ice cream, he brings it to my lips, surprising me by feeding me. I'm not sure if this is hot or just plain weird.

"Tell me what you think of this."

Sliding the ice cream off the spoon with my lips and tongue, I let it start to melt in my mouth. Mmm, lemon. The texture is incredibly creamy, and the taste heightened and fresh. My thought is that this is probably from some local small-batch creamery. The initial sweetness finishes with a pleasantly tart flavor toward the back of my tongue.

"Mmm, lemon. One of my favorite flavors."

"I thought you might be a lemon fan." He brings another spoonful to my lips, teasing me with just the tip of the spoon. "So, what do you think?"

"I think I want more." I open my mouth awaiting the loaded spoon.

"What do you think?" he asks again, still holding back. "You like it?"

"Yeah, it's really yummy, very creamy, nice rich texture."

He moves the spoon away and deposits the ice cream in his own mouth. "You're right. It is good." There is a look of joy on his face. "Want more?" He's giving me a playful look, his eyes locked on mine.

"I do." *As in, much, much more.*

Digging out another spoonful, he brings it to my lips.

"I know I have a broken ankle but I'm fully capable of feeding myself." I reach to take the spoon from him and his hand jerks, depositing ice cream all over my lips.

Leaning forward, he catches me by surprise as he licks the ice cream from my lips and the corner of my mouth with a slow swipe of his tongue. "It tastes even better on you and you're not even toast."

I don't know if I'm more shocked that my Griffin Chase look-a-like just licked me, or that when he licked me, he made a weird toast comment that I'm totally not comprehending.

"You licked me." I think my mouth is hanging open, which is probably not a good look.

"I did." His smile tells me he's not sorry.

But that other thing. It's crowding my mind and jettisoning the little focus I have left after this crazy day. "You eat ice cream on toast?" Maybe he didn't say that. Could it be all the drugs in my system just catching up with me? Yeah, it could.

"No. But I do eat avocado on toast, as you have witnessed firsthand." Slowly, he turns the ice cream container toward me, showing me the name and brand.

Lemon flavored avocado ice cream. What? Avocado ice cream? Who even knew there was such a thing? In my world, there's Blue Bell Ice Cream, made just up the road a piece from Houston. They have cows on their containers, not ugly, bumpy green fruit.

Finn is now sporting a shit-eating grin as he takes in my reaction. The son of a bitch just fed me avocado and licked it off me.

Avo-freaking-cado ice cream? Where the hell am I? Briefly, I wonder if I'm hallucinating as I stare into a set of very amused pale blue eyes that make me want his tongue on me again. Shit, this guy is handsome. I need to be careful. I really do or I'm going to find myself in that position we talked about earlier. But he licked me...

"You tricked me."

"You liked it. Admit it, you liked it."

"That imposter ice cream or being licked?"

"Both."

Opening my mouth to deny all claims, Finn ensures I don't have the opportunity as he leans in, this time with a kiss, soft at first until his hand cradles my neck, pulling me into him. He ends the kiss by swiping his tongue along my lips again and then sitting back with a smile, leaving me both breathless and speechless.

"There. All the offensive avocado ice cream has been expertly removed." He appears very amused with himself.

"You broke my leg and kissed me. All in one day."

"I licked you, too."

"Yes, you did. You licked me." And I want more. More ice cream and more Finn, not necessarily in that order, but it doesn't deter me from reaching for the spoon standing erect in the container. Scooping up a spoonful of the pale yellow whatever-the-hell it is and slowly bringing it to my mouth, I savor a portion of the frozen treat, leaving half of it on the spoon. Taking my hand by the wrist, Finn maneuvers the spoon back to his mouth and I jerk my hand just as it reaches his lips, ensuring his lips are now covered in it.

As he releases my wrist, this time it's me reaching out, my hand sliding behind his neck and pulling him to me. Slowly, I swipe my tongue across his full bottom lip before softly pressing my lips to his and opening my mouth slightly, an invitation that even I'm surprised to be extending.

He tastes like the surprisingly delicious lemon avocado ice cream.

Putting his forehead against mine after breaking our kiss, his voice sounds thick, "I think it's best I head out to the couch now."

"I feel bad that you are sleeping on the couch."

"Well, I feel bad that I broke your leg," standing, he reaches down to cup my cheek, "but I think we'll both survive."

Crooking him with my finger until he is inches away, I can't help but smile at him. "You didn't say goodnight."

Placing his lips on my forehead, he kisses me softly and then picks up the duck on the nightstand. "Take care of our girl," he instructs my little surfer friend before leaving the room.

Finn's bedroom is bright when I open my eyes, although there is no direct sunlight coming through the window. I need to pee badly, and it's not until I attempt to get out of bed that I realize two things: my leg is in a cast and I hurt all over.

Propped against the nightstand are my crutches. Finn must've brought them in while I was sleeping, which means he is already awake. Placed under the duck, is a note.

Good Morning.
I didn't want to wake you. I'm leaving for the gym and then I'll stop off to pick up some breakfast tacos for us. There's juice in the fridge and hot coffee. Help yourself to whatever looks good. Call me if you need anything. – PJ

PJ.

Parker Jameson.

One kiss and his customary Finn signature has disappeared.

Maybe this is why, until yesterday, I felt that I couldn't get a good sense of who he was. Yesterday, he shared some very personal things with me, and it wasn't only about his history. It was his actions, they were caring and protective. If that's not Griffin Chase, I don't know what is.

And today, he's ready to introduce me to PJ.

Hobbling out of bed, I cross to his dresser where the Costco bag with my stuff is sitting. Rifling through the bag for clean clothes it occurs to me that this man has seen my underwear. *Ugh.* As I dig deeper into the bag, I feel the heat rise in my face.

My red lace teddy.

He found it.

And he brought it.

So that was where his 'whole little red' comment came from. It now made sense. That stinker!

Maybe it was time to color PJ's world.

Finn

Shifting packages from my right hand to my left to unlock the door, I can hear the soft twangs of country music from inside my apartment. That's certainly a first. Frankie's sitting at the kitchen table, laptop open, coffee mug nearby. I want to describe my feeling as happy when I see her, but it's more than that. I'm just not sure how to label it yet. Her smile is the perfect greeting and her beachy waves are pulled back.

"You're up." I join her at the table, depositing the bag with the tacos and grabbing us some plates and a mug of coffee for myself before I sit down.

Kiss her good morning? It's what I want to do, instead I do this weird pet of her hair and tug on her loose braid. "This is cute."

"Yeah, you like it?" she asks, with a smile looking up at me.

"A lot." I return her smile as I sit down and start pulling the tacos out of the bag. "What are you working on." I motion to her laptop.

"Just editing the last chapter I wrote. I didn't have your internet password, so I couldn't get online. Which was probably a good thing. Forced me to work."

"Is this your next book you're working on?"

"It is." Her eyes light up.

And why is it I was never attracted to blondes before?

"Is there a part in there for me?" I say, half-teasing, as I take a long swig of my coffee.

"There very well might be. It's kind of a big ensemble cast. Lots of characters."

"Oh, really, what's it about?"

"It's about the occupants of an apartment building and all of their stories and then an over-arching arc that ties them all together."

"That sounds interesting. Will it have the same kind of social relevancy as *Fleeing an August Moon?*"

"Yes, because there will be a lot of diversity in the characters, but the overall theme is that we have more in common than we have separating us, and that we're all in this together."

"So, it's not a romance this time?"

"Some of the story arcs are very romantic and look at love in different phases, from young love to seniors. From people who've been there for fifty years to newlyweds just moving in."

"Sounds like there will be more of a chance of a part for me." The minute it is out of my mouth, it sounds so desperate, even to me. I know I'm coming across as just working her for the Griff role. Attempting to change the subject, and not making the situation any better, out of my mouth rolls, "So, what inspired *Fleeing an August Moon?* When I first started reading it, I thought it was just your basic love story, but as I got into it and saw where you took it, the scope and the message were just so much wider than what I thought at the beginning of the book." I'm talking fast and I know it. Nervous. Trying to bury my comment from earlier. And I can't take my eyes off her lips. I want to taste them again.

"Living in south Texas, immigration is obviously a huge issue. And it's an emotional issue. People feel very strongly, and I've seen some families really destroyed, people's lives decimated, and so I thought if I could create two characters whom readers could relate to, bond with, and ultimately, fall in love with, that I'd be able to take the politics out of it, and humanize what goes on. We're all people and to not love someone or want to save someone because they came from across an imaginary line, is crazy to me. We're all just people and we're all in this together."

"So, there is a common thread running through both of your books," I comment. "We're all in this together." Although the theme is positive,

I'm still processing what she said about knowing people whose lives were destroyed. "Do you draw your writing mojo from a place of pain?"

"Sometimes, I guess. *Fleeing an August Moon* more so than my other books because it was inspired by something that happened to a friend."

"You're going to have black eyes," I change the subject. Her skin is a pale, translucent purple under her eyes.

"This guy told me if I don't give him the part, he'd beat me up." Her nose crinkles when she smiles at me. "That's what I'm going to tell them at the studio."

"We need a better cover story than that. One where I don't get blackballed all over town for beating up on everyone's favorite author," I pause. "She is an A-Lister, you know."

"A-Lister." She laughs. "That's really kind of funny, isn't it?"

"Eva was clearly very threatened by you." I wouldn't call Frankie naïve in any sense of the word, and I'm sure she can certainly hold her own, but Eva definitely plays dirtier than her.

"But why?"

"I think she was intimidated. And she had no idea that we knew one another."

"Really? You didn't tell her you'd auditioned?"

Shaking my head, I clarify, "It's kind of a bad luck superstition thing to tell anyone. So no, she didn't know."

She unsuccessfully tries to contain a small smile as she finishes her taco. Her silence makes me feel like I need to speak.

"And she clearly picked up that I wanted to kiss you." I surprise myself the moment it comes out of my mouth.

"You wanted to kiss me?" She chokes on a sip of coffee.

Reaching over, I pat her gently on the back as she continues to cough. "I looked for you at the after-party," I admit. What the heck, I've already licked ice cream off her, I might as well go all in.

"I looked for you, too." Looking down, she appears embarrassed to be sharing that with me.

Reaching behind her, I grab her braid, gently tugging on it, and pulling her toward me. "I would have slept better had I known that."

She looked for me. Fuck you, Maverick Dailey. You may be a superstar, but the girl was thinking about me. Sliding my fingers up her braid, until my hand cradles the back of her head, I let my thumb glide along her jaw. "Now, if only you'd found me, we probably could have avoided the broken ankle and black eyes."

"This makes a better story."

"We have a story. I like that." My lips are on hers possessively with senses initially focusing on their softness, followed by the pleasant taste of coffee and toothpaste.

"Yeah, well, I like this." She leans in for another kiss.

"Chapter one," I whisper, impatient for our lips to meet again.

"Shit, you'd think they'd have better directions than this." I sit on the floor with pliers and screwdrivers of all sizes assembling Frankie's little scooter.

"I can't believe they call this partially assembled." She's been reading the instructions to me.

"Partially assembled, my ass," I grumble, definitely not looking like a cool Mr. Handy.

Her laugh comes out almost like a giggle, tearing my eyes away from my task to look up at her on the couch, knowing I'll catch her smile.

"What's that look you're giving me?" She wants to know.

"It's the I-like-having-you-here look. You are a very positive energy, Frankie Simonelli," I tell her as I tighten the last piece, feeling very confident about my mechanical prowess and not looking like a total loser. Perfect time to shift the conversation. "You ready for a test drive?"

She nods and I stand to help her off the couch and over to the scooter, supporting her as she gets her leg situated, before taking off across the living room.

"This is pretty easy and I love the backpack up front."

"You can throw your purse and laptop in there."

Cocking her head to the side, she asks, "Are you sure I can't reimburse you for this?"

"Absolutely not." I shake my head and take a seat on the couch. "I broke your damn ankle."

"Then, will you at least let me buy you dinner." She scoots back over to the couch and sits down next to me.

"Are you asking me out on a date?"

"I guess." Her cheeks blush almost immediately as she says it. This woman writes damn hot, graphic sex scenes and she's blushing asking me out to dinner.

Shaking my head, I offer, "No."

"No, what?"

"No, you can't buy me dinner."

"You don't want to go out on a date with me?" She is clearly surprised.

"I didn't say that." I'm just fucking with her now.

"I'm confused."

"No, you can't buy me dinner."

"Why not?"

"Because if we're going on a date, I'm going to be buying you dinner."

"That works, too." She smiles. "Even though I'd like to repay you for this contraption."

"Just heal well so that you can get back to running. That's the only thing I want from you."

"That's the only thing you want from me?" She laughs.

"Yeah, well, maybe not the only. But it's up there."

"Top three?" she asks.

"Solidly." *Yeah, a movie part and wanting to nail you most definitely beat out your ankle healing.*

"Well, I appreciate that." She clearly knows what numbers one and two are. "Will you be able to take me back to my hotel tomorrow? I told the studio I'd be back to work on Thursday."

"Sure. Will you need a ride to the studio? I can pick you up."

"Thank you, but the studio is sending a car for me. They've rescheduled a bunch of stuff around me, and my agent is coming to town next week. I know there's going to be a big powwow with investors." She rolls her eyes, then jumps a little when her phone on the coffee table buzzes with a message. Picking up the phone she smiles at a picture of what looks from my angle like a horse. "Jua," she exclaims, tapping the picture and starting the video.

And there is the unmistakable voice of Maverick Daily. *Fucking awesome.*

Francesca, our friend wanted to send a get-well message... She taps her phone screen again and stops the video.

"You can watch it. It's not going to hurt my feelings. Unless, you want to watch it privately."

"No. No," she protests. "It's not anything like that. This horse is a rescue, she was injured in one of the fires. She's rehabbing now and Mav adopted her."

"Wow. That's really nice of him." *What can I say bad about this guy, that's a really awesome thing to do.*

Frankie laughs. "This is funny, she is a possessive little thing. She gave me the stink-eye and wanted to make sure Mav's attention was all on her."

"Are you talking about this horse or Eva?" I kid.

Slapping me playfully on the arm, she sputters while laughing, "The horse," and then stops to think for a second. "But it could be Eva."

"So, you've met this horse?"

"Yes." She nods.

"Finish watching the tape."

She's met his horse. Okay, but she kissed me and told me she doesn't care if he went home with Eva. *But his horse? The man is slick, I'll give him that.*

Looking back down at her phone, she restarts the video.

...To cheer you up. Tell her what you told me you were going to say.

The horse lets out three loud whinnies as if she's saying something.

She knows what it's like to be hurting and wants you to be walking again soon. I'll call you. Say bye, Jua.

And the freaking trick horse lets out another loud whinny.

Smiling at her phone as the video ends, I can see that made her feel good, so there's no way to dog the guy for going out of his way to make Frankie smile.

It's been three days since she's been gone, and it feels like triple that amount of time. Three freaking days and I can't get her out of my head. Coming back here after dropping her at the hotel, I found the little gift she'd left for me as soon as I walked into my bedroom. Thumbtacked to the wall, right next to the TV was that red lace number. No way I could miss that.

And yeah, I'd love to nail you in that against the wall was absolutely my first thought.

Pulling out my phone, I shoot her off a text.

Finn: Thanks for the present.

It was only about five minutes later, but it felt a whole lot longer, when I got her response.

Frankie: You need color in there.

Finn: Well, this is a very respectable first piece of art.

Frankie: Respectable? Hmm, I might pick a different adjective. ;-)

Finn: Question for you…

Frankie: Ask at your own risk.

Finn: Have you worn this "art"?

Frankie: Not yet.

I went directly from that text into the shower.

And now three days later, I've had enough of not seeing that sweet smile and only exchanging texts and emails. With three warm cowboy cookies and a small bottle of cold milk on the passenger seat, I'm ready to surprise her at the hotel. In the pocket of my leather jacket, the red lace bodysuit is folded up. Surprise number two.

I've missed her laugh and her energy in my apartment. Which is actually the strangest thing of all, having her blend so seamlessly into the flow, and me not wanting my own space. Just the opposite, I wanted to be wherever she was. Even if it was in my own bed on top of the blankets reading, while she lay sleeping under the covers on the other side. I didn't touch her, and yet, it may have been one of the most intimate moments I've ever spent with a woman.

But that wasn't the only thing that surprised me. Helping her and taking care of her was not just a guilt thing. I *wanted* to help her. I took over and she let me, and it just worked for us. And now driving to the Casa del Mar, I'm excited to see her, to surprise her, hear her voice, and kiss her again.

The kissing. Holy crap, who'd ever believe that? I can't remember the last time I just kissed a woman and didn't have sex with her. High school? Middle school? One long-ass time ago. It was freaking hot. I have not felt this wanting probably ever in my adult life.

And that has made these last three days hell.

Strolling through the hotel's grand lobby, I know I've got a goofy smile on my face as I walk past the people milling about on a busy Saturday evening. As I pile into a crowded elevator, a grandmotherly woman comments, "Something sure smells good," and I hold up the paper bag, revealing I am the culprit.

It's been three days since I've walked down this hallway, last time using her keycard to let the two of us into her suite. Knocking on her door, I'm wondering if she can already smell these cookies on the other side. The warm, dark chocolate is killing me. I want to taste it almost as much as I want to taste Frankie's mouth and lick the molten chocolate from her lips. It won't be the first time I've licked her. I find myself chuckling out loud.

Hearing movement inside, I feel my anticipation spike as she makes her way to the door. I know it will be slow, either with the scooter or her crutches. It is going to take a moment for her to get to the door. I can't help but smile picturing her as she approaches. That is, until the door opens, and I'm face to face with, you guessed it, Maverick freaking Dailey.

"Hi. I remember you." He gives me the movie-star smile and I can tell he's wondering what the fuck I'm doing there.

"Yeah, good to see you." My tone is a little more dismissive than I intended as I walk past him and head toward Frankie on the couch.

"Finn." She's smiling, but she's got this *oh shit* look on her face.

"Warm cowboy cookies and cold milk." I hand her the bag with a smile, grasping her gaze and holding it tight. *Shit, Frankie, I hadn't even considered this as a possibility when I got in my car to come surprise you.* "Hey, I don't want to intrude. Just wanted to drop off your favorite cookies."

Yeah, I said favorite cookies, you douche. I know what her favorite cookies are. Do you? Doubtful, asshat superstar.

Sticking my hands into my jacket pockets, my right hand immediately touches the lace bodysuit, which I had forgotten was in there the moment I walked into this shitshow. Now I ball the garment into my tightening fist. Two ways to play this scene with this little lace number. One is for him. The other for her. Easy choice. The dude doesn't get to steal our moment — unless I let him. And I'm not. This is going to be for her. For us.

"Do you want to hang out?" she asks, already knowing what my response will be.

The slight shake of my head and the expression on my face confirms the answer. "Enjoy the cookies." I smile, mostly to let her know I'm okay, and turn, making my way back to the door, passing Dailey on the way. "Have a nice night," I say to him, keeping my tone even, without any attitude creeping in.

Endless is how I'd describe the walk back to the elevator and the wait for it to open on the third floor to get me the fuck out of here. I was cool in there, though. Kept it short and sweet. He and I are both acutely aware that we are at war for two things — the part, which I assume he's figured out I'm interested in, and the heart. No assumption needed there. And I just keep thinking this is a classic David vs. Goliath match-up and I've got a red lace slingshot.

Straying off the grand lobby into the Terrazza Lounge, I am badly in need of a drink after that little scene. Grabbing an ocean-facing, caned-back stool at the bar, I tune out the crowd around me, focused only on getting the bartender's attention. Quickly.

"What can I get you?" He lays a napkin on the sand-colored granite before me.

"Bombay Sapphire martini shaken."

Staring out at the silhouetted palms poetically framing a now-dusky ocean, it's impossible not to think about what is going on in the suite three floors above me, a suite overlooking the very same expanse of ocean at which I'm now staring. Do I think there's something physical between them? Could be. It's Maverick Dailey, for God's sake. But Frankie, she just doesn't seem like the type to go from one man to another. There's a depth to her and she doesn't need him for anything. It's him who needs her, and that's what I don't trust here.

I know his motives. Too well.

And right there is the truth.

"I know you." It's a jarring invasion of my thoughts and my enjoyment of the martini I'm quickly draining. I turn to the brunette who has stealthily slid onto the barstool next to me.

My eyebrows raise questioningly. I don't recognize her, but that means nothing.

"Well, I don't know you, know you. But I know who you are. I was a big fan of your show." She touches my arm as she says that.

"Thank you. Appreciate the support." I smile back, but not too broadly. I'm not ending up in a room with this woman, no matter how many martinis I down. With a flick of my finger, I signal the bartender for a second.

"Will I be seeing you in something soon," she asks, trying to keep the conversation alive.

"Nothing I'm at liberty to share yet. Just keep watching." The two scripts I got from Sebastian earlier today were a nice surprise, along with the news that Sherri knew of another film they would soon be casting that she thought might have a part with a good fit for me. Yes, there would be life after *Fleeing an August Moon,* whether I landed the part or not.

What are you doing up there, Frankie? What are you talking to him about?

As I'm nearing the bottom of my second martini, and pondering a third and an Uber home, there's a flurry of activity. Women are entering the bar excited, chatting loudly, with a few squeals thrown in for good measure.

Two women approach the bar and the woman next to me asks them what all the commotion is about. "Maverick Dailey was here. He stepped out of the elevator and stopped to sign some autographs on his way out. He was just here."

"I can't believe I was so close to Maverick Dailey and I missed him." The woman next to me looks crestfallen and upset with herself for wasting her time on me when Mav Dailey was merely feet away.

"Who was he with?" I ask one of the squealers, who still has not gotten the bartender's attention.

"No one. He was just by himself."

Most excellent.

I nod and pick up my drink, quickly draining what is left on the bottom. Catching the bartender's eye, he makes his way down the bar. "I'm ready to settle up," I tell him, handing him my credit card. "And put these ladies' next round on my card."

"Thank you," they call after me, but I'm already halfway out of the bar.

So, Mav is gone. Looking at my phone for the time, it appears he stayed about thirty-five minutes after I left. The elevator doors are just closing as I approach, and I manage to slip in sideways. I wish I had a breath mint or something, I know I smell and taste like booze.

Exiting on three, the hallway still seems as long as it did a mere forty minutes ago as I head down to Frankie's suite for the second time tonight. A deep breath is in order as I knock on her door.

"One minute." I hear her call from inside and wait an interminably long twenty seconds.

"What did you forget?" she says, laughing as she opens the door, only to be stunned into silence when she sees it's me, and not Mav, standing there.

"I forgot what your lips taste like after you've eaten cookies."

Her response never quite makes it out of her mouth and ends up mingling with my tongue, as my hands slide down her back to that delectable ass, lifting her up as her legs encircle my waist.

Our lips break for a moment as I get whacked by her cast. "Ouch, you're dangerous."

"You taste dangerous tonight," she comments, as I walk her into the bedroom. Fuck the couch she sat on with Dailey. Not going there.

"Mmm, I've had a few." Lying her down on the bed, I stand by the edge gazing down at her. "So, it seems it was you who forgot something."

Removing my hand from my jacket pocket, with a quick snap of my wrist, I hold up the red lace bodysuit by its spaghetti straps.

Her eyes widen and she goes to speak, but not a word is produced.

"I'm going to fuck you in this," I inform her, fueled by gin, vermouth, and an unhealthy dose of testosterone.

"And here I thought you just came up to have milk and cookies with me."

"I'll bet you get that same satisfied smile when you write a great line." Her intelligence and wit have been such a turn-on. And now here she is lying back, propped up on her elbows smiling at me.

In one fluid motion, Frankie reaches forward and swipes the bodysuit from my hand. "Help me." It's an order.

"With pleasure." I help her off the bed.

"Shit, there's really no way for me to strut gracefully into the bathroom to change into this." She starts to hobble toward the bathroom, looking over her shoulder to tell me, "This cast is ruining my style, you know."

"Nothing could ruin your style, lady."

Stepping out into the living room, I toss my jacket onto one of the pale-striped couches and head to the mini-bar. Pulling out a cold bottle of wine, I notice the milk is now in the refrigerator unopened. Turning, the cookie bag is sitting on the table and I've just got to know — did she share them with him?

Unrolling the top, I peer inside the brown paper bag. *That's my girl.*

With the wine and glasses in hand, I re-enter the bedroom, just as Frankie steps out from the bathroom, her hair wild and loose and nothing on but red lace and flesh.

"Red is an excellent color for you." My mouth has gone dry. "Wow, just wow." I manage to put the wine and glasses on the night table without taking my eyes off her. "Frankie, you look — wow." I'm too blown away to even articulate and not stumble over my own words. Not very impressive, I'm sure, but there is nothing hidden, and that body that tortured me when she was in running shorts and a tank top is beyond delectable.

And I plan on tasting every part of it.

She still hasn't said a word, continuing to silently stand before me, her dilated pupils obscuring most of the blue of her irises.

"Here, let me help you." I plan to have her lean on me and surprise myself, and her, when I pick her up. As soon as her arms are around my neck, I tell her the only thing I've been thinking about for the past three days, "I have really missed you."

"Yeah?" She's fighting a smile.

"Yeah," I whisper, setting her down on the bed and sitting down next to her.

"Finn," she pauses, looking very serious. "I think you're a bit overdressed."

Laughing, I kick my shoes off and swing my legs up onto the bed. Turning on my side toward her, I reach out, letting my fingertips lightly trace the pattern of the lace.

"You are exquisite." I finally have words and I'm marveling at what I'm seeing within the lace as my fingers find one of her pale pink nipples and follow the lace's ridges around it. Her nipple immediately hardens under my touch, and I roughly run my thumb over it. "I'm going to fuck you in this," I repeat my promise from earlier.

"You're going to fuck me when I'm out of it," she corrects me.

Shaking my head, "No, I'm going to fuck you in it. And then I'm going to take it home and hang it right back on the wall. I might have to nail you against a wall, too." I smile at her, now rolling her nipple between my fingers, twisting it until I can see the pleasure on her face. Our eyes remain locked.

"Take your shirt off." Her voice is sexy and husky.

Reaching back by my collar, I pull my shirt off over my head without unbuttoning it, and then let it trail to the floor.

"Better?" I ask.

Making a face, she scrunches up her nose and shakes her head.

"No?" My chest automatically expands, showing off what I work hard on every single day, for probably too many hours.

"I want to see more. You have an unfair advantage here." Slowly, she swipes the back of her fingers across my chest.

Catching her hand as it moves across my left pec, I move it down to the zipper on my pants, placing the metal tab between her fingers. She tries tugging it down, but my hard-on is jamming the zipper.

"Let me help." I laugh. "You've done enough damage already."

"Damage?" she asks, coyly.

"Yeah, damage. I can't get you off my mind. It was impossible not to think about what you'd look like in this thing." Reaching out, I slip my finger under one of the silky straps and let it trail down. "And reality is even better than my imagination." With my zipper now down, I grab her hand again, guiding it, my eyes closing the moment she makes contact, her fingertips teasing with a gentle swipe along the length of me.

She doesn't stop stroking as she says, "Yes, I'm on birth control. I'm healthy. And I don't want to break your heart if things don't turn out..."

I let my fingers stray over the lace pattern again, gently caressing her breast. "I'm healthy and I'll be disappointed, but my heart won't be broken."

"If it were up to me..." I can see the sincerity in her eyes as she says the words

"But, it is up to you, Frankie. *It is up to you.* Control. You do have control."

"Maybe, the contract says I have control. But you know you've said it to me, and I can feel it at the studio, that maybe I'm just being afforded the illusion of control." She continues to slowly stroke me. "But I'm more focused on the lack of control I have right now."

"So, if you were going to write this, which is where you have total control, what would happen?" I ask.

"You want to act it out?" She appears amused.

"Acting? I'm your man."

"Put your shirt back on and zip up," she directs.

"My shirt?" Is she kicking me out?

"Mmm-hmm." She's nodding, and I do as she instructs. "Tuck it back in your pants."

"Everything's going back in my pants," I grumble. I don't think I'm going to like this chapter.

"And stand by the end of the bed."

Okay, now this could be interesting. I'm not getting eighty-sixed so quickly.

Getting to her knees with her back to me, she slowly shimmies backward toward where I'm standing.

"Try and picture this without a cast on my leg," she says over her shoulder looking up at me through her lashes, her smile almost apologetic.

"Sweetheart, I'm not looking at your leg." Thong-backed, the red lace strap is nestled in her butt cheeks, and I'm already jealous of it. Sweet. I've been admiring that ass since the first time we ran together. And now, I'm getting harder by the second just looking at it.

Moving her long hair to one side, she sends it over her shoulder, letting it rest on her right breast. When she reaches the edge of the bed, she stops and turns her head to look up at me, leaning back into me.

Bending down to trail my lips down her neck to her shoulder, I feel her shiver at my touch, launching my own excitement into the stratosphere. It's powerful being able to do this to her. Snaking an arm around her body, with my hand ending up between her legs, I pull her against me. Her soft moan makes my dick throb. I've got to get out of these pants.

With my other hand below her chin, I tip her head back, bending down to kiss her. "So, what happens when you're not controlling the script?" I ask when our lips part.

Her brows furrow as she considers my question. "I guess I have to get out of my own head."

"Let's go off script." My fingers find their way into her bodysuit, gently stroking her wet heat. Letting go of her chin with my other hand, I hastily unzip my fly again, releasing myself from the constraining pressure. I want to just move the lace strip of her bodysuit to the side and take her from behind, while I'm still fully dressed.

With her head tilted back against my chest, Frankie smiles at me and delivers this surprise. "I think those few days we spent at your apartment should be considered our foreplay. We've done that already."

"Uh-huh. Are you telling me that you think foreplay is overrated?" My fingers continue to explore her, and I get a little bolder.

"Shh, don't tell my readers."

This woman has me laughing during sex. "Do you want me to stop?"

"No. Definitely not. But tell me something."

"What?"

"Do you think it's hot to fuck me from behind with your clothes on?"

"Fuck, yeah, it's hot."

"And do I look good?"

Shaking my head, I laugh. "Yeah, you look great, babe. You know you do."

"Okay, well, hold onto that image."

"Why?" She has me totally confused now.

"My leg is starting to really bother me in this position." Her mouth has formed a defeated pout as if she's sorry to disappoint me.

"Hey, turn around." I remove my hand from her bodysuit, so that she can get off her leg. "Raincheck on this position for when you are not in that cast, because it is very hot, and I need to fuck you this way so you can write me into that scene many times."

"Deal," she agrees, and I know both of us are silently wondering will there be a time after her cast is off? Will we still be a part of one another's lives? Or will this just be a memory of another Hollywood escapade?

Putting my hands under her ass, I pull her to the very edge of the bed, moving her legs to my shoulders. "Try not to kill me with that thing." I motion to her cast.

"No promises. It's going to depend on how good you are," she teases.

"How good I am?" Pulling the red strap to the side, I nestle the head of my cock against her. "How good I am?" I repeat, plunging deep into her, delighting in watching her eyes widen and hearing her gasp, before feeling the searing pain in my right ear as I get slammed by her cast.

"Oh my God, I'm sorry," she apologizes, when she catches her breath.

"I'm not." I sink deep into her again and again and again.

"I'm not, either." And I know she's not talking about slamming me with her cast.

"Hey, take that thing off," I tell her.

"Now that we're done having sex you want me to get naked?" Her hair is a sexy, wild mess from me plowing into her.

I nod and she slowly shimmies the spaghetti straps down her shoulders.

"Let me help." Reaching down, I peel the red lace from her revealing the creaminess of her fair skin. Removing it, I fold up the garment and put it back into the pocket of my leather jacket.

"You really are taking it?" She is surprised that I wasn't joking. "But you fucked me in that."

"That's what makes it so special."

Pulling a pillow to herself, I can see she's suddenly not comfortable with being so exposed, I guess especially while I'm not.

"How about some milk and cookies?" I suggest and with her nod, leave the room to go retrieve them. Finding a small microwave near the coffee pot, I put the cookie bag in for a few seconds to get them gooey and fragrant again.

"Will you grab me a t-shirt?" Frankie asks. "You already know where they are."

Yes, I do. I've been through every dresser drawer in this suite. Heading right to the correct drawer, I pick a cropped t-shirt, and with a smile, toss it over to her.

"Figures you'd pick this one," she mutters, slipping it over her head. It covers her breasts, but not much more. *Excellent choice.*

"Mind if I get comfortable?" I smirk at her.

"Be my guest."

For the second time tonight, I pull my shirt off over my head, but this time I toss it playfully to Frankie, who surprises me by bringing it to her face and breathing in.

"Mmm, it smells like you."

"Is that a good thing?" Suddenly concerned that it's not.

She nods, smiling, bringing the shirt back up to her nose. "It's the same scent that was on your pillows."

"And that's a good thing?" I ask again.

"It is. I like your scent. And I liked smelling it when I was sleeping in your bed."

Sitting down next to her, I pour the icy cold milk into the two unused wine glasses on the nightstand. Cookies and milk in bed. I don't think I've ever done this with a woman before. Maybe because there are no cookie-eating women in LA. Or maybe because I feel so comfortable with this particular woman.

"Why don't you take off your pants and stay awhile," she chides me for still being half-dressed, while she's half-bare.

"I think I will." Standing back up, I slowly unbutton and unzip my pants, letting her enjoy the show and leaving on just my gray boxer-briefs. Sitting back down, I swing my legs up onto the bed and hand her one of the glasses of milk and then put the cookie bag between us.

"Oh my God, they smell so good."

"Worked up an appetite?" I open the bag and tip it toward her.

"You did all the hard work." She's now smirking back at me as she pulls a cookie out of the bag and hands it to me, before diving back in for her own. "And thank you for bringing these."

I lift my milk glass to make a toast. "To meeting you. Unexpected and excellent." I shrug. "I'm better when scripted."

Almost choking on a bite of her cookie, she washes it down with the milk. "I'm really glad we ran into each other, Finn, and that we've gotten to know each other. Pretty cool that we just happened to be running on the same beach at the same time. And you know what?"

"What?"

"I've loved getting your emails and talking through the characters and their motivations. It's been fun for me, too. I like knowing you're out here. I don't really know many people here in LA, and it's comforting to know you're here." A furrow forms between her brows. "Is that a weird thing to say?"

"Mmm-mmm." I shake my head. "Not at all. I'm glad you feel that way." Leaning forward, I kiss her softly. "I've been dying to taste cookies on your lips for three days now. But who's counting?"

"You were so sweet to bring them."

"Any excuse to come see you." *Hmm, is that telling her too much?* "And I got Maverick."

"I'm sorry about that. You're like two dogs circling each other."

"Did he kiss you?" I have no right to be territorial, and look at me. *God, I'm an ass.*

Tilting her head, she shakes it slightly. "Are you asking me if *I* kissed him?" She is now shaking her head more vigorously. "No, I didn't. And do you want to know why?" She pauses and gently runs a finger over her bottom lip. "Because the memory of what your lips felt like on mine was still so fresh. And that's what I wanted, not another man's." She reaches out, pushing the hair from my forehead, the move, intimate, comfortable, and yeah, comforting. "So, he came here tonight to see how I was doing and to tell me something pretty strange, which I think you'll find interesting. And I would have told you the moment you walked through the door, but we got a little sidetracked."

More than a little.

"Okay, I'm listening." *Why do I have the feeling I'm about to go from cloud nine to a barf-stained gutter?*

"So, on Friday we cast Griffin's father. Paul Waters is going to play Ashton Chase."

"Excellent casting. I can totally see him in that role."

"And Maria Cruz has signed on for Briela's mother."

"Another great choice." This is a primo cast. To work alongside these great actors would be the dream of a lifetime, and I'm already aching just listening to this.

"Mav wants to come in and read this week."

"Have you cast Briela?" That was the plan.

"No, we haven't."

"I thought you wanted to cast that role first."

"That was the plan."

I just said that in my head. I know a bomb is about to drop. Putting my glass of milk onto the nightstand, I don't want to spill it all over her bed after she tells me what the fuck Maverick Dailey was doing here in her hotel suite.

"Frankie, just tell me."

"He wants to audition with Eva. It appears they've been working together running lines."

This is not what I expected her to tell me. I don't know if I feel angry. Betrayed — by Eva, not Frankie. But even that's crazy because

Eva doesn't know for sure that I read for Griff's part. She probably assumed, or how the heck would I know Frankie.

And fucking Maverick Dailey. The dude just keeps pissing all over my shit.

"Wow. I did not expect you to tell me that. Surprising, but not surprising, right?"

"Well, I didn't expect him to tell me that." She takes another bite of her cookie.

"How do you feel about it?"

"I don't know. Honestly, a mixture of emotions. Probably most of them I shouldn't be feeling." She takes a sip of her milk. "How do you feel about it?"

"A mixture of emotions. Probably most of them I shouldn't be feeling." I parrot her sentiment.

She reaches out, wiping chocolate from the corner of my lip and then sticks her finger in her mouth, sucking it off.

"What shouldn't you be feeling?" I need to know where she's at.

"Eva. She's your... whatever she is." She gestures with a shrug and I grab her free hand.

"Hey..." I want to shut down whatever it is she thinks might exist between me and Eva, but she plows on.

"And there's just a weird vibe between us. Me and Eva, that is."

"Frankie, she needs you. You don't need her. Just remember that. Look, I know she's a big fan, so I don't know why she acted so weird to you."

"Really, Finn, you don't know? Eva needs to have every man in the room in love with her."

"Yeah, you definitely pegged that right."

"And she sensed something between us."

I like hearing her say that, admitting that there's been something between us.

"Babe, you don't even need to be perceptive to know there is chemistry between us. She knew it. The minute she walked up to us, she knew."

Frankie nods. She looks lost. And I'm about to lose myself in this admission.

"Frankie, she knows me well enough to know that the moment I saw you there, I didn't want to be with or talk to anyone else. She knew I had feelings for you, and that's a threat to her, even though there is no longer anything between us."

"I just keep telling myself I need to be professional — with Eva," she clarifies.

"And with me?"

She nods. "But the reality is, I'm sitting here half-naked with you eating post-coital cookies." She laughs and repeats, "Post-coital," clearly amused.

"So, maybe we should just refer to them from here on out as fucking cookies. As in, I brought you your favorite fucking cookies."

"You can bring me my favorite fucking cookies anytime." She reopens the bag and looks in. "Well, we can split this last one or save it until morning." Looking up at me, she raises her eyebrows suggestively.

"Are you asking me to stay?"

Her nod is accompanied by a questioning look with a hint of a smile. She really doesn't know how I'm going to react.

"I was so worried about you the last few days," *God, what am I doing admitting that to this woman?* "Wondering how you were getting along going to the studio and all with your leg and that damn scooter." Reaching forward, I slide my fingers through her thick hair and offer yet another admission, "And I hated that you weren't in my bed the last few nights. I really liked waking up and having you there, even though I was on the couch."

"Thank you, you made me feel very comfortable."

"Yeah, well, you made me feel very uncomfortable." Her eyes widen at my declaration, and I finish my thought. "I had a freaking hard-on the whole time."

"Did I do that to you?" she asks innocently. And when I nod, she mouths, "Good."

Wrapping an arm around her shoulders, I pull the both of us down to the pillows and once again get to taste the sweetness of cookies on her lips.

"How would you feel about me calling you PJ?"

It's unexpected and seems almost random. "I'm okay with it. May I ask why?"

"I really couldn't get a good read on you when we first met. During the audition, I was so focused on if you were Griffin or not, that I didn't see you."

That's still my fear — and she just voiced it. *Does she see me or does she see who she wants me to be? A product of her imagination. And those are shoes no man can ever fill.*

"And then when we ran into one another running and went out to breakfast," she continues, unafraid to make direct eye contact, "I mean, you were nice enough and all, we had a really pleasant time, but I still walked away feeling like, who is this guy? I just couldn't get a handle on you. I seriously could not pin down what was the essence of you? And it was only through our emails after that morning, where I kind of was getting a sense of who Finn was."

"And?"

"And," she reaches over, again pushing the hair from my eyes, "obviously I liked the guy you were showing me. But it was this week, when I got hurt, that you let me meet PJ, and I think you felt it, too, and that's why you signed the note to me that way."

A quick response is not rolling off my tongue because there is so much I could say to that, but she continues before I fully formulate and attempt to articulate any of it.

"Finn is a character for you, isn't he? He's your Hollywood shell. Your persona. But PJ is a lot closer to the real you. PJ is the guy who comes out when the door closes behind you in your apartment and you're finally alone." Looking down for a moment and breaking eye contact with me, she lets out a small sigh before gazing back up. "I want to get to know PJ."

"No one has wanted to get to know PJ for a very long time."

With a smile, she shrugs. "Their loss."

"You know, you are the most *real* person I have met in years. And it's really refreshing."

"Ah, you just like my great ass," she kids.

"It is really exceptional." Reaching down, I cup one cheek in my hand, pulling her closer to me, my body reacting immediately to her warm skin pressed against me.

"Hold that thought." She traces my lips with her finger, before rolling away out of my grasp and grabbing something off her nightstand.

Turning back to me, she holds out a hotel room keycard. "Why don't you put this in your wallet."

Taking it from her, I pull her in for a kiss. That gesture said a lot. Frankie Simonelli wants to get to know me, not a character or a persona, but actually me for who I am.

I only hope that reality is not a huge letdown for her.

Frankie

A swarm of executives are milling about in our area on the studio lot today, some people I haven't seen in a while, and quite a few whom I'm meeting for the first time. The energy feels off today. Tense. It gripped me the moment I scooted in, quickly evaporating my Zen-like high after waking up next to Finn for the fourth straight morning. He knew today was the day Maverick and Eva were to read a very emotional scene between Griffin and Gabriela. Eva hadn't shared the news with him, but I had.

"Keep an open mind," he urged me, being a total professional. "We'll talk later, I'm going to be reading through the two scripts Sebastian sent me last week."

I know he's thrown that in because he wants me to feel that landing the part or not landing the part, he will survive, that this is just another day in Hollywood, and the next script might be *the one* if he's not Griffin Chase.

To say I'm conflicted is an understatement. I have put myself in a really bad position. And why? Because I couldn't resist this big, handsome guy with eyes bluer than robin's eggs. Parking my scooter behind the table, I take my usual seat and an assistant comes by with a large tumbler of coffee as I'm pulling my notebook from my bag.

Nervously flipping through the pages, the notes I've written about each of the actors and their attached headshots jog the visuals in my mind of their auditions.

I'm really apprehensive about seeing them. Seeing Eva and Mav, that is. *Hey, Eva, I'm fucking your ex. Oh, and Mav, you know that guy you keep running into — yeah, well, I'm doing him and he's auditioning for the same role as you. Break a leg. Oh wait, ha-ha, I already did that for you.*

"So, I see you've already managed to get yourself into trouble out here." I'm caught off-guard, but that New York accent is unmistakable, and if I'm not mistaken, my agent, Caryn Crane, is not supposed to be out here in LA for a few days.

What the heck is going on?

"Caryn." There's surprise in my tone. Yes. I am surprised. I reach up to give her a hug since getting out of my chair is cumbersome with my leg. "You're out here early."

"Yeah, I understand there's an important audition today." She takes the seat next to me, and catching the assistant's eye motions to her that she would like coffee, too.

"Yes, a little later, we've got some other folks reading first."

I have not spoken to Caryn in a few days, so her learning about the audition schedule, and then getting on a plane and flying out, means someone has been feeding her information with the goal of insuring that her client, one Francesca Simonelli, chooses Maverick Dailey for the role of Griffin Chase. I'm no dummy, that is definitely what is going on here, and now my agent's presence, which I usually enjoy, is making me feel like I am being boxed into a corner.

Everything feels very *off* today, and it is not a figment of my very fertile imagination.

"Where are you with the new manuscript?" she asks, after guzzling nearly the entire tumbler of coffee in two quick swigs.

"It's coming along, a lot of interesting characters and they're beginning to really coalesce."

"When can I have the first fifty pages?" Amped up on caffeine, she spits out the request in the rapid-fire-style speech of a cable TV political pundit.

"Not yet. I haven't even gone back and done my first read through. Lord knows what it says on those pages." And I haven't looked at my manuscript since Saturday because I've been having non-stop sex with a hot man on every single surface, horizontal or vertical, in my hotel suite. Bed, couches, chairs, windowsill, and yes, nailed against the wall just like he promised. And damn, it was fine!

"I don't want to miss the deadline."

Geez, she's in a mood. "Have I ever?"

"Let's keep it that way." Her tone is testy.

"Is there something you want to say to me?" I keep my voice low so that no one can hear our conversation, which is bizarre, at best. Caryn and I generally work well together. Lord knows I've made the woman a fortune over the past few years. So, why the attitude with me now? And what the heck is she doing out here early? Something is going down and I think it's called *Project Railroad Frankie*.

"I don't know. We'll see."

A sharp pain stabs the lower left side of my gut as I realize that it's all about the bottom line and not what's best for the film, even with Caryn.

Turning my chair to face her, I consciously try to will away the agonizing distress which is now migrating toward my chest, dragging with it an overwhelming trail of sadness and a stifling feeling of isolation. I knew today wouldn't be easy, but I had no clue it would get ugly this early.

"Well, then, let me say it to you. If you are not here to support me, there is no reason for your presence." I can't even believe these words are coming out of my mouth after all Caryn and I have been through together with this book. But I'm her client and it's my back she should be guarding.

"There are a lot of people who have a lot at stake here."

"And the odds are in their favor that each and every one of them will make a killing on this film, and that's just based on a percentage of my readers going to see it."

"So, what's your beef with Mav?" She cuts to the heart of it.

"Beef with Mav? I don't have a beef with Mav. I think he's an amazing actor and a truly terrific person."

"Then why are you putting everyone through this?"

I'm stunned. Yet, I'm not. She has been summoned to LA to *manage* me. And the only thing I need to manage at this moment is my temper, because I'm about to blow like an oil well in west Texas. And that shit is messy.

"Because I don't look at Maverick Dailey and say to myself *he is Griffin Chase*. My gut says it would be a gross miscasting and no one really cares about that, but me. And all the people who are so concerned about it, well, their names are not out there. This is not their brand. They'll make their money, but they don't have the name exposure with this project that I have. Maybe I'll feel differently after seeing him and Eva Armeni today. I'm keeping an open mind, Caryn," I assure her.

Everyone is beginning to filter in to start the day's work, and at this point, I'm just so annoyed with Caryn and whoever the hell told her she needed to come out here and talk to me. Actually, I'm not annoyed, I am seething. Flipping through my notebook, I busy myself looking at bios of people who will be auditioning today so that I don't have to have a conversation with anyone around me.

I knew today was going to be funky with having to deal with Mav and Eva, but I really didn't anticipate this turn of events souring the day so early. The morning had started out so well with an amusing conversation with Finn as I stood before the bathroom mirror putting on extra make-up.

"Hey, mind if I shower while you do your make-up?" he asked, coming up behind me and kissing my shoulder. Looking at me in the mirror, he tilted his head, questioningly, not used to seeing me with a heavy layer of foundation on my face.

"I'm not going to see your ex with two black eyes that you gave me. " I answered his unasked question, addressing his reflection.

"Tell her that I did it to you attempting a new yoga sex position."

His smile was both delicious and evil, and I'd have given anything just to crawl back into bed with him and spend the day there.

"Yoga sex? Is that really a thing?"

Feeling his arms wrap around me and watching his muscles hide my arms, had me smiling. "I have no clue." He laughed. "But I do know that she'll think it's the new hot thing and search everywhere for it."

"Downward dog," I had snickered.

"Save that thought for later." He then kissed the side of my head before disappearing into the shower.

Looking through my notebook now at the studio, my eyes see nothing on the pages, my internal lens remains focused on the scene in my head with Finn.

Cleanse. Finn can't be here now. Compartmentalize.

Two actresses fill the morning with their auditions for Gabriela's part, and both women are good, believable, and possibly worth a second look. It almost feels like I'm the only one paying attention and everyone else is just biding time until the main event. There is no doubt in any of these people's minds that Maverick Dailey should play Griffin Chase in *Fleeing an August Moon*. No doubt at all. Their only question is who will play Gabriela and they are anxious to see Eva read, because Mav's request to bring another actor in for a role like this is unprecedented, so sight unseen, they are convinced she is Gabriela.

And the buzz has already started. It is the only topic at an interminable lunch in the executive dining room with the table's occupants talking as if it is already a done deal. Their only question appears to be if Eva is the right actress to play opposite Maverick.

I feel anxious. I so want to be openminded about this audition, for Eva as much as Mav. I'm sleeping with her ex and it just feels like she'll know, even though I'm sure Finn has said nothing to her about us. I don't know why I'm so nervous, it's not like she's going to smell him on me or anything. I can't help but smile thinking about sniffing his pillows and blanket those first days when I was convalescing in his bed. If I close my eyes, I can recreate the scent.

"What are you smiling about?" Richard Lesser, the film's director asks.

"I'm just thinking about this audition. It's really exciting for me to see Maverick Dailey perform a character of mine. Especially such a beloved one," I explain my smile and see Caryn just observing me out of the corner of her eye.

As we settle back into the audition room after lunch, I check my phone. No messages. I want to send something to Finn, but what could I say. Everything seems inappropriate under the circumstances. Putting my phone back in my purse, I look up just as Sherri is ushering in Mav and Eva. The room erupts with greetings. The first thing I note is that they are both dressed for the part. Mav is in a suit, shirt open at the collar, silk tie loosened, and Eva has toned down the glam to almost nothing. Her make-up is minimal, exposing her natural beauty and in-line with Gabriela's character.

Making his way through the greetings, a pro at working the response to his presence in a room, Mav shares lots of back-clapping and kisses before finally making his way to where I am sitting.

"Francesca." He smiles at me, taking my hand and not letting it go.

"Maverick," I answer as formally.

"How's the leg doing?"

"It's definitely hindering my style." I laugh. He still hasn't released my hand.

"You'll have to fill me in on the details of how it happened."

"Bad position during yoga sex." My delivery is deadpan, and it slips out naturally just as Eva sidles up next to Mav.

"Yoga sex, what is that?" Her eyes are wide. "I think I need to know about this."

Smiling at her, I warn, "Just be careful. It can get rough." Mav's eyes widen, and catching his gaze, I add with a shrug and a widening of my smile, "Rough can be good." And we both laugh.

"We need to spend more time together, Francesca."

"It could happen," I flirt back.

Looking over Maverick's shoulder, I notice a film crew is beginning to set up, cameras are placed, lights on high poles brought in, and assistants are checking light meters. This is the first time I've seen this during the audition process, and it dawns on me that this is an actual screen test we're going to see this afternoon. The stakes have just risen immeasurably. This is real. Very real. The rise of excitement swells in my chest, grabbing oxygen's place in my lungs, my breathing becomes fast and shallow.

"It never gets old." Mav gives my hand a squeeze.

As if the curtains in a darkened room have been ripped open, I see before me a reality that never seemed real. Not until this moment. And it is certainly not lost on me that one of the biggest movie stars of our time is standing before me, sharing the moment.

His hand moves to my shoulder. "Excuse me, I'm just going to go into another room for a few minutes and get myself ready."

Nodding, I understand what he's saying to me. He needs to go off and get himself into that place, his raw place. I remember the fevered pitch of my emotions when I wrote the scene he and Eva are about to perform. I'd finished writing it at four in the morning and curled up in my bed, knees hugged to my chest, destroyed by Griffin and Gabriela's heartache, and desperate to let go of the pain I'd internalized.

"You and Maverick seem to get along nicely," Caryn is by my side again, commenting.

"Yeah, we do. He's a really good man." *Keep an open mind, Frankie. Keep an open mind.*

"Eva is very pretty. I've only ever seen her looking very stylish. She really looks better with a natural look. I'm glad she came in character to play Briela."

"Me, too." I'm so keyed up I'm finding it hard to speak.

"It'll be interesting to see if she can hold her own with Maverick. He's such a powerful actor."

"We shall see." And once again, I remind myself. *Keep an open mind, Frankie. Put out of your mind that she is Finn's ex. With benefits, as she put it.*

Richard stops next to me. "I'm still in awe that you asked him to do this and even more blown away that he's here doing it. We're in for a treat." As an afterthought, he mutters, "I hope she can hold her own." That seems to be the overwhelming consensus of the room, the same exact phrase spoken twice in less than a minute.

"We're ready," an assistant informs Richard, who instructs another assistant to let Maverick and Eva know that we're ready for them.

As everyone sits down, the production team takes their places. I'm glad this is being filmed, and have a feeling I will be studying it as soon as I can get my hands on a copy, and then watching it obsessively.

Mav and Eva stroll in hand in hand, Griffin and Gabriela walking through the night toward a spot at the border where it will be easy for her to cross into Mexico without authorities stopping her and demanding documentation that does not exist. They stop in the middle of the floor before the cameras and stand there, staring out blankly as if the darkness of night looms before them.

Gabriela: I don't see a line. Where is the line?

Griffin: You know where the line is?

Gabriela: Where? (looking around)

Griffin: It's here. Right here. (Mav's fist goes to his chest) *A thick, relentless black line, ripping me in two. That's where the line is, Brie. It's here.* (Mav pounds on his chest) *It's right here.*

Gabriela: I don't think I will ever be ready to say goodbye to you, Griffin. I'll never actually be ready. (Eva pauses, letting out a short, derisive laugh) *You know, I feel like I've been saying goodbye to you my entire life.*

Griffin: This time is by far the hardest. We never went our separate ways with the thought that this might be it. There is a very distinct chance that this is our forever goodbye and I want to stop you. But, I know I can't. So, let me be by your side. I need to make sure you get there safely.

Gabriela: I can't let you take that risk. I can't let you give up everything. You know that. I would never let you give up everything.

Griffin: I am giving up everything, Briela. I'm giving up you.

Gabriela: You can't walk away from everything you've built, everything you believe in, and have fought for. The work you are doing, it's too important. Especially now, with the world blowing up around us.

Griffin: It's not just my fight. It's ours. One we should be fighting together. Not apart. Not with the specter of you never returning.

Gabriela: You have a mission, Congressman Chase. And I have one, too. Unfortunately, at this time, a border and the law are not yet on our side.

Griffin: (Putting his hand on her cheek) *I don't know that I'll be able to get you back into the country when you are ready to come back. Living with that uncertainty and being too far away from you to ensure your safety...*

Gabriela: I'll be okay. This guy I grew up with taught me how to take care of myself when I was seven years old. (She smiles at him and reaching up, lays a hand on his cheek) *You have a fight to lead. Please don't question that because of me. You can't walk away, and I understand that. People need you, Griff, a lot more people than one girl who watched you grow up to be an extraordinary man. I've had you a lot longer. They need you now.*

Griffin: That doesn't make this moment any easier.

Gabriela: And that makes me love you even more, Griffin Chase.

Griffin: (Taking her into his arms) *I'll wait for you, Brie. You know I'd wait forever to have you back in my arms again. I promise I will do everything in my power to make that happen. You have my vow. Right here. Right now.* (He looks up) *Standing here under these stars. You have my vow.* (Wrapping his arms around her tighter) *I'm going to hold you again, you know that, don't you? If I don't do anything else in my life, I will hold you in my arms again.*

Gabriela: (Tears streaming down Eva's face) *You need to let me go.*

As I watch the scene unfold, I'm in awe of the two of them. The emotion is palpable, and as the scene progresses, I feel it just ripping at my chest as the lump in my throat expands and grows denser.

Their gestures are both intimate and believable and it's evident that Maverick and Eva have been working together, perfecting their timing into explosive, punctuated beats that dictate the breath of everyone in the room. And it's Eva whom I can't take my eyes off of. Mav is Maverick Dailey, he doesn't give a performance short of brilliant. But, it's Eva who is drawing me in, siphoning my emotions, and wringing me dry. I'm riveted.

Is she out-acting Maverick Dailey? The Maverick Dailey! How could that be? Am I the only one seeing this? I wonder.

With the scene nearing its climactic end, I'm reaching down into my bag for tissues. Caryn nudges me to give her one. Caryn Crane crying is probably a sight very few people have ever seen. She is tough New York bitch, personified, and right now she is trying to hide her tears.

Mav and Eva end the scene as he watches her turn away and start walking. The surprise is Eva actually walks out of the room as he stands statue-like watching her leave. The room is silent, no one is breathing. Everyone is with them on a desolate stretch of land illuminated by moonlight. Maybe forty-five seconds pass before Maverick moves and the character of Griffin Chase is gone, just like that. A few moments later, Eva re-enters the room to spontaneous applause.

Maverick Dailey as Griffin Chase. I'm probably the only one in the room still questioning if he truly is Griff. His performance was masterful. No one expected anything less, even me. Yes, he could be Griffin, but he's not my Griff. Eva, on the other hand, as much as I hate to say it, Eva Armeni is Gabriela Sotomayer. The guy I'm screwing's ex is the perfect actress to play the female lead in the film of my book.

The guy I'm sleeping with's ex. My character. My movie. Methinks this town is incestuous.

I wish I was alone to let this sink in, because processing it in a roomful of people is not working for me. My emotions are ping-ponging, as they have been since my first breakfast with Finn, accentuating the confusion I've been having about stepping over lines and deciphering what's real and what's just living out fantasy in a town that serves up fantasy the way it serves up avocado toast.

"What'd you think?" Caryn whispers in my ear.

"I think she out-acted him," whispering back, I put it all out there for her.

"Yeah, me, too. He was great and they are great together. Good chemistry. But she was the shocker here."

Looking up to find Eva heading straight toward us, I smile at her. "You did a great job. I can't wait to see the tape."

"Thank you. I was so nervous. I mean, it's such a huge role and all. And obviously acting with an actor of Maverick's caliber was really stressful. Plus, this is your character, you created her, and I hope you saw her in me."

Well, her tune has certainly changed since the night in the ladies' room when it clearly wasn't clicking in her brain that I was the gatekeeper to this role, and that her future in this film boiled down to me. Her main focus was that her ex with benefits and I had a visible connection. Tactical error on her part.

But, she is the best Eva I have seen to date.

"I did. You were excellent," I reassure her.

Clutching her chest, she closes her eyes and smiles. "That means the world to me, Francesca." And now her acting is over the top, her insincerity not masked the way she's hoping it will be.

I do not like this woman. Mustering a smile as insincere as her declaration, I just can't bring myself to answer.

"So, did I do okay?" Mav is now by Eva's side and I can turn my attention to him.

"Do you ever not?"

His smile is both disarming and charming. "Probably more than I'd like to admit," he shares, breaking into laughter. Reaching out, he takes my hand, threading his fingers through mine. "Thank you. I appreciate you allowing me to read for Griffin."

"You know everyone thinks I'm nuts." I look around, clearly referring to making a superstar audition.

"It was actually a good experience for me. Gets me back to my core, so I'm actually glad you did." At least when he speaks, I feel the sincerity. Leaning in, he admits in little more than a whisper, "I had fun."

The smile crinkles at the corners of his eyes, make me smile. There is something so likable about this man. Maybe he's acting and it's all part of the ploy, but my gut tells me he's not, and I hope that he and I can actually maintain a friendship when this is all over.

"Give Jua a kiss for me." I squeeze his hand.

"Will do. Let me know if you want to take a ride up there. I'll come pick you up."

"I don't know if she'd like that. She's kind of possessive of you. I saw her give me the stink-eye." And from the corner of my eye now, I see Eva's doing the same. It's obvious that she is not fond of my friendship with Mav. *Is it bad that I wonder how she'd react if she knew I was involved with Finn?*

Within moments of Maverick and Eva's departure, Marlena, the Executive Producer, announces a dinner meeting. In attendance will be me, Caryn, Richard, Sherri, and the head of the studio himself. If I had to venture a guess, I'd say that I'm the only person learning about this dinner meeting for the very first time.

Now Caryn's early arrival makes perfect sense. They figured they'd humored me with Maverick's audition and that was done.

I'm about to get squeezed.

Finn

Pulling off the bubble wrap, I'm immediately struck by the energy burst I feel from just a cursory glance at the abstract red and yellow swirls flaming across the canvas.

"Yeah, baby. You will look fine on that far wall. You'll be the first thing I see now when I walk through the front door," I tell the painting as I carry it toward its new home.

I really had not noticed how barren my apartment was until Frankie pointed it out to me, and now it's all I can see. The emptiness. The void. Is that me? Have I had the hue of life erased from my existence? I really have to question if I've been living in limbo waiting for my life to happen? I hadn't even thought about having lost myself somewhere along the way, at least not until recently. Not until I crossed paths with her did I question who I really was in all this.

Finn. PJ. Parker.

She liked Finn and I've shown her PJ and she seems to like him, too.

Maybe Parker someday. Maybe not. I have the perfect mask to hide him under. People out here generally don't want to look past the blond hair and blue eyes, my biceps and long legs. And that's just fine with me. Just fine, indeed. Maybe I am the perfect vessel for Hollywood. Maybe I am.

From two large bags sitting in the middle of the floor, I begin to unpack the rest of the colorful things I purchased at HomeGoods, unwrapping them from their protective tissue paper and placing them around the apartment, stepping back each time to take in their placement and make sure it feels right. Sometimes a piece works where I thought it would, other times not so much. The color pops of red and yellow set off the multiple cobalt blue pieces.

Standing in the middle of the living room, I do a slow three-sixty. The transformation is greater than I expected and now I'm looking at the bare spots and thinking they need to be filled in. *I am my mother's son.* Yes. I am.

"Mom, you would like this." I say, stepping back from my newly hung painting

Picking up my phone, I shoot a few photos, my first thought is Frankie's going to love seeing this. Even though the colors are prime and bright, they warm up the place and it feels like me. This is who I am.

Where have I been?

I'm excited to show off the transformation. Yes, that translates into I really want Frankie to see this. She's the catalyst, opening my eyes to the stark reality I've created for myself and hidden within. Maybe it's an extension of the Finn persona. What is it I'm missing in me as a person? Or trying to hide? Whatever it is, most likely I'm trying to hide it from myself. And have obviously been pretty successful.

I wonder if my inability to land parts for the past two years has been because if I can't connect to myself, how am I to connect with a character who needs to be able to connect with the audience? Missed connections all around.

Yeah, I want to reach out to her. But I can't. She's probably with Eva and Dailey. *Fuck. I am dying to know what is going on. Does she see Griffin in him?* Leaving her hotel this morning was like stepping out of our bubble, and that rainbow-glinted sheath dissipated the moment we said goodbye.

Will things be the same between us after today's auditions? And if I'm really being honest, I'm obsessing more than a little bit wondering if I am still a contender? But I really like her, too. There's no doubt about that.

My phone torments me, mocking in its silence, screaming my imagination's worst fears. Losing the part *and* the girl. That would be pretty freaking shitty, because these last days with her have been some of the best days I've had in almost as far back as I can remember. I have told her more shit about my life than I think I've ever shared with any other woman. She listens and she's empathetic, but doesn't let me off the hook. Which makes me think about stuff I haven't let myself think about. Maybe ever.

I wonder if it's because she's a novelist that she's always looking for what the motivation is behind the actions. Or in my case, inactions.

Text me, Frankie. Give me something here.

As I flick her room key mindlessly against my palm, I wonder how I should play this. Give her space? Wait to hear from her? Show up in her hotel room and bring her cookies and me? Grab her by her wavy mane of hair and pull her head back and kiss her. She totally gets off on having her hair wrapped around my hand and tugged.

Watching basketball on TV is not cutting it tonight, and I pick up my phone for the umpteenth time, somehow expecting a message to be there, although I've had no alert.

I just need to know.

Finn: How did it go today? Taking matters into my own hands, I then try to refocus on the Lakers game when my screen remains blank.

I jump slightly when it finally buzzes twenty minutes later. Man, am I ever strung tight tonight.

Frankie: It's still going.

Wow. Not the answer I expected from her. But it makes me feel better. She's not avoiding talking to me because she doesn't want to deliver bad news. That shit was all in my head. Thank God!

Finn: You still at the studio?

Frankie: Yes. Took a bathroom break to answer.

Finn: Break from auditions? Could they still be running auditions at this hour?

Frankie: No, meeting. Everybody and their brother. Including my agent.

Finn: Your agent? I thought she was coming out in a few days? Oh, man, this is where they squeeze her to get their way. Make her think she's in control and that the decisions are hers. But the reality of this is, they will get the outcome they want. They brought her freaking agent out. Shit. Hardball time. That's a manage your client move if I've ever seen one.

Frankie: Me, too! But today was ambush Frankie day.
She gets it. She totally gets it.
Finn: Holding up okay?
Frankie: They are slick. But yeah, I'm okay. I'm wearing one shit-kicking cowboy boot and a very hard cast.
Finn: That's my girl. Why the fuck did I type that? Especially in this situation. Am I that manipulative a fuck?
Frankie: Gotta go back in now.
Finn: Good luck.

What the fuck is wrong with me? *That's my girl.* It just came out, but boy that was inappropriate. She doesn't need more pressure, and certainly not from me, of all people. I want to do something to make it better. Leave something for her in her room? No, that's creepy. If I really want to do something for her, I need to leave her alone.

Time to look at those other scripts.

"Boychick," Sebastian sounds like he's had three cups of coffee and needs to be scraped off a wall. And I'm on the couch, where I evidently passed out reading. What the fuck time is it?

Wiping the sleep from my eyes, I look at the clock on my DVR box. It's 7:52 a.m. *Damn.* A pre-8 a.m. call. This is a first.

Bad news on an empty stomach. I try and ignore the disappointment beginning its vicious churn in my gut.

"I just got off the phone with Sherri."

"And?" I cut him off.

"Let me get straight to it."

Do it.

"They want you to come back and do an actual screen test."

A wave washes up me, moving up from my lower abdomen neutralizing the bilious fear that had so quickly snaked through me.

"A screen test?" Oh, man, Frankie, what did you pull off, babe?

"Yeah, it appears that they did an actual screen test with Maverick Dailey and your friend, Eva. Brought in a crew and filmed them."

"Wow." I'm at a loss for words.

"Now, I'm not supposed to know this, but Sherri and I go way back. You know how us native Angelenos have each other's backs. It's you and one other guy being called back for a screen test."

Who was it whom I saw in her notebook that she liked? What is that guy's name? I rack my brain. I can see his face in my mind, but his name eludes me.

"So, me, this other guy, and Dailey all get screen tests."

"That's what she said. And Mav's is already done. The studio wants this done yesterday. They want you in at four o'clock."

"Today?"

"Yes, today. Do you have a more pressing engagement?"

"No, I mean, that's fine. I'll be there. Just surprised."

"Surprised they want to screen test you or surprised it's today?"

"Both."

Frankie, nice negotiating.

"Well, here's another surprise, you'll be reading with your buddy, Eva."

Holy fuck! What did he just say to me?

"Did she get the part?" The astonishment in my voice cannot be concealed. Eva as Gabriela?

Eva.

Holy shit.

She must've been brilliant for Frankie to be moving forward with her. Frankie bristles at the mere mention of her name.

"I haven't heard anything officially. But if she's screen testing with the final round of actors being considered, I'd say yes." The surprise in Sebastian's voice is evident.

"Wow." My words are not coming easily this morning. "Does she know she's going to be reading with me?" That's going to be a little bit of a mindfuck since we'd never talked about me auditioning for the role. Although, she might have already put it together, she's no dummy.

"Not sure. I've emailed you the scene. I know it's short notice and not a lot of time with the script."

I've had more time than he knows. "Not a problem. I'll call you when it's over," I promise, rushing him off the phone, a reversal in patterns for us.

Finn: Awake? My text to Frankie is off the moment the call disconnects.

Frankie: Yes, writing. Two cups of coffee in me.

I smile at her words, picturing her at the desk overlooking surfers greeting the incoming tide and runners lost in the beats from their earbuds as they pound the cold, soaked sand. I'm imagining her hair in a loose braid and an oversized Rice University t-shirt.

Finn: Just got off the phone with Sebastian.

Frankie: ;-)

Finn: Yeah, I've got one of those smiles on my face, too. Why didn't you call me?

Frankie: Because that was a moment you and your agent needed to share.

Finn: And Eva?

Frankie: Nodding my head, yeah, Eva.

Finn: Wow! Just wow!!! Does she know that she and I are doing a screen test together?

Frankie: Not unless you've shared it with her.

Finn: LOL no. I never told her how I knew you.

Frankie: Then I don't think she knows. Unless her agent was told and he told her. Does that happen?

Finn: Probably not. Unless you're reading with Maverick Dailey.

Frankie: She didn't need her agent to tell her that one.

Finn: LOL, true. Okay, I'll see you later. And Frankie. Thank you.

Frankie: No need to thank me. You are being brought back because your first audition was excellent. Looking forward to this one.

Finn: Me, too.

Me, too. I'm going to knock your socks off, lady.

Opening Sebastian's email, I find myself saying, "Yes!" rather emphatically. My rendering of the scene may be more reminiscent of

Frankie's words than the script, but I've got plenty of time to go in and see how it wavers from the source material.

But first, there are a few things that need to be taken care of.

You ain't seen nuthin' yet, Ms. Simonelli.

Frankie

Scott Burke.

I can feel the people around me in the room, the ones who weren't at his first audition. I can feel their thoughts. See their internal eyeroll. I know they are thinking, *WTAF were they thinking letting the author be the decision maker on this? Her agent should be commended for striking a crazy good deal. Crazy being the operative word. But seriously — this guy? For the Griffin Chase role? They should never let outsiders have that much power.*

But Scott Burke is going to blow their minds. Of that, I am sure. He and Eva are standing off to the side talking. They've literally had no time to run lines together or anything like that. Which surprises me. But, on the other hand, it doesn't. The studio is placating me. They are throwing two actors in there, totally cold. How could they ever stack up under such circumstances to the great Maverick Dailey? And so, after yesterday, and seeing the well-rehearsed chemistry between Mav and Eva, they are sure there will be no doubt in my mind that Mav is the one. He is Griffin Chase.

And look, it was who Francesca Simonelli chose for the part, after all.

Finn warned me about this game, and he was totally on the mark

In my head, I start sending out good thoughts to Scott and to Finn. I want to see both of them knock it out of the park. I want all these people to see what I see. But I don't know that they can see anything beyond the bottom line.

And yes, I understand that.

But that's not what I want.

And I just pray that one or both of these guys totally kills it today, and everyone in the room sees Griff. My Griff.

Moving to the center of the floor, the lights dim and they begin.

Gabriela: I don't see a line. Where is the line?

With the first words out of his mouth, Scott is commanding. The tenor of his performance different than Maverick's. *More primal?* In a very chameleon-like way, I can see Eva meld to his intensity. Yes, that's what it is. She's allowing him to lead her, like a skilled dance partner.

Laying down my pen in the open spine of my notebook, I just sit back to watch. No notes. No thoughts. My full attention on Scott and Eva. He's upping her game and she's rising to meet him. He has totally marshalled the scene. And I think, this very-unlikely Griffin Chase is winning over this room with every single line he delivers.

What would my readers' think? I know this is not who they had in their heads for Griffin and there might be a significant portion who would say they will not see the film with Scott in the lead role. It's going to be based on what they see in head shots and Google searches. But maybe when trailers are released, they'll be more accepting of a different Griffin Chase than they'd pictured, because this guy definitely nails the soul of the man.

As the scene builds, I take a quick peek at the others in the room to try and gauge their reactions in the dark. He has seized their attention, that's for sure, and he's not being overpowered by Eva's performance. I can't wait to see the videos of these auditions. I think that will tell me a lot and hopefully give me something close to the visual I see in my head.

Again, as I did when Mav and Eva played the scene, I reach into my bag for a tissue. Caryn nudges me again and I hand her one, secretly taking delight that Scott's performance has moved her. I knew I wasn't wrong about this guy. He has got heart and soul, and he's a damn fine actor.

With this reading not being choreographed like her previous go-round, Eva isn't quite sure how to end the scene, and she and Scott stand there, him with his hands on her arms until the lights come up and a spontaneous round of applause punctures the rapt silence.

I can see Eva's lips form the words, "You were wonderful. Thank you." I can't see what Scott says back to her as he dips his head close.

After Scott has left, Richard asks Eva, "Are you ready to do this again?"

"As many times are you need me to." She smiles at him.

"We've got one more in about thirty minutes, if you need a break or some water."

"I'm going to step out and make a phone call. I'll be back in just a few." She grabs her purse and wanders out to the hall.

Caryn tilts her head toward me, "I'll bet you ten dollars she's not calling her agent."

"That's like robbing me." I laugh.

"I bet she's sleeping with Maverick."

I need to get off that subject. "So, what did you think of Scott?"

"The guy can act. That's for sure."

"You worried what my readers will think?"

"It would take them a moment to accept him, but I think he'd win them over. She didn't out-act him," she adds in little more than a whisper.

Nodding, I know she's thinking what I'm thinking.

See, Frankie's not so cray-cray after all. Now I just hope she'll support me when the rubber hits the road and we don't both end up as Hollywood roadkill.

As Eva re-enters the room, I can't help but check her out, she is really beautiful. I can totally understand Finn's attraction to her. That hair. It's shampoo-conditioner commercial hair. The sheen under the lights accentuates the brilliance of its silky texture. I'm immediately envious of her frizz-proof tresses. Humidity and rain don't turn this woman into a walking, talking Chia Pet and that alone is reason to hate her. And she's Finn's ex. And his type. And I'm about to make her a household name. The irony of this is not lost on me.

I know I need to pull my personal crap out of this. I've created this conundrum for myself.

Sherri takes a phone call and nods her head before hanging up and whispering something into Richard's ear.

He, too, nods and then directs Eva. "Eva, please take your mark."

She looks at him quizzically as the next actor auditioning for Griffin hasn't entered the room yet, but follows his direction and takes her mark in the center of the room as the lights are lowered, simulating the dead of night.

Oh my God, she doesn't know it's Finn.

"And we're recording in 5, 4, 3, 2, 1..."

Out of the shadows, Finn Parker takes his place next to Eva Armeni and the shock is momentarily evident in her eyes, before she recovers and flawlessly delivers the scene's opening line.

Gabriela: I don't see a line. Where is the line?

Griffin: You know where the line is? (He puts an arm around her shoulder and draws her into him)

Gabriela: Where? (Looking around)

Griffin: (Taking her hand, he lays her palm flat on his chest) **It's here. A thick, relentless black line, ripping me in two. That's where the line is, Brie. It's here.** (He gives her hand a squeeze and then opens his palm flat over hers) **It's right here.**

Caryn leans into me and whispers, "Oh my God. This guy is exactly how I pictured Griffin would look."

I stay silent, not wanting to miss a beat of this, but I'm thinking *you and me both, sista.* And today more than ever before. Finn has cut his hair. It's still a little long on top, but much more conservative than it's been. And there's no scruff on his face. He is totally clean-shaven. In a navy blazer, khakis, and a white shirt open at the collar, Finn Parker *is* Congressman Griffin Chase. Damn, he has totally transformed into the man about whom I wrote.

Gabriela: I don't think I will ever be ready to say goodbye to you, Griffin. I'll never actually be ready. (Eva pauses, searching his face. I don't know if it's the shock of seeing Finn or if she's looking for answers) **You know, I feel like I've been saying goodbye to you my entire life.**

Griffin: This time is by far the hardest. Nothing has been like this. Ever. (He's now following dialogue from the book and not the screenplay!) *We never went our separate ways with the thought that this might be it. This might be our never. There is a very distinct chance that this is our forever goodbye and I want to stop you. But, I know I can't. So, let me be by your side. Take you there. I need to make sure you get there safely. I have to make sure you are safe or I will never rest easy.* (He has her face in both hands, his voice pleading, his eyes boring into hers, she is transfixed as he goes into an off-script riff)

Gabriela: You know I can't let you take that risk. I can't let you give up everything. You know that. (Finn brushes her hair from her face in a very intimate and loving gesture) *I would never let you give up everything.* (Her voice is already beginning to crack)

Griffin: I am giving up everything, Briela. I'm giving up you. You are my everything.

His last line is an anguished whisper and Caryn grabs my arm, her perfect manicure digging into my skin. I don't think she realizes she's doing it.

Gabriela: You can't walk away from everything you've built, everything you believe in, and have fought for. The work you are doing, it's too important. Especially now, with the world blowing up around us. People need you, Griff, a lot more people than one girl who watched you grow up to be an extraordinary man. A lot of people need you to fight for them.

Griffin: It's not just my fight. It's ours. One we should be fighting together. Side by side. Not apart. Not with the specter of you never returning.

Again, a nice riff that is not in the script. This is like the fourth time he's gone off-script. Risky, but seriously, oh so effective.

Gabriela: You have a mission, Congressman Chase. And I have one, too. Unfortunately, at this time, a border and the law are not yet on our side.

Griffin: (Staring intently at her, a thumb lovingly brushes her cheekbone. Their intimacy is on display for all to witness) *I don't know that I'll be able to get you back into the country when you're ready to come back. Living with that uncertainty and being too far away from you to ensure your safety...* (Taking off his blazer, he wraps it around her shoulders, protecting her from the night air, his hands remaining at her shoulders)

We are watching lovers. And we ARE watching lovers, but besides them, I am the only one who knows that. Caryn's fingernails have now successfully punctured my forearm.

Gabriela: I'll be okay. This guy I grew up with taught me how to take care of myself when I was seven years old. (She smiles at him and reaching up, lays a hand on his cheek) *You have a fight to lead. Please don't question that because of me. You can't walk away, and I understand that. They need you. You are their hope, Griffin.*

Griffin: That doesn't make this moment any easier.

Gabriela: And that makes me love you even more, Griffin Chase.

Griffin: (His hands go back to her face as he draws her to him. Their touches are so intimate. These two are very much in sync. Lovers understanding one another's nuances) *I'll wait for you, Brie. I need you back in arms, even if it takes forever, I will wait for you. And I promise you, here and now, that I will do everything in my power to make that happen. You have my vow, baby. You will always have my vow.* (Pulling her tightly in his arms) *I'm going to hold you again, so don't you ever doubt that? I won't be whole until you are in my arms again.* (Kissing the top of her head) *And you will. You will be back in my arms again and it's going to be forever. I promise.* (He whispers)

He has totally gone off script and substituted dialogue from the book. Lines we laid in bed and talked about at length, and my heart is soaring. He so gets Griffin. He listened to my responses when he asked me deep and insightful questions. And now he doesn't just look like Griffin Chase. He is Griffin Chase.

Gabriela: (tears streaming down Eva's face) *You need to let me go.*

Griffin: (Releasing her from his arms, he takes her hand in his and kisses the inside of her wrist before taking a step backward and letting her hand slip slowly from his)

Gabriela: (With a shrug, she begins to remove his jacket and he shakes his head, causing her to halt the motion and pull the jacket back around her) ***Griff...***

Griffin: (Reaching for her hand again, he pulls her to him for a deeply emotional goodbye kiss, and then resting his head into the crook of her neck for a moment, before straightening up to take her face in both hands. Eva is sobbing as he presses a hard kiss to her lips) ***It's time...***

Gabriela: (Nodding, she wraps his coat tightly around herself again. Eva is shivering. Slowly, she turns from him and walks away)

Emotion? Or is she actually there in that desolate field with him in the chill of night?

Griffin: (Finn just stands there watching her go and then hangs his head to his chest, his fisted hands hang at his side before shoving them into his pockets and lifting his head to stare out into nothingness)

And it's freaking powerful.

One beat. Two beats. Three beats. Four beats. I can't breathe. No one is breathing.

And as the houselights come on, Eva and Finn are greeted with resounding applause, which gets louder when Eva steps back into the center of the room and stands next to him.

"What did we just see?" Caryn whispers in my ear as the noise level is still celebratory and she finally releases her death-grip on my arm. Now I have an injured leg and an injured arm.

"We just saw Griffin and Gabriela together for the first time."

"Oh my God. The emotion between those two," she's breathless as she speaks. "They are so believable. I could feel their pain."

Over Caryn's shoulder, I see Finn approaching, my emotions well with each step. I want to throw my arms around him, but no one can know. They can't know anything.

"You clean up nicely," I kid.

"Ha, my mom used to tell me that." I see the flash in his eyes.

She would have been so proud of you, PJ.

"I just wanted to thank you for this opportunity," he continues. "I hope I did justice to Griffin Chase." His comments and demeanor are professional, and no one would ever suspect that our relationship is more involved.

"You were excellent," Caryn chimes in and extends her hand. "Caryn Crane, I'm Ms. Simonelli's agent."

"Very nice to meet you." He's holding her captive with his mesmerizing blue eyes. I've stared into them across a pillow, talking and laughing in bed. "Finn Parker." He takes her hand.

Eva works her way over and playfully punches him in the arm. "I can't believe you didn't tell me?"

"Surprise," he delivers with a breathtaking smile.

"You two know one another?" Caryn asks, just as Richard and Sherri join us.

"We're friends," Finn offers.

"He's my ex," Eva admits at the very same moment, the two of them talking over one another.

Please don't say with benefits. Please don't say it.

Richard's eyebrows momentarily catapult as he looks at Sherri and then focuses on me, with a quick, furtive glance. My gut tells me he's thinking this would make for great press. What a PR story they could develop about the real-life Griffin and Gabriela. I know he saw the power in both of today's auditions, and that's probably already causing him strife. While Maverick Dailey is a brilliant actor, he is not the best person for this role. But a real-life love story, that's a public relations pot of gold. I feel clairvoyant, as if I'm reading both his and Sherri's thoughts. They're figuring the spin for the money people and studio execs, if they need one.

"I can't believe you didn't tell me you were auditioning for this role." Eva is standing too close to Finn as she presses him again on it. "That crazy superstition of yours." She shakes her head, smiling at him with familiarity.

With a smile planted on my face, I watch, witnessing the truth of the situation. She knows him so much better than I do, so much better than I probably ever will, and this moment is a glimpse, a peek through a crack in the front door of a club where I'm not a member. Finn and Eva. I might be putting them back in one another's arms. Me. I might be responsible for that.

Thank me later, you two.

Suddenly, I feel very tired, and a wave of nostalgia rushes over me, and in this moment, I want nothing more than to be back in the squalid humidity of Houston and away from all things that feel painful, even though intellectually, I know this shouldn't be.

I'm suddenly feeling less than. And that's clearly my shit. I'm nowhere near as beautiful as Eva. I'm not a woman who knows Finn well or deeply.

Snap out of it, Frankie! You're being stupid and letting insecurity rain down on you. They both want parts in *your* movie. You are holding all four aces.

"So, this is how you two knew each other?" Eva looks from Finn to me and back to Finn again.

"Yes, we met during his first audition." The smile is still plastered on my face as I answer for him.

"I should have guessed." She still hasn't taken her eyes off him. I get the distinct impression she is not happy with him for not telling her. Seriously, it really doesn't take a brain surgeon to figure out why he would know me.

His eyes aren't on her, they are on me. And his response doesn't acknowledge her. It acknowledges me. "Thank you for giving me the opportunity to read for this part today. I really appreciate it."

Nodding, I assure him, "You earned it, Finn. It was a pleasure watching you." I pull my eyes from him to make eye contact with Eva. "It was a pleasure watching both of you. I'm looking forward to seeing the footage."

And I am. I want to study the videos from the three auditions. I want to watch each through to get the entire feel. Then do a round two to zero in on Mav, Scott, and Finn's performances. And on the third, but, maybe not final, round, I want to focus on the nuances of Eva's chemistry with each of the actors. My brain is already floating away thinking about the checklist I want to create in my notebook to rate and rank the performances. I think it's going to be a long night.

Eva removes Finn's blazer and hands it to him. "Walk me out?" she asks.

"Sure," he answers quickly and turns back to me. "It was really good to see you again."

"Good to see you, too." I smile at him, acting very professional, and then set my sights on Eva. "Great seeing you today, Eva."

"I'm just so thrilled you've asked me to read for Gabriela, Francesca." Francesca. She's been hanging around Maverick.

"Take care of that leg." Finn gives me a mischievous look.

"I won't be running for a while," I quip, enjoying the connection of our inside joke.

"Are you a runner?" he asks, and I can see he's having fun with this.

"Well, I was. Before my accident."

"He's a runner, too." Eva touches Finn's arm, staking possession. *She really does need to be the only woman in the room.*

"I miss it." I push away her overture and start glancing around the room. I need this conversation to end. Turning to Caryn, "Are we getting a break before the next meeting."

Finn immediately picks up on my discomfort and on the cue to leave.

"Again, thank you. And good to see you." Looking at Eva, he asks, "You ready?" And although I need them to leave, it hurts to see him go, but not as much as it hurts to see them leave together.

Richard has told the assistant to have dinner delivered.

"Make sure there is no avocado anywhere in that food," he directs an intern. "Ms. Simonelli is highly allergic to avocado."

Allergy? Okay.

"Well, then, Mexican's out." Sherri shrugs and shakes her head, her wry grin giving it all away.

"Go print us out a few copies of Providence's menu." Richard tells the intern.

"Providence delivers?" she questions him, surprised by his request.

"No, but you do," he snaps, sending her scurrying from the room. The moment she's gone, he turns to me and smiles. "I'll bet you five dollars in thirty minutes we'll be able to find on Twitter that you are allergic to avocados."

"It'll probably be trending." Sherri laughs.

"My readers are a communicative bunch. Love them!"

Marlena enters the room, closing the door behind her, and joins us at the conference room table. "Alright, we have a little time, and I mean very little, before half this studio descends on this room. So, let's get this figured out."

"I would really like to see all the videos first to confirm or refute what I'm thinking. I can't, in good conscience, say anything until I watch the three clips." I immediately throw my two cents in.

"The reel with all three will be ready for us in the next few minutes." Richard says and sends a text to someone. "They know to bring it here."

"You've got a good eye." Marlena's delivery is dry, but I'm assuming she's complimenting me.

"Score one for the crazy author." I shake my head.

"You do know there's going to be a lot of pushback and pressure." She's preparing me.

"I do. I know that. And that's why I'd be remiss if I didn't watch what this looks like on film before saying anything."

"You don't have to be so politically correct. We were all in that room for the past two days." Turning to Richard, she adds, "How long until we can see them?"

There's a knock on the door and the assistant is back with a stack of papers. "They're ready for you in the viewing room at the end of the hall." As we all begin to get up, she asks, "What should I do with the menus. I have the menus from Providence."

Richard points to the table without saying a word as we leave the conference room and he leads us down the hall, with me pulling up the rear on my scooter.

The lights in the viewing room are dimmed as I approach a seat on the aisle of the first row, easing onto the plush cushion of the theater-style chair. As I settle in and let the soft padding cradle me, I feel it absorbing the tension radiating from my spine, relieving the burden I appear to have internalized as I run scenarios in my head about how the evening is going to go once we open up the casting discussion.

A voice over an intercom asks if we're ready and Richard raises his right hand to indicate they are okay to start, and the room immediately darkens.

Crap! My notebook is on the table in the conference room. I'll have to remember to jot down my initial thoughts when we get back.

On a large screen in front of us are Maverick and Eva. Shot in the darkness of the soundstage to simulate the hour just past midnight on a moonlit night, it actually appears there is nothing to distract me from thinking they're not in the middle of nowhere, down along the barren Texas/Mexico border.

Maverick Dailey in on a screen playing one of my characters. I think I'm finally having my *holy crap* moment and realize my smile is so wide my cheek muscles are quivering. Divorcing external thought from my mind, I let my senses absorb, trying to take in as much as I can visually, aurally, and emotionally. The depth of what the lens picks up in non-verbal communication, shows me how much I missed even being there witnessing it.

They are good together, Eva and Mav, but it feels very packaged and she's definitely stealing the scene from him. I wasn't imagining it. I try and clear the thought from my head, so I can fully focus on their performances and let myself just feel.

When their reel ends, the room's dim lights come back up and I'm wiping my tears with the back of my hand.

Yes. They made me believe.

The intercom voice speaks again. "Let me know when you're ready for the next one." Richard gives him the signal.

Let's see what Scott and Eva look like together and if this is believable or not.

Where is the line? I don't see a line.

It's Finn. I was expecting Scott. *What the heck?* Eva's not the only one with a surprised look on her face. I'm just glad I'm sitting in the dark so no one can see my shock.

I guess we're not seeing them in order.

Even in the darkness, the clarity of Finn's eyes is mesmerizing. The camera truly loves this man. The shorter hair and clean-shaven face transform him physically into the perfect Griff, but I'm going to miss him rubbing his scruff across my stomach to make me laugh. I have a feeling I'm going to be missing him, in general. No matter how this goes.

Push those thoughts away and focus.

The chemistry between these two is making me ache. Finn and Eva burn up the screen together. Viewers will be enraptured by their longing and desire. The believability factor is off the charts. There's a truthfulness in their emotion. Whether they are conjuring up moments from their shared past, or just deeply entrenched in their roles, it is impossible to discern. We are all voyeurs rubbernecking on a dark, dusty road to steal a glance of their emotional carnage.

Fuck me.

Seriously, just fuck me.

I am sending him right back into his ex's arms in a pair of emotional roles that is going to change both their lives. They will be in their own world together in two different realities. A screen reality they create, and a reality they create for lovers of the screen. And they were lovers. Exes with benefits. Who, if we move forward with the two of them, will be a PR person's wet dream. Two ex-lovers falling for one another again while playing this pair of modern iconic lovers. It's a story everyone will love as much as they adore the romance on the screen.

And it will be the studio's coup, creating this narrative that the public will eat up.

Fuck me.

I really, really like this guy. Wow, there's an admission from the girl who has made an artform of burying her own emotions.

Just fuck me.

As the third reel roles with Scott and Eva, I fight to get out of my head and observe. I owe them that. I owe that to this talented actor. I owe it to everybody, including myself. But it's impossible to get the specter of Finn and Eva out of my head, even as I watch Scott's brilliance and deftness as he responds, thrown into a scene with a partner he's just met. The man is quick, nimble, and powerful.

As lights illuminate the room, I feel drained, as if someone has pulled the plug on my energy pack and we haven't even begun the serious discussions that will ensue from these performances.

Richard stands and faces us, his brows are drawn together giving him the appearance of scowling, but I think it's actually a look he gets when multiple thoughts are careening around his brain. "I think it's going to be a long night," he begins. "Let's go back to the other room, order dinner, and start to sort this out. By the time we go home tonight, this movie will be cast, and we will have everyone from the head of the studio down on board with what we are doing."

Finn

I am officially a stalker. I'm trying to come to terms with that as I sit in the lobby of the Casa del Mar.

Where are you, Frankie? Eight hours ago, I was saying goodbye to you after my audition, as if you were a stranger. And now I'm sitting here in your hotel lobby at 10:30 p.m. waiting for you to return. I shouldn't be here. I know that. I really do. I need to give you space. You have to make the decisions that are right for your career, not mine.

What am I doing here? This was truly a bonehead move. *Go home, asshole.*

Rising from the plush chair, I dig for the car keys in my pocket. I can always text her later and see how she is. Or maybe, I'll even hear from her.

"Going somewhere?" I hear the question just as my fingers loop the key chain and I pull the keys from my pocket.

It's impossible not to smile at her. This woman. This woman who has made me feel like I've emerged from a long, dark tunnel is now before me on her little scooter.

"I was just leaving." I shrug. "I realized it probably wasn't the smartest thing to come here and crowd you."

"Leaving would not be the smartest thing." She looks tired.

"Well, you are the smart one in this relationship," I quip, surprised to see her eyes widen as soon as the word relationship tumbles from my mouth with ease, and even more surprised that I actually uttered the R word. Again, I want to kick myself.

I am suddenly overwhelmed with the admission that I am in a relationship with this woman, and that I want to be in a relationship with her, which might even be more significant, as it unleashes the pervasive fear that the wave of emotion I'm feeling in this moment might be either fleeting, non-reciprocated, or based on selfish intent.

"PJ." She reaches up from the scooter and takes my hand.

"I should go, right?" What am I doing here except putting her in an uncomfortable position? *What is it I expect her to tell me? I'm sorry but I couldn't give you the part.* This was totally selfish and shallow of me. *Welcome to LA, baby.*

She shakes her head.

"You sure?"

This time she nods and her eyes mist. She's in pain. *Why is she in pain?* Because she doesn't want to hurt me?

"C'mere." Reaching down, I pick her up in my arms. Holding her like I did after the accident. "Let's go ask the front desk to have someone bring this up to the room." I eye her scooter.

"Let's tell them to bring it by in the morning." Her voice is punctuated with sighs as she tightens her arms around my neck.

"That's an even better idea," I whisper as I carry her into the elevator, my mind already spinning off, wondering if this is the last time I will enter her hotel suite.

I don't want to talk. Not yet. I don't want to know. And I certainly don't want to say goodbye, but that's clearly inevitable no matter how this all shakes out. If the part goes to Mav, most likely Frankie and I will be going our separate ways immediately. I know she'll feel like shit about letting me down, even though I knew this was a long shot. Right now, I want just one last moment in our little bubble before it bursts and dissipates, initiating my retreat to the space I was in before I got the first call to audition for Griffin Chase.

God, that feels like a million years ago.

Entering the room with her in my arms, I can feel the unspoken goodbye waiting just on the other side of this moment, and I'm overcome by this need to prove how memorable I can make it. I don't want her to forget. Not now. Maybe not ever.

Sitting on one of the plush couches, I pull her onto my lap, straddling me. "Frankie…" Searching her eyes, I look for silent words that I want her to write. Does she know anything? Would she tell me?

"Shh." She puts two fingers to my lips and shakes her head before leaning in for a kiss.

Splaying my fingers through her thick, wavy hair, I give a slight tug and receive the moan I've waited all night to hear. My body reacts to the guttural sound as I press her down on me, my hardness greeting her.

I'm aching. Aching to be inside her, sure, but that's not what is causing this discomfort. As I unzip and push her underwear to the side under her splayed skirt, I'm overwhelmed by the sadness born from knowing that this may be our last time. Sinking deep into her, I press her down, not letting her move. I need to be deep within her, as if my mere presence is going to invade places I don't usually think about invading. A place I need to invade. I'm surprised. My heart aches as I struggle to impale hers, wanting her to feel that ache she often writes about. I want to be the real one. It's me.

Can't she see that?

Or does she still just see him? Has she always only seen him?

But her eyes aren't telling me that as I pull her head to my shoulder a nanosecond before being thrust from our bubble as it is pierced by the shrill ring of my phone on the couch next to us.

"It's Sebastian," she informs me, peering over at my cell. Pulling her head back to add, "You should answer that." Her look is serious and I'm reading it as somber. "Answer it," she urges again.

Reaching for the phone with my right arm, I use my left arm around her waist to hold her tightly onto me.

Is it insane to still have hope?

"Hey, what's going on?" It's late for him to be calling me.

"Just got off the phone with Sherri. Nothing's official, nothing's in stone, but she told me we might want to be thinking about a range of acceptable numbers."

"What?" I can feel my eyes widen as I search Frankie's.

"She said your performance today was amazing and that your chemistry with Eva is off the charts."

"Wow. I'm just speechless." And I'm buried deep in the author right now. *Holy shit.*

"I'll let you digest this, and we'll talk in the morning. I want to push Sherri on what she thinks the upper limit is. I think she'll help me to some extent. Congratulations, boychick."

Frankie is now moving on me, and a slight moan escapes my lips. I need to end this conversation with Sebastian immediately. "I'll talk to you in the morning." Tossing the phone onto the couch, I look at a smiling Frankie in my lap. "There's so much I want to say, but it's going to have to wait until I've fucked every last brain cell out of that adorable head of yours." I tell her as I hold her on me, and rise from the couch. We head toward the bedroom, our connection still intact, the physical being the less important at the moment.

Lying her on her back, I place both her legs on my right shoulder so that the cast is not next to my head, and bury myself deeper into her, my pace starting slow, thrusting all the way in, slowly pulling out and watching her composure begin to crumble.

"Touch yourself," my request is brusque as I quicken both the pace and intensity of my thrusts.

This isn't goodbye for us. So, why can't I let go of what feels like pain. I need to let go of pain. I need to learn to let go of pain. The tide is turning. Go with it.

Closing my eyes in an attempt to focus on the opposite of pain, I feel Frankie grabbing for my hand and threading her fingers with mine, tethering me, keeping me from being alone.

"Let it go, PJ." I hear her whisper and feel the pain start to dissipate at the sound of her voice. "Let it go." She knows so much. Without my ever having to tell her, she knows so much.

As a stream of tears comes out of nowhere, I'm horrified. I'm fucking this woman and crying. *What the hell is wrong with me?* Driving into her harder, as if that's going to hide my weakness of emotion, I finally open my eyes to find Frankie with her eyes now closed, tears streaming out of the corners, and I muffle an odd, sob-like sound fighting to escape me. Squeezing her hand tightly, as I finally let go, coming deep within her, I battle my need to turn away, so unnerved that she sees me this vulnerable.

Letting her legs slide down from my shoulders, she yanks my arm, pulling me down onto the bed next to her and rolls to face me.

"You've had a lot pent up, haven't you?"

"I guess more than I've realized. Sorry," I apologize, wiping my cheeks with the back of my hand. *How freaking embarrassing.*

"Nothing to be sorry about," she assures me.

"Can I ask you a question?"

She nods and gives me a small, reassuring smile.

"Am I getting the part because of this?" With my hand, I indicate the two of us.

"No." She shakes her head. "You're getting the part because of this." Sticking out her right arm, she perches it right under my nose. "See that?"

"See what?" I pull her hand and bite down on the heel of her palm.

"Ow!" She yanks it from my grasp, twisting her arm so that I can see the top. "See that?"

"Yeah, what happened?" There are four small, crescent-shaped scabs. I pull her arm back to my mouth, softly kissing her where the cuts are.

"You happened. It was you. Your performance with Eva caused that."

"How's that?" I'm confused now.

"Those are the marks of my agent's fingernails. She dug them into me watching you perform." She stops and smiles, explaining, "Your performance made her maim me." Then dramatically adds, "What you did today made her scar me, PJ."

I can't help but laugh, immediately enjoying the cloud of self-doubt lifting, as she blows it away with her soothing story.

Pushing her wild hair from her face, I tell her, "You make me feel good, Frankie. I really did okay today?" I want her to tell me what it made her feel. I need to know if it ripped her to her core, the way it did to mine.

"Do not doubt your talent. You are so good. You took everyone on a journey with you today. It was mesmerizing. It really was." She swipes a hand softly across my now clean-shaven cheek. "You really look like him now."

My flinch is involuntary, but I can see she feels it and caresses my cheek again.

"And you like that." It's not a question. I know her attraction to me was based on my looks, which is something I've been accustomed to with women my entire life. But this one was a bit stranger because she liked my looks because I look like someone in her head. Someone with a heroic personality that can only be found in fiction. She didn't like me because I'm PJ Finn. Well, at least, I know she didn't initially.

And I wasn't interested in her because she was some cute blonde who made me laugh and think and feel and look at myself.

Well, at least, not initially.

Have we really both moved off our initial motivation?

"I like it both ways. You look great like this. But I loved your scruff." She continues to softly rub my cheek, which is still sensitive from being totally bare.

"Two days you'll have scruff back." She liked my look for me, not just the Griffin look.

"Good," she mouths the word.

"Can you tell me what happened after I left today." I nudge my leg between her thighs and pull her closer.

"We went into a screening room and watched several screen tests. It was really interesting to look for different things. How did it feel overall? Chemistry with Eva."

"Hmm." It escapes before I can stop it.

"You two have chemistry, PJ. There's no denying that."

"And how do you feel about that?"

"I think it will translate brilliantly to film."

I can feel her emotional retreat. Although, with my leg between hers, I'm physically restricting her from pulling away from me.

"How do you feel about it, Frankie?" I'm not letting her off the hook.

"PJ, I'm not going to lie to you. It was very hard to separate myself out of this and really look at what was best for the film. You had to give the best performance and have the best chemistry with Eva for me to say to everyone, 'He's the one.' And you did. And they all saw the same thing I saw. They saw someone who was perfect for the role."

"Well, thank you." I lean forward to place a kiss on her nose. "It's because of you, you know. You let me pick your brain and gave me so much insight into the character. You put up with my crazy, nit-picky questions, and I know I went into that screen test with a better understanding of Griffin Chase than anyone else could have had. But, Ms. Author, you still haven't answered my question."

"How do I feel about you and Eva?"

I nod.

"Again, I had to separate myself. Do what was best."

"But not necessarily what you wanted?" I need to hear her say that.

"I would have been more comfortable with her playing opposite Maverick. But that's my shit. You were the best person for the role, and I did what was right. For everyone."

She kind of said it, but not really.

"But not necessarily right for you?"

"PJ, soon you are going to be off filming and doing a lot of pressers and it's going to be all about you and Eva and selling a love story. I'll be back in Texas most of the time, writing. Doing what I do."

I feel like she's trying hard to sound casual about it. But, maybe I'm wrong. "You won't stick around through production?"

"I'll be there for key things, or as needed. But I've got deadlines and editors waiting on me." She shrugs.

"You can write out here." We both seem surprised by my comment. "You should get a place. Rent something." I quickly recover, trying to seem more casual about it.

"I don't know. This is not my home. I'm not an LA person."

And, unfortunately, I have to agree with her. Too much time here would gnaw at her soul, dim the light she's unaware she even possesses. I would hate to see that. Although, I'm drawn to her light and I'm beginning to realize just how much I like having her around.

"Well, if you need a place to stay when you're out here," I whisper, mostly because I loved the days she stayed with me, and I'm hoping that subtly lets her know there will be nothing going on between me and Eva.

And I have this feeling that I'm going to miss her. Which is not a typical emotion for me and the women who have been in my life. I've made an artform of not missing women.

What she's not saying is blaring, a loud noise between us shrouded in a sad silence. We're both feeling it. I can tell. It's like we've come to the end of something and there's no apparent beginning stretching before us.

"I appreciate the offer."

"I liked when you were there. And there's been some decorative changes you need to see."

"Decorative changes?" She laughs.

"You're just going to have to come over to see them. I'll make you dinner one night before you head back to Texas." Pulling her close, I kiss the top of her head. "I'll even have your favorite avocado ice cream for dessert." I'm smiling as I tease her.

She looks up from my chest with a huge smile, her eyes misty, hopefully from remembering our first kiss. "Am I ever going to get back my lace bodysuit?"

"No. That's part of the permanent décor. If you want to wear it, you can come over, but then it stays."

I can't help but think her smile doesn't look happy. The bodysuit stays, but she doesn't. The film has been cast, and that is what she was out here to do.

I want to tell her to stay. But maybe this is all we were ever meant to be. Maybe it was all about Griffin Chase for both of us and we each actually got what we each wanted and needed and it was time for our chapter to end.

Maybe we were just a short story.

What a difference a week makes.

From the moment the trades got wind that *Fleeing an August Moon* had been cast, the studio public relations team went into overdrive and the paparazzi heeded their call. Now, as I sit several seats away from Frankie at a long, blond-wood conference room table and pretend there is nothing between us, a whole dramatic story about me and Eva is being created for both the press and the public. I wish I had sat down next to her so that I could be pressing my thigh against hers as all this talk about me and Eva reconnecting is being discussed, but all I can do is watch the muscle tinges in her cheeks as she remains cool and professional, taking notes in that little notebook of hers.

Eva and I are going to be seen everywhere. A whole world is being created for fans, one that has no bearing on our current reality, but will become the narrative that builds the excitement for this film. The story of two people who found each other again through Griff and Briela.

You can't make up this shit.

Frankie will give a few interviews with us, initially, but then the public relations focus will be on just me and Eva. It really is hitting home that Frankie putting us together as the leads really was a testament to her professionalism. Or maybe it doesn't affect her that much and I was just her personal Griffin Chase stand-in.

Nah. Just being insecure.

Mindy, the publicity guru, looks down at her ringing cell. "I need to take this. Let's break for twenty." She grabs her phone and is the first one out of the room.

I've never been part of press and PR planning in this capacity before, not even with the streaming show. It's amazing how orchestrated everything is, little tidbits of information leaked out to tease the public, right down to Twitter posts that Eva and I will tweet at predetermined times, reservations made at restaurants to ensure paparazzi is camped out in full force. The level of detail is extraordinary to spin this yarn about me and Eva and our rekindled love affair.

"There's my girl." I find Frankie standing outside the building. She's not checking her phone or anything, just staring at the buildings on the lot.

"Hey." She looks up at me with a smile.

"Why didn't you tell me you were going to the doctor. You know I would've taken you." Her foot is now in a boot.

"It was fine, and I knew you were tied up in meetings." She shrugs.

We have avoided each other in the presence of everyone associated with the film so that there's no talk of impropriety or our affair being the reason I got the role. We both know that nothing good can come of that for either of us, if that is what the studio and investors think.

"Plans tonight?" I inquire.

She shakes her head.

"How about that dinner I promised to cook for you?"

With the first bright smile I've seen in too long, she nods. "I'd like that."

"I know you just want to skip to dessert."

She laughs. "The avocado ice cream?"

"No, me."

"Well, then, I plan to overindulge."

With a smile, I turn and walk back to the building as one of the producers approaches her.

We're okay. She's doing okay with all this.

I'm actually worrying about a woman.

It feels good.

"Oh my gosh, PJ, this place looks beautiful. You are so good with color. I'm going to have you come and decorate my place."

"You like?" I'm loving her response to my apartment's renaissance.

"Yes! You really have an eye for this. I could never bring a place together to look like this and have it all work. I'm very impressed."

"I can thank my mom for this. This is definitely her influence."

"I like that. I'll bet it feels different when you walk in here every day."

"Totally. And I have you to thank. So, thank you." I give her a little side hug. "I didn't even realize I'd been living the way I'd been until you pointed it out."

Walking around and checking out all the pieces, Frankie turns to me and smiles. "I get such a sense of PJ from all this." She picks up a metal vintage airplane sculpture splattered with bright blue paint. "You have such a great eye, and I think an artist's soul."

"That might be the nicest thing anyone has ever said to me. Now let's see what you think of my cooking." I wave her into the kitchen.

"It smells good. What are we having?"

"Spaghetti with homemade vegan meatballs and sauce. I cooked last night, so it will be even better today."

"You are pulling out all the stops."

"An easy way to say thank you."

"You don't have to thank me, PJ. You were the right actor for the part. That's why you got it." She seems annoyed that she has to tell me that again.

"Yeah, but Frankie, we both know that I bugged the crap out of you to understand the character. So, thank you for letting me do that."

"You cared enough about the role to want to know. And I appreciate that."

Stirring the sauce, I pull the spoon out and hold it out to Frankie for a taste, before bringing the spoon back to my mouth.

"Mmm, that is good. Gotta love a man who can act, cook, decorate, and is damn good in bed."

"Bed, huh? I like that thought, let's go have that dessert course and work up an appetite for dinner." Taking her hand, I gently pull her toward the bedroom.

"Here I thought I was the main course."

"Baby, you are a dish. That's for sure. One that needs to be eaten slowly and savored."

Coming to a dead stop as we enter the bedroom, Frankie halts me. "Oh my God." She laughs at seeing the red lace bodysuit tacked to my wall next to the TV.

"You can put that on for me later tonight. Right now, we've got to get everything off you." Pushing her blouse from her left shoulder, I lean down to run my lips from the arch of her neck to the curve of her shoulder, her slight quiver having quite the effect on me.

"I'm going to miss this," she moans.

I'm going to miss this.

Straightening up, my hands go to her shoulders as I look down at her.

She's leaving.

Not that I didn't know that. But still, hearing it is like a sucker punch. "When?"

"Saturday morning."

It's not the news I wanted to hear. "Will you at least let me take you to the airport?"

"I'd like that." She smiles.

"Well, I'd better make this good, huh? Give you something to remember me by." Unbuttoning her blouse, I push it from her shoulders.

"Mister, you are not forgettable." With a not-so-soft caress, she rubs me on the outside of my pants, and I acknowledge, hardening against the pressure of her touch and the rough fabric. Unbuttoning and unzipping my pants, she lets her hand dip in. "Commando." Her eyes light up at the discovery, matched by a wicked smile.

"Well, I knew you were coming. So to speak."

"I like a man who is ready." She gives me a squeeze and it's impossible not to respond even more to her touch.

Putting my hand over hers, I guide her up and down the length of me, squeezing her hand to tighten around me, and as we lock eyes, I return her earlier sentiment. "I'm going to miss this, too."

In case you haven't guessed it, that's Parker-speak for, 'I'm going to miss you, Frankie.' Though that's much harder to admit.

Even to myself.

Pushing my pants down, I step out of them and give them a good kick.

"Impressive," Frankie comments with a smile when they land clear across the room, and then looks down at the glistening head of my cock crowning her enclosed hand. "Very impressive." She affirms with a smile.

"You haven't been in my bed in way too long, let's change that." Taking the hand that has been stroking me, I pull her to me as I tumble back, and she lands beside me. Reaching over, I tug her skirt down. "Commando." Now it's my turn to be amused at her little surprise for me.

"Well, I knew I was coming. So to speak." Gently slinging her leg over me, her eyes are smiling, as she says, "I can do that now without maiming you," referring to her now cast-less leg.

With my hand spanning her thigh, I pull her close to me, immediately warming my hard cock against her smooth skin.

Closing her eyes as a small moan escapes her smiling lips, she positions herself, and slowly, very slowly, slides down, pressing herself to me, surrounding me like a sheath.

"You don't really have to go, do you?" *I am going to freaking miss this.*

"Why? You going to miss me?" Her grin is positively evil as she tightens her muscles around me.

"What do you think?"

"Well, I hope you miss this." Very deliberately she moves up and down on me.

"You know I will." Grabbing her ass, I thrust hard up into her for the first time. "And I hope you miss this." For effect, I thrust hard again. "Maybe I'll even get a chapter." I whisper into her ear.

"You'd be a most interesting character."

"Me?"

"Yeah, you'd make a great character." She nods, with a smile, not missing a beat as she slides the length of my cock.

"Because I can make you come fifty ways to Sunday." It's not a question, it's my cue to make sure she misses having my cock slamming into her.

"Well, that, too." The words barely surface as she begins to edge.

Backing off on the pace, it's time to reel her in, make her hang until I get there. "Too? What else?"

"You know, we've talked about it. I met this aloof, guarded guy named Finn. A blank palette, or so I thought, but it turned out he was the person to introduce me to PJ...this guy who is warm and funny, with a whimsical eye for slashing the palette with color. And now I'm leaving, and I haven't met Parker yet."

I can't believe we're actually having this conversation while fucking. And what's even more unbelievable is how we're allowing our vulnerabilities to be exposed.

"Parker" My name comes out in what sounds like a grunt. "I think my dad and brother and sister are the only people who know him. I don't even think I know him anymore."

"Did Eva know him?"

I stop thrusting and hold her still to me, taking a moment for my eyes to focus on hers. I'm surprised that Eva has made it into bed with us. It's like a red flashing light in my head, and obviously even more alarming than that, she's in Frankie's, or she wouldn't have brought it up.

"No. Eva doesn't know Parker." Pushing her hair back from her face, I shake my head. "Frankie, Eva doesn't even know PJ." I continue running my fingers through her thick waves. "If you referred to me as PJ, she would not know who you were talking about."

Pulling her in for a kiss, I begin to drive into her hard, as if my rough pounding is going to punt Eva very far away from us. I need Eva out of our bed and out of Frankie's head. And the only thing I can do now is fuck her away from us.

In that moment of clarity, I know why Frankie is going back to Houston.

And the only thing I can do is get lost in this moment, while we're still in it, because it is soon about to become a sweet memory.

"What do you mean you haven't told your dad, PJ? That is crazy." Her nose is scrunched up as I hand her back the ice cream container.

We're back in bed again, but that red lace number is still hanging on my wall. Which is not acceptable.

"My dad has never supported me or my dreams, Frankie. He just thinks I'm a dreamer and a bum and that I need to man-up and get a real job."

"Well, you need to tell him about this movie," her tone is adamant and just the mention of the movie is elevating.

"You're hogging the ice cream." I reach to pull it from her hands in an attempted deflection. Talking about my relationship with my dad is never comfortable. Never has been, and I'd venture to say, it never will be.

Giving up the container, she smiles, then looks down at her now-empty hands before sending me back down on the see-saw. "You should talk to your father."

"It's not so easy."

"And that's what will make it so worthwhile." Inch-worming closer to me on the pillow and aligning the tip of her nose with mine, she shakes her head, our noses rubbing. "PJ, you have the chance to still be in one another's lives. That's a gift. Don't miss the opportunity to reopen that door."

"It's really complicated, Frankie. It hasn't been good since my mom..." It's hard to even finish the sentence.

"I know. And I can't even imagine what that was like for you, but I never got to say goodbye to my dad. The last time I saw him, I was running out of my parents' house to get back home because I had to get in my writing word count for the day. A word count I'd created for myself. It wasn't because I had anything due to an editor or publisher or anything, it was an arbitrary goal I gave myself. I blew him a kiss goodbye. I didn't think anything of it, and I was out the door. But if I had known. If I had known I would never get to hug him and kiss him goodbye again, I would never have blown him a kiss from across the room. I mean, really, what was I thinking?"

Pulling her to me, I can't hear this story without holding her tight. "What happened?"

"My dad worked for an oil company. There was a catastrophic fail on the rig he was on in the Gulf."

Houston. The Gulf. Makes sense.

"I'm so sorry," I whisper.

"Thank you. Make sure you have no regrets, PJ. They are a bitch to live with. So, this is my advice to you."

"You have lots of good advice, Frankie Simonelli. You are like no other woman I have met before." Sitting up, I feed her a spoonful of ice cream.

"Is that a good or a bad thing?"

"It's a great thing."

This is not going to be easy to replace. I know that. A grueling shooting schedule is going to make it easier, that's for sure. I'll be able to get lost in my work. Come home, crash out. Do all the press things. Not have time to miss this. And I'll see her again. It's her movie. She's going to be involved. It's not like we're not going to be a part of one another's lives – at least, tangentially, for a while.

It's just that I got spoiled with her being right up the beach from me.

"You're going to miss avocado ice cream." I feed her another spoonful.

Leaning in to kiss me, she purrs, "It might end up being among the top five things I miss."

"Hold this." I hand her the ice cream container and swing my legs off the bed. Looking back at her, I smile. "It's time to get this freaking thing off the wall. I swear, it's torturing me. I need to see your gorgeous ass in it." Removing the thumb tacks, I run the bodysuit through my hands.

"Do I get to take it home after tonight?"

"Not a freaking chance." I toss it to her. "Now put it on."

"It was really nice of Richard to do this for me." Frankie is telling those of us standing in a group near her at a Friday evening going-away party hosted at the home of our director. As we watch the sun rush to greet the ocean, all of us are in awe of the sweeping view from the hilltop of his Malibu home. "It's not like y'all aren't going to see me again."

Searching for a word to sum up my feelings, the only thing I can come up with is surreal, and even that fails to describe how my life has changed. And how rapidly that has happened. The studio has booked me and Eva onto late-night talk shows, daytime shows, print magazine and digital press interviews, podcasts, and special events, keeping our calendars full until the start of production. Seeing their buzz machine at full-throttle is a thing of beauty. They've got this down to a science.

What I can't believe is that we've gotten through to this point and no one has a clue about me and Frankie.

Pretty amazing.

Caught in the illumination of the setting sun's warm, golden rays, strands of Frankie's wild hair glow and beg to be smoothed in the humid air, but it's not like I can walk over to her and run my hand through an unruly lock. As I nurse a gin and tonic, I can't help but check out her toned legs and how perfectly her little round ass fills out her short, flouncy turquoise skirt. Would she be so bold as to attend commando? Even with her leg in a boot, she still looks hot. *But is she commando?* That would be a nice gift on her last night here, and immediately I wonder if maybe I can inspire a scene for her next book, set in one of Richard's ten-thousand bathrooms.

Catching her eye, I nod my head, motioning toward the house, and excuse myself from the group. Making my way into the house, I wander in search of a restroom, but I'm quickly distracted when my eye catches a large, cobalt blue piece of artwork hanging in the hallway. On closer inspection, the piece appears to be an etching marrying subtle elements of architecture and cartography, but what's so striking are the vivid colors and how well it works in a home overlooking the Pacific.

"This is definitely your taste." Frankie is beside me.

"Absolutely, but definitely out of my league." I laugh.

"That's not true any longer. I understand your agent is quite the negotiator." Playfully, she elbows me in the ribs.

Taking a quick glance around to make sure we are alone and out of view of any of the catering staff, I slip my hand under the back of her skirt, cupping a firm, bare cheek, before discovering the lace string of a thong.

Leaning down, I approvingly whisper, "Lace. Oh, yeah. That's my girl."

Still staring straight ahead at the bold etching, she smiles at my words. "Lace strings are your specialty, after all."

Giving the string in between her cheeks an upward tug, her sharp intake of air has the same effect on me as if she had just rubbed the front of my pants.

Grabbing her hand, I pull her after me down the hall. Opening the first door, we discover a coat closet. Looking at Frankie, I shake my head and we continue down the hall to the next door. This one is a bathroom. I nod and she smiles, returning the nod.

"I've been wondering all night if you were commando." I admit, locking the door behind us. "But lace thong will do." Lifting her onto the white marble vanity, I assess the height. "This'll work," I comment, pulling her toward me with her legs spread.

"I'm glad you have long legs," she giggles, and I feel like a mirror, I can feel that happiness and I'm wondering how the heck I can hang onto it, onto this moment.

Leaning forward to kiss her, she twines her arms around my neck.

"I can work with this."

"Well, then, get to work," she volleys back.

"Yes, ma'am." I'm smirking as I pull my zipper down.

Three, two, one... and right on cue, Frankie whacks me in the shoulder with the back of her hand. "Ma'am? What the heck!"

Slinging an arm around her shoulder to her waist, I pull her closer to the counter's edge, my other hand slowly grazing her thigh as I head toward the lace string and the mission of pulling it to the side.

"We fuck a lot fully clothed, have you noticed?"

Maneuvering the lace, I can feel how ready she is. "Who has time to take off clothes."

"Good point," she says, reaching out and guiding me to her. As the tip of my cock brushes against her, she smiles at me. "Even a better point."

And that's all I need to hear to drive the point home. The whole evening, leading up to this moment, pretending there is nothing going on between us, was our foreplay. Finding each other's eyes as we were engaged in conversations with different groups of people, both knowing we would find a way to make this moment happen, had my balls aching all night.

Burying her face against my shoulder to muffle her sounds as I bury my cock deep in her. "PJayyyyy..."

"Shh." I hold her head tighter to my chest. I've never talked more during sex than I do with this woman, but right now I need her to keep silent.

"Then fuck me faster and harder." She loses breath halfway through the sentence.

"Someone wants to come fast tonight."

She responds with a mewling sound, and with both hands, I pull her to the very edge of the vanity.

"Squeeze me, Frankie," my whisper is gruff and the moment she bears down on me, I bring one hand to the front, pressing my thumb hard on her clit.

As her breathing becomes ragged, I know I've got her on the edge, and start to rub her in a counterclockwise motion, not letting up on the pressure as I plow her deeply.

"Oh God, PJ." A spasm runs through her entire body, every muscle, vibrating and setting me off, my own grunt probably too loud.

Wrapping my arms around her, we stay still, until breathing isn't so labored.

"Does that get in the next book?" I'm still holding her head to my chest and I can feel her nod.

"We just had sex in the director's bathroom. This is so Hollywood."

"Couldn't let you leave town without being properly indoctrinated." Grabbing a plush, monogrammed towel, I comment, "This is probably rude to do with someone's good towels," and run a corner of it under warm water, using it to clean Frankie and then myself before helping her down from the vanity.

"Let's see if we can get out of here without getting caught." Her smile is wicked as she reaches for the door, unlocking it.

The moment the lock clicks off, the door swings open. I can hear Frankie gasp and her whole body jumps at the shock of another person opening the door from the outside.

"Sebastian." My tone is definitely not calm and cool as we stand face to face with my agent.

"Well, this is a surprise," his tone is as amused as his face. "I didn't know you two were..." Neither of us answer, and to fill the awkwardness of the dead air, he adds, "Well, I guess when I told you where she was staying, you took the opportunity to..."

I know he doesn't miss the alarm on my face as I stand behind Frankie, nearly pressed into her ass.

"When did he tell you that?" Frankie turns to me, the crevasse between her eyes something I'm seeing for the first time.

Is it shock? Confusion? Anger? Not sure.

Caught off-guard, nothing rolls off my tongue as either a cover story or the truth. I can tell from the energy shift in the air, this is not going to end well.

She looks back at Sebastian, who has now realized he's said too much.

"When did he tell you where I was staying, Finn?"

Finn. *This definitely is not going to end well.*

"Shortly after the first audition," I confess.

"So, before the first time we met on the beach?" The devil is in the details, her specialty as a writer.

"Yes." There's no reason to lie. This is already bad enough. I sat there at breakfast and pretended that day that I didn't know she was staying at the Casa del Mar.

"Well, that certainly answers a lot of questions that have been hanging out there." As she nods, the distance in her eyes is clearly evident as I wait for the veil to fall... three... two... one... and there it is. Her gaze shifts to a spot on the bisque-colored walls. "Well, alright." Turning, she brushes past Sebastian, leaving me standing in a bathroom with my agent.

If she had wondered if any of this was real, she is now no longer wondering, because this damn well looks like I set her up, just another Hollywood hack willing to sell his empty soul for stardom. Bing-fucking-o.

Heading back out to the lawn, I pass by the group of people she is now talking with and stand there for a moment. She purposely does not look my way, and I move on toward the bar.

Looking out over the ocean as I wait for the person in front of me to order their drink, only a few streaks of pale red light shred the darkness as day seeps into night.

How do I make this right? Not just because of the film, but between us.

The nagging question always at the back of her mind is never going to stay put again. It will always shroud everything. As I reach my turn at the bar, the sky has totally exsanguinated the last vestiges of the sun's color bounce.

"You are looking particularly handsome tonight." Slipping her arm through mine and standing too close, her overpowering perfume displacing the scent of Frankie that has been wafting up from my shirt. The darkened sky feels like more than just nightfall. As is becoming habit, Eva's timing is impeccably bad.

Looking back over toward Frankie, she is no longer with the group. Extricating my arm from Eva's grasp, I take off back to the house to look for her. We need to talk. She's got to know that this wasn't all a set-up to get the part. That, yeah, I did know where she was, but running into her that first day was truly a coincidence and not me stalking her for a part.

She is never going to believe that. Do I?

Richard is walking out of the house as I'm about to enter it. "Have you seen Frankie?"

"I just put her in a car back to her hotel. She said she wasn't feeling very well."

Finn: It's not what you think. I text her a few minutes later, standing off in a corner of the massive white and stainless kitchen.

Frankie: Finn. Just don't. Okay.

We are definitely back to Finn, huh. In my mind, I see a door slam shut.

Finn: No, Frankie, not okay.

Frankie: Well, that's a fucking understatement.

Finn: I'm going to come to the hotel. We need to talk.

Frankie: Don't come. I'm going to get a new room key, so don't even try.

Finn: So, you don't even want to talk to me, hear what I have to say?

Frankie: We started with a lie, Finn. You are a very good actor and it landed you the part. This isn't a total surprise. I'm not stupid.

Finn: Frankie, you can't leave like this.

Frankie: Actually, I can. I'll see you when I have to see you for press stuff. I'm turning off my phone now. I've had enough for one night.

I wait until 6:20 a.m. before texting her again. I am supposed to pick her up at 7 a.m. for the airport.

Finn: Coming to get you.

It's five minutes before my text alert sounds.

Frankie: I'm already gone.

I somehow knew that long before I even sent the text.

She walked away from me. She fucking walked away from me.

"Hey, Dad, it's me." He picks up after the first ring.

"Parker?" The surprise in his tone makes my heart hurt a little.

"Yeah."

"What a surprise. Is everything okay?"

"Yeah, yeah. I just wanted to say hi. See how you were doing?"

"It's been a while."

"Umm, yeah, I know. I'm sorry about that."

"Are you working?" he asks me.

"Not yet, but I'm about to start on a film. A big one." I feel the need to explain and justify myself, as always. "Leading man," I add, as if that's going to win his approval and pride.

"Do you need money?"

I know that is the reason he thinks he's hearing my voice.

"No. No. Nothing like that. I'm solid financially. Really." There is something I need from him, but it's not his money. "Dad," I can hear the hesitation in my own voice as I begin. "I think I fucked up."

Frankie

I think I might be OCD.
... Or maybe, I've got some kind of pervasive thought disorder. I'm really not sure. But there is definitely something wrong with me. Oh, shit, I hope it's not like a brain tumor or anything.

Who am I kidding? Brain tumor, pfft!

It's a wounded ego.

I got caught up in it. Caught up in him. That handsome face, those ungodly clear blue eyes, the muscles in his thighs when he was running.

I got caught up in my own fantasy. Beginning and end of story. I got to be the heroine instead of the author for a brief moment where the role wasn't just in my head.

It was intoxicating.

Every single moment of it.

And now I can't get it out of my head.

It's been difficult to see the daily rushes that Richard's PA sends me. I freaking see him every day. I didn't make a mistake casting Finn and Eva. Their chemistry is iconic. This couple will remain with people for a long, long time. The casting is on point. I know that. And I know I flinch every time he kisses her or holds her in his arms. I know what he smells like, and when I see Eva's face against his chest, I swear I can smell that. I know what he feels like against her cheek.

I know. I know.

I need to watch the rushes. Make sure everything is working. It's part of my job. But what I don't need to watch are the talk shows. I don't need to read the magazine or the online stories about the exes who found themselves in love again through their on-screen characters. I just can't. Whether it's manufactured or not, there's only so much shit I can subject myself to.

It's better here in Rockport than at home in Houston. It's just a much more conducive place to finish off the first draft of this new book, even though this house is a vessel overflowing with memories. The ones that stand out in my mind most are fishing with my father, whether from the dock behind the house, or on Pappy's boat out on the bay. The echoes of my mom yelling at him that I was getting too sunburned haven't dissipated with the years, and it was here that my love for running on the beach was born, as I pounded the surf-smoothed sand, eavesdropping on voices in my head that I was yet to recognize were characters begging me to tell their stories.

The house had been my grandparents, the home where they raised my father. A little boy more at home on the water than on land, it was no surprise to anyone who knew him growing up in this seaside town, that he would eventually go to Texas A&M for Petroleum Engineering and live half his days on an oil rig in the middle of the Gulf.

The pace in Rockport is slow and the fish run fast. Tides are the only thing that change with regularity. And there's comfort in that. Change with predictability. Curled up in an oversized Adirondack chair, wrapped in one of my Gran's crocheted afghans, I watch nightfall claim the bay. Somewhere, hundreds of miles to the east, I like to think my father enjoyed a spectacular last sunset. In my version, Dad and his team ate a hearty meal of barbeque Gulf shrimp and jalapeño grits, before settling in for a rousing game of Texas Hold 'Em, never realizing how high the stakes actually were that night.

I just pray it was over in an instant and that he and his team didn't suffer.

Wrapping the blanket around me tighter, the stars begin to present themselves along with a stiff breeze off the bay.

Hey, Daddy, I'm almost done with the new book. I really like it. It gave me the chance to stretch myself and try something very different.

I think I'm about three or four days away from sending it to Caryn and to my editor. I was going to go home, but now I'm thinking maybe I'll stay here and do some remodeling on the house. It's still got a lot of vintage Gran and Pappy stuff, and it would be nice to make it look new and bright. Update the kitchen and bathrooms. Redo the floors. Put in some new windows. Get that hideous flowered wallpaper out of the kitchen.

I can hear you laughing. Yes, that wallpaper should be burned. I certainly have more than enough money to get a great architect and a contractor and a designer, so I think I might stay down here and do it. Rebuild.

Maybe I'll make this my primary residence when I'm not traveling. I feel closer to you when I'm here. And I like that. Do you feel it, too?

I don't know if I ever told you this, but when I was little, I used to pretend that the ghost of an ancient sailor lived here. He'd sailed here on a galleon in the 1730s and the ship was wrecked in a violent storm in the Gulf. Probably a hurricane. He washed ashore on the beach right here, land-bound, unable to get back to where he came from. I vowed to help him find his way home, but we had to find the portal for him to breach the space-time continuum. When we finally found it along a cove of rocks, he decided not to go. He didn't want to leave me.

It's no wonder I became a writer, right?

So, now, here I am, all grown up, and a pretty darn famous author. And part of me hopes you don't want to go through the space-time continuum, but most of me wants you to, if it means you'll be able to rest in peace.

Is it selfish that if you're out there, somewhere, that I don't want you to totally leave me? If it's selfish, I'll stop wishing it. But just thinking you're out there, and that you can hear me, makes me feel not so alone. And yet, here I am in Rockport, hiding, because I want to be alone. If I'm alone, no one can hurt me. I just don't give them the chance.

I really fell for him, Daddy. I really did. I should have known. I had red flags, I knew I was mixing business and pleasure, and that is never a good thing. But I just loved being with him. In some weird way, it felt like our energies healed one another. Like I was helping him come back from a self-imposed dark place and he was helping me live among, and love among, real people. Not just people who only exist in my head.

But I was dumb to believe it was real. There is no real in Hollywood. I know that now. I was a movie-industry neophyte and I was naïve. And I wanted to live my own love story. Which is no crime, but it turned out it was as make believe as the ones in my head, but only worse, because at least those have a happy ending. And I am anything but happy right now.

I feel like I'm totally OCD, Dad. Was I always like this? Not being able to move on. Maybe I was. It just feels so much more acute this time. I confused reality with fiction. I blurred the lines and couldn't tell one from the other. How pathetic is that? I feel like such a loser.

As we went along, I thought I was special to him. And I thought I was falling for him and not a character I created. But it turned out not to be a love story. Not a real one. And I guess I'm grieving. It's like another death. And I know that sounds trite saying that to you. But, Daddy, my heart really hurts with this one.

I'm trying to think what you would say to me. I think maybe you'd say, "Frankie-Girl, the best way to get over a broken heart is to fall in love. With someone else."

And, yeah, I know, I know, I know, I'm not going to meet someone else hidden away in front of my laptop here in Rockport.

Maybe my ghost sailor will pay me a visit. He didn't want to leave me. Maybe he's still lingering around here somewhere.

Pulling out my earbuds, I hit pause on my screen, finally silencing Thomas Rhett after listening to "Crash and Burn" on repeat for over an hour, the repetition of the melody putting my brain into a groove, smoothing all the jumpy edges naturally and allowing me to focus. I'm so close to the end of the chapter I'm writing, and even closer to hitting my word count goal for the day, and it's only late afternoon. I've been rewarding myself with short runs, nothing to stress my bones, but a great way to continue to build the muscles and ligaments that provide the scaffolding.

The ding of a text on my cell phone pulls me away from my manuscript.

Maverick: How far is Schulenburg from Houston?

I find myself smiling at a surprise text from Maverick. Wow. Maverick. Just the thought of him brings back warm memories. Is he here?

Frankie: About ninety minutes. Are you in Schulenburg?

Maverick: I am.

Frankie: Well, I'm guessing it's probably not to see the painted churches. LOL.

Maverick: What painted churches? LOL

Frankie: Filming? Horses?

Maverick: The latter. Came to look at some horses that were abandoned in the floods last year.

Frankie: :-(So many animals were lost. It was terrible. You are a nice man, Maverick Dailey. How long are you in Schulenberg?

Maverick: Just today. I'm arranging transport for three of the horses. Was thinking after that maybe I'd hop over to Houston to see my favorite author (flying out of Houston tomorrow).

Frankie: Somehow doubt I'm your fave. I'm down on the Gulf in Rockport. Probably about two hours from Schulenberg. I can come there or you can come here.

Maverick: Rockport sounds good. Never been. Can be there this evening. Dinner?

Frankie: Best offer I've had in months! Will seafood, a great whiskey menu, and a water view work?

Maverick: Send me the address.

Frankie: I can't wait to see you!

Well, that was a surprise, to say the least. Kind of ironic that my self-imposed exile ends with a visit from Maverick Dailey. Quite the way to be dragged back from the edge of oblivion, I laugh.

Looking in the mirror, I see myself for the first time in weeks, maybe months.

Frankie-Girl, you need a shower. You'll scare Mav if he sees you like this!

Even with a baseball cap pulled low on his brow, there's no denying that gorgeous profile. His perfectly straight nose and strong chin are unmistakable, even the uncharacteristic dark scruff can't render him incognito. As he lifts his whiskey glass, I'm halted in my tracks. This is who I'm meeting, and the warmth I'm feeling is more than a little surprising. I was always so conflicted about him and now, just seeing him, without *Fleeing an August Moon* hanging over us, the friendship piece of our relationship envelops my heart as I walk the few feet to his barstool.

Turning his head slightly as I approach, he puts down the whiskey and rising from his barstool, opens his arms for me.

"Francesca." He pulls me to his chest.

Holding him, probably longer and tighter than is socially acceptable, I'm drowned by what feels like all that's been lost, memories repressed of the sunshine and squalor of LA.

Finally letting go to gaze up at his handsome smile. "Maverick Dailey, you are a sight for sore eyes.

"I'm glad you feel that way." He doesn't bother to hide the surprise on his face.

Sliding onto the barstool next to his, I can see the bartender is very interested to know who I am, now that the famous movie star's date has arrived.

"I'll take whatever he's having." The illuminated bar behind him lights up the array of caramel shades filling the bottles on the shelves behind him. With ease that appears to be muscle memory, he grabs a bottle from the third shelf and pours a generous neat whiskey, then refills Mav's glass.

Lifting my glass, I begin a toast. "Welcome to Texas. To friends."

"To friends." He clinks my glass, his eyes sparkling in the dim light.

"So, three more horses?"

"Yeah." He laughs, shaking his head. "We'll see how Miss Jua responds to her new paddock-mates."

"How is Miss Jua?" I take a sip, and let out a little "mmm" as the first wave delivers a sensual burn.

"Ornery as ever."

"She didn't like me."

"Nothing personal. She doesn't like women."

"Women? Or women with you?"

Laughing and taking a sip, his grin turns wolfish. "Astute, Francesca."

"So how many of us did you bring to meet her."

"A few." He shrugs.

"Oh, man, that is totally a douche move. Totally. Playing on women's emotions that way."

"Busted."

"Geez, Mav. Well, I'll bet that got you laid."

From the tilt of his head and laugh, I can tell I hit the nail on the head.

"So," I continue, "how many women who have met Jua have slept with you?"

"Everyone. But you."

With a shake of my head and an exaggerated sigh, I can't help but tease him. "And here I thought I was special." Although I'm joking, I feel as if I've just been robbed, I thought taking me to meet Jua was something just us two shared. I should've known, nothing is quite as it seems in Hollywood. *That,* I learned in spades.

"Ah, but you are special. Very special." The man is a thief of hearts.

"As special as Eva?" It is out of my mouth before I even know that I'm going to say it. *WTF, Frankie.* That was some insecure woman shit, and not a good look at all.

His hazel-green eyes are piercing as he silently regards me. "Eva." He sneers.

I immediately want to fill the silence, but intentionally remain silent to listen. I figure he's at least one drink ahead of me. That should have loosened him up.

He doesn't disappoint.

"Much more special than Eva. She's not in your league, Francesca. She's..." He takes a moment to think. "Hollywood."

I shrug, indicating that I don't know what that means.

"They all kind of blur together."

"You kind of took her under your wing." I can see he's looking for a response, so I fill it in for him. "Gives good head?"

Slapping a hand on the bar, his burst of laughter has me laughing. "I've had better."

"So, what was it with her?"

"She was pushy. Physically good for the part, she looked like what I had pictured Gabriela would look like, and it turned out she could actually act." He takes a sip. "And she gives decent head."

"Gives, as in present tense." Now I'm prying. If she's still sleeping with Mav, maybe she's not sleeping with Finn. I know all the news stories are part of the PR, but they are together everywhere. Even I'm buying the storyline, it feels so real.

"Not recently."

Not the answer I want to hear.

"Well, maybe with the new horses you can lure her back into your lair, or paddock, or mansion."

"No, those new horses have a much more noble purpose."

"Oh, and what is that?"

His face lights up, "Let's get a table. I have lots to tell you." Turning to the bartender, he asks, "Do I need to close out, or can this go on our bill?" He points to the restaurant side to indicate we're going to be staying for dinner.

"No, you're good." And he replenishes both our glasses before we walk toward the hostess to be seated.

"I'm totally fangirling." The hostess can barely speak.

"Does that mean I get a table with a good water view?" Mav flirts with her.

"Yesss," she drags out the word. "Can I get a picture." She's already digging around on the hostess stand for her phone.

"I'll take it," I offer.

"Oh no, I know who you are. I want you in the picture, too." She flags down a waiter to take the shot.

Mav is on her right side and I go to flank her on the left, but he slings an arm around my shoulder, pulling me to him.

"Well, that'll be all over the Internet in minutes." He laughs as we sit down in a section of the dining room that is more secluded.

"Nah, probably just her Instagram."

"By the time we finish dinner, we'll be all over the media outlets."

"You think?" We're in a fish and whiskey joint in a little town on the Gulf coast. I can't imagine this will make it past the hostess's personal social media pages.

"We'll check after dessert. If I'm right, you have to meet me for avocado toast next time we're both in LA at the same time."

"Wager's on," I agree to the terms, knowing I won't lose this one and be forced to eat the nasty, green mush.

"So, tell me about the noble cause for the horses," I urge, after we've ordered.

"Well, with these three, I'm going to be up to seven rescues. The first step is to make sure they are all nursed back to full health, and then I'm going to have trainers work with them. The horses I've adopted all have really mellow temperaments."

"Jua?" I interrupt.

"Jua might be my exception." He laughs. "She's my alpha mare, but the other six I think will do well."

"What are they being trained for?"

"Hippotherapy." The smile on his face might be the most real I've ever seen from him, filled with passion and clear joy. "The horses will work with people with disabilities and people who have had injuries and strokes, to help them rehabilitate."

"Mav." My heart is swelling. This is a man never to be underestimated.

"It'll be therapeutic for both the horses and the riders. The horses know when they are helping, and it gives them purpose. As for the riders, especially kids, they tend to bond with animals in ways sometimes they can't bond with humans. It's a very spiritual kind of relationship. A win-win for everyone."

Wiping a tear from my eye. I certainly didn't expect this. "You are one impressive man, Maverick Dailey."

"I'm assuming, Ms. Texas Girl, that you know your way around horses."

"I grew up in a saddle. No surprise there."

"So, if I do a benefit fundraiser auction-type thing, will you help?"

"You know I will. Anything I can do. Just don't leave me alone with Jua. I bet she kicks and bites."

"Only women." He laughs.

The waitress arrives with a tray of oysters, placing it between the two of us.

"May I have a wine list?" Mav asks her.

"Sure, let me grab one." She turns, and without taking a single step, grabs one off the empty table behind us.

"Pinot grigio?" he asks me.

"Are you staying down here tonight?" Whiskey and wine, not a good combination for the road. I nod to the waitress that the wine selection is fine with me.

"I've got a flight out of Houston tomorrow, so I'll probably drive back up there tonight."

Shaking my head, "No. Not happening. I've got plenty of room. You'll spend the night at my house, and you can drive up to Houston in the morning.

"Stay at your place? Is that why you ordered oysters?" Smirking, he cocks an eyebrow, taking one from the silver tray and loosening it with his seafood fork.

How can I help but not laugh, although my gut is not chuckling with me. "Eva gives better head than I do." I attempt to deflect, a tactic in which I'm experienced.

"Did her boyfriend tell you that?" He's still smirking as he slurps his first oyster.

I open my mouth to answer, but nothing comes out. *Does he know about me and Finn?* I thought we'd been really discreet. *Does everyone know?*

"Eva was convinced he was sleeping with you," he continues.

"Is that why she thinks he got the part?" Picking up an oyster shell, I'm a bit panicked at the moment, feeling exposed and in need of defending myself and feeling the guilty weight of Mav not being my first choice.

"That was definitely her theory."

"I see." *Well, she had one part right.*

"You know what I wonder..." He focuses on loosening another oyster from its shell.

"What?" I'm seriously afraid to hear.

"I wonder if those two set us up."

I'm begging you, oyster, do not come back up. Stay down. Slide right down into my stomach where you were meant to go. No returns!

"What do you mean?" My throat has constricted to pinhole circumference.

"Everyone in Hollywood knew the movie was casting and you had final say so. It also wasn't a secret that I was in talks."

"Mmm, no, I don't think so, because I didn't know I'd be at the Golden Globes with you, so there was no way they could have known."

"That's true. But something just doesn't feel right about the whole thing."

"I don't know." I shrug. *But I do know.* I know good and well that Finn running into me was not purely coincidental. He knew how to find me and then led me to believe he didn't know I was staying at the Casa del Mar. "Do you think she used you to ensure she got a chance to audition?"

"Oh, absolutely." He slurps another oyster. "These are delicious, by the way."

"Fresh from the Gulf."

Uncorking the bottle tableside, the waitress pours a taste into Maverick's glass and he promptly hands it to me to taste.

"It's wonderful." I nod to the waitress and she finishes pouring, taking her time, clearly not wanting to leave our table.

"Here's what I think." He washes down his oyster with the pinot. "I think she thought you would not be interested in her reading for the part, and I was a shoe-in to get her there and she would do anything to make that happen."

"I believe that's true. She knew you could get her access."

"Would you have not brought her in for an audition."

"I don't know. I'd just met her that night for the first time. Honestly, Mav, she kind of overwhelmed me." Picking up my wine glass, I look at him with a smile. "I think she and Jua have something in common."

"I think you're right." He laughs. "You're a threat to her, Frankie. You've achieved a level of success in your field that she's only dreamed of in hers."

"Yeah, but that's what I don't understand. I was in the driver's seat to help her make that dream come true. She should not have been antagonizing me."

"She was really antagonistic?" He looks amused. "I think if it was just about the part she would have been smarter, but she let her need to be the only woman in the room get to her. Frankie, there was palpable tension between you and Finn. She couldn't handle that."

Palpable tension? Oh, fuck. "The woman is stunning, I can't even imagine..."

"There you were, in your cowboy boots, the new girl in town." He cuts me off mid-sentence. "Successful, smart, beautiful, and her date wanted to bang you."

I choke on my wine, sputtering it up. Half-laughing, half-freaking out.

"I'm sure they'll both do a great job in their roles. From what I've heard and seen, they burn up the screen together and the whole exes coming back together to play this couple is truly brilliant and has the world shipping for them already."

He slurps another oyster. "But something about those two is just not sitting right with me. I feel like we were double-teamed."

"Well, I hope not," is all I can say.

With each passing day, my time with Finn has seemed less and less real, and now Maverick's words have darkened any memory of the joy of living life in the moment with him. I'm not sure if it's anger, sadness, or embarrassment, or some combination of the three that I'm feeling, but the loss shouldn't feel so devastating and so fresh for a short relationship with such a dubious foundation. But the pain of the burn is excruciating. Why does something that I should have been able to walk away from like a good-time fling feel so bad?

I have been dreading, even before tonight, the point where I have to step back into things for pressers with them and the talk-show circuit. And now, after listening to Mav's gut feelings, my apprehension has ratcheted up a few notches.

How could it have felt so good and right with us and been totally nothing? Could that possibly be? It's not Griffin who causes these feelings of emptiness, it's Finn. Actually, it's not even Finn, it's PJ. Whatever it was that I felt between us is not leaving me. I'm haunted and I'm hurting, and I want to tell someone, but if anyone knew, I'd be skewered by the studio and the investors.

Picking up his phone when it buzzes, Mav lets out a hearty laugh. "I definitely should have upped the stakes on this one."

"What is it?" I'm also laughing, because he's so hysterical, although I have no idea what I'm laughing about.

Handing me his phone, I see the headline on the *Hollywood Hotline* app, **Mav and August Moon Author Getting Cozy on the Gulf Coast.** Below is the picture we took earlier, except the hostess is cut out, so it's just a picture of Mav pulling me into him.

"Wow, forget about waiting until after dessert," I comment. "We haven't even had the main course."

"Well, since we didn't even make it until dessert to get outed, I say why wait until LA. I think you're going to be having avocado toast for breakfast, my friend."

"They're doing a table read now," the production assistant explains to me, gesturing to the laptop in front of her, as I stand looking over her shoulder in the film's administration trailer.

I can see that they're in a room that doesn't look like it's housed in a trailer. "Is this on-site here?" I can't take my eyes off Finn as he reads his lines.

"No, that's about a half-mile down the road. Driving in here, you passed by some warehouse buildings. It's in there."

I'm half-listening, I zoned when she said it was a quarter mile away. I'm a quarter mile away from Finn. And Eva. And they are both right in front of me on this laptop screen.

"They've been using the facility for indoor shots. Tonight, they'll be filming the scene they're rehearsing now on location, which is about fifteen miles south of here, down near the border."

"Did Richard want me to come to the table read?" I'm hoping not. Being in a room with Finn for the first time, with everyone else there, including Eva, is making me feel anxious and I've got enough anxiety as it is about seeing him again for the first time

"He said, if you wanted to, I should bring you over or if you wanted a tour of what we have here and then to wait for him in his trailer, he was also fine with that. It's up to you."

"A tour sounds nice." I put my purse and notebook down on a table and follow her out, taking a last glance at the computer. It appears they've finished a scene and are about to take a break. Eva lays her head onto Finn's shoulder and his arm drapes around her affectionately as he pulls her closer and kisses the top of her head.

I really did not need to see that.

"Let me show you where all the make-up magic happens. After the table read, cast will be in here having make-up done. Tonight is going to be a long night."

Freaking understatement. It's going to be a long night indeed.

I'd asked Richard prior to making the drive down to south Texas not to let people know I was coming, explaining that I didn't want it to distract anyone's flow. He understood and I think was relieved.

Standing off to the side, in the dark, watching the set in full action is a rush. The lights, the booms, the cinematographers. It really does take a village to blow life into all of this. I just sit at my little desk and scribe the things coming out of my head. But it's just me, alone with a cast living in my mind. I see all the places that will be up on the big screen, but the screen in my mind is comprised of visions I translate to words. It's such a bare, minimalist process in comparison to all of this. This is truly a production.

It's hard to believe this is my book that I'm watching as the story is unfolding in front of me. The feeling is surreal and made even more so watching Finn, who has completely transformed into Griffin Chase. He is the person I've seen in my head for years. And he looks very similar to a guy who used to be in my bed. It makes me wonder if in my head and on the pages of my books are the only two places I can successfully maintain a relationship. My real-life experiences, including the one with Finn, haven't worked out as well.

An assistant approaches and hands me a *Fleeing an August Moon* baseball cap. Merchandising, wow, now that makes it feel real. Pulling my hair, thickened by the night's humidity, into a ponytail, I thread it through the back of the cap and pull it low to my brow. The illusion of being incognito is calming as I dread the first meeting with Finn, whom I have successfully avoided since my arrival. If I could script it, we wouldn't be face to face for the first time with Eva around.

Shaking his shoulders out as they finish the scene, someone hands Finn a water bottle, which he nearly finishes in one draw. Here I am, maybe a hundred feet away, standing in the shadows, silently watching. Eva's being touched up by make-up. Finn runs his hands through the top of his hair, and what strikes me is that that is a Griffin mannerism, not a Finn mannerism. And for some reason that makes my heart hurt, blurring my ability even further to identify and admit to things that are painful. Seeing Finn is painful. Walking away from whatever it was we had hurt like hell. Hurts like hell. Present tense. Although, I haven't really let myself do a good job of feeling it. I am a master of burying reality and resurrecting it as fiction playing out on the pages of someone else's life, someone who is not real. I can transmit the pain to them, write about it and never, ever have to recognize it in my own life.

Done with the touch-up of her make-up, Eva walks over to where Finn is standing. Putting his hands on her shoulders, he says something to her. She smiles up at him and shakes her head. I can see his smile as he pulls her to him, holding her close for a few moments before loosening his hold. Taking her face in both his hands, he kisses the tip of her nose.

The gesture is very intimate.

I've seen enough.

Finn

Three days. I have three freaking days all to myself.

No shooting. No crazy hours. Not being surrounded by a gazillion people. Three days' worth of clothes packed in a rental car and I have no clue where I'm going. Santa Fe? Austin? Houston? That's probably not the best idea. An airport? Dunno. Don't care. I have three days and I am one burned-out motherfucker. I need to just get away from everyone and recharge.

Stepping into the admin trailer, I'm greeted by Abby's smiling face. "You out of here?"

"I am." I know I'm grinning at just the thought.

"Where are you off to?"

I just shrug and shake my head.

"Nice," she drags out the word.

"When am I on the schedule next?"

"Let me check." She looks back down at her computer screen. "Not until Tuesday mid-day for a table read. So, you've actually got four-and-a-half days."

"You just made my day." Maybe I will drive to Santa Fe after all.

"Glad to be of service." She laughs and reaches for a file on the desk. As she lifts it, the shock of what is underneath pounds in my chest.

What the fuck?

"Is Frankie Simonelli here?"

"Oh, shit, I keep forgetting to mail that." She pops her forehead with the heel of her palm.

"She was here?" I ask again, my mouth dry.

"Yeah, she left it on my desk."

"When was that?" I'm trying to act cool, nonchalant, and I'm failing miserably.

She thinks for a second. "Earlier in the week. She was here in the afternoon and then went out on location for that first night of night shooting. You didn't see her?"

"No, I must've missed her. Too bad, would've been nice to say hello." I've regained my equilibrium.

Rifling through some pages of notes on her desk. She sighs with relief. "Here it is." She pulls out a padded envelope and addresses it before slipping in the worn leather notebook with Frankie's initials, and then sealing the envelope.

Without even thinking about it, I reach down and pick up the envelope. "I'll mail it for you on my way out of town," I promise. "If anyone needs me, call my cell. Have a great weekend." I need to get out of there before she decides that she has the responsibility to get this back to Frankie.

Tossing the package onto the car seat, I glance over at Abby's neat handwriting and plug into the car's navigation system an address in Rockport, Texas.

Three hours and nine minutes.

Sorry, Santa Fe. Destination Rockport.

The name sounds familiar and it only takes a moment to remember why. That's where she was photographed with Maverick Dailey. In Rockport. Fucking guy. He'd better not be there in three hours and nine minutes.

Turning onto US-281, two-hundred miles separates me from Frankie. It's been hard enough during location filming to know that I'm in the same damn state as her. Each day, I've been waiting for her to show up. And fuck me, she did. Came and went without me even knowing it. How could she not let me know that she was there? It doesn't seem like the Frankie I know, who is pretty much a straight shooter. Why the heck would she do that?

Not sharing this whole experience with her feels like the sun is not quite making it to the apex of the sky. It's breaking the horizon, showing me how beautiful everything is around me, how fortunate I am to be surrounded by it all, but that golden glow never brightens to where I bask in full sunlight, awakening and warming all that is numb in my darkness.

So, what is it I'm going to say to her when she opens the door? I've got three hours to figure it out. Three hours to find words that aren't scripted for me to try and show her that she can trust me, that what I feel for her is freaking killing me.

The world has been opening up before me in a way it never did before. At least, not before being named as the actor chosen to play Griffin Chase. I can't go anywhere anymore without being recognized, without paparazzi following me around.

I now have everything I always thought I wanted, and it all feels so empty. I feel empty. Which I now realize was the norm of my existence until she came along. And I don't want to go back. But the truth is, hours that I'm not on set working, I am back. One-hundred percent back. No matter what bright colors I put on the walls of my apartment, it doesn't penetrate this dark shroud that's surrounded me since she left. The same one that was there before I first read for the role. The one that I've dragged along with me since my late teens. Even though I never realized it. I didn't know it was there before. It's just the way it always was. And now it feels like Hell.

Frankie, Frankie, Frankie... I hope I can find the words to make you understand...

Cutting east toward Corpus Christi and the Gulf, I can feel both the excitement and dread in my gut. Was this spontaneous road trip totally ill-conceived? Will she be happy to see me? Will she even be there? Will she be alone?

Fucking Maverick Dailey. Seeing them together on *Hollywood Hotline* was freaking shocking, to say the least.

Maverick Dailey, what the fuck is he still doing in her life?

And Lord knows, Eva didn't make it any better.

"Did you see who's shacking up in Texas together?"

"What are you talking about?" I had responded.

Pulling out her phone, she already had the picture of Frankie and Mav pulled up, waiting to gauge my reaction, which I tried to temper as much as possible, but the woman knows me well, and is a master of eliciting reactions, which is exactly what she wanted.

"Hmm," I responded, "I wonder why she didn't give him the role. You'd think she'd want her boyfriend in her movie." I then handed Eva back her phone and walked away.

Later, a chair in my trailer took some abuse when I kicked it into the wall. Sitting down on the couch, I pulled up the picture on my phone, where I could study it closely in private.

What the hell is he doing with her in Texas?

And in this moment, I need Griffin Chase more than anyone. The man is truly my savior, my escape from the pain. The place I can go to be great.

The green sign for the Rockport city limits reads population 8,846. I wonder if she's moved here from Houston to be closer to the water. Maybe she's running on the beach again. I hope so. Another thing to feel guilty about, taking away what she did as her release.

A market on my right catches my eye. *Yes. Perfect.* I pull into the parking lot. Getting out of the car, it feels good to stretch my legs. The air is dank and heavy, but the unmistakable trace of salt on the breeze reminds me of running on the beach with Frankie in Santa Monica.

I am so close.

She's so close.

I'm surprised to be surrounded by water and palms as I drive onto Key Allegro. Canals and a deep-water bay corral the streets that fan out like splayed fingers. No wonder she stayed out in Santa Monica rather than closer to the studio, she needs to be on the water.

I get that.

Pulling up the short, gravel driveway, I park next to a red Mustang Cobra convertible.

It fits her. I can imagine her wavy, blonde hair whipping around in the breeze, driving along the water with the top down.

On the seat next to me sits the envelope neatly addressed to Frankie and the bag from the store. Opening the envelope, I reach in, pulling out the notebook and then grab the grocery bag.

With the gravel crunching under my feet, I start counting the steps to her door. Now is as good a time as any to ask myself if this ill-begotten road trip was really the best path to her heart. As the walkway brings me face to face with a marine blue front door, I realize it's a bit too late to now be wondering if this is a mistake, and with her notebook in my hand, I press the bell with my knuckle.

And again, I start counting. One. Two. Three. Four. With a loud, creak the door swings open.

She's looking at me. Shocked. And it is so freaking good to see her. I knew I missed her. I didn't know it was like this. This is an avalanche and it's all crashing down on me. I just hope I come out alive.

I must be smiling, because she's searching my face and tips her head and gives me a smile. I have just groaned. I'm not sure if that was in my head or not. It could have been. But maybe not.

Holding up the notebook, I ask, "Missing something?" *Or someone?* I'm afraid the answer to that one I might not like.

Her eyes widen, the surprise now complete.

"How..." she stutters.

"I saw you'd left it and thought I'd deliver it to you."

"Wow. I hope they're paying your mileage," she quips.

Her grin is playful, and in that moment, I can feel the anxiety slightly loosen its grip and I know we'll at least talk. Holding up the bag in my other hand, I return her grin. "Are you going to invite me in before this melts?"

"Of course." She steps to the side to allow me entrance, and I hand her the bag as I pass into the living room in what appears, by the décor, to be her family's beach house. A little dated and really comfortable.

Pulling the container of avocado ice cream out of the bag, she laughs and makes her way into the kitchen. As she pulls open the freezer, I'm right behind her, pressing it closed and catching her by surprise, my body so close behind hers that the citrusy scent of her soap prickles my nose.

"We need a spoon," I bend down and whisper.

"Okay." I can hear the hesitation in her voice as I feel her body stiffen, thrown off balance by my physical proximity.

When she goes to grab two spoons, I correct her. "We'll only need one."

Dropping one back, she continues plucking the other one from the drawer. Handing it to me, I follow her back to the living room, where she sits at the far corner of the couch and lays the notebook on the glass top of a driftwood-based coffee table.

Sitting down next to her, probably closer to her than she'd prefer, I remove the lid from the ice cream. Indicating the tabletop, I ask, "Can I put this here?"

She nods, and I put the lid topside down onto the table before digging in and scooping out the first spoonful. Letting the ice cream melt in my mouth and swallowing, I sort of wag the empty spoon at her. "You know, I had it all worked out in my head. I just spent three hours driving here, figuring out exactly what I was going to say to you." Looking back down at the container in my hand, I scoop some more for myself.

"And?"

Pausing to again swallow, I shrug. "I got nothing." I take my third spoonful of ice cream.

"Then why are you here?" She's not looking so pleased to see me anymore.

"I had to return that to you." I point to the notebook on the table.

"Did you read it?" Her arms are now crossed over her chest. Forcefield engaged.

Shaking my head, I take another spoonful. "Not this time," I admit.

"Not this time?" Her tone is becoming indignant and the timbre of her voice rises slightly.

"When I picked it up from your hotel room the night of the accident, I might've glanced at a few pages." With my admission comes a shit-eating grin.

Her eyes narrow, and in that moment, she appears more feline than feminine and I fear being pounced on and scratched.

"C'mon Frankie, stop giving me that look. I know that you already don't trust me." I scoop out another spoonful and deposit it in my mouth, letting it melt before I swallow and start wagging the empty spoon at her again. "But you know what, maybe it's me who shouldn't trust you."

"What do you mean?"

"Do you see me? Do you see Parker or just your boy-toy version of Griffin Chase?"

"I've never met Parker." Her teeth are clenched, her jaw motionless, but yet the words are enunciated perfectly.

"He's sitting here right here in front of you. If you'll open your eyes, you might see him."

"My eyes are wide open."

"And what do you see?"

"Some uninvited, rude son-of-a-bitch sitting on my couch, eating a pint of ice cream and not even offering me any."

I can't help but smile at her. *Damn, I've missed this woman.* Digging back into the container, I pull out a spoonful, extending it to her. Her lips part for me and there isn't a spot on my body that doesn't ache in that moment.

"It was real, Frankie." My voice is soft. I didn't plan to say that, but it just came out, so I go with it. "I know this, because fake doesn't hurt. And this hurts. I hurt."

"Badly?" She smiles.

"Yes, badly. This is funny?"

She shakes her head, points to the spoon and opens her mouth. I'm happy to oblige, delivering more of the lemon avocado ice cream. It's not lost on me that this is what was all over her lips the first time we kissed.

"Not funny. Just a misery-loves-company kind of thing." She pauses, and I know what she wants to ask me. "Finn..."

"Don't call me that," I cut her off."

She ignores me, not going to give me the satisfaction of calling me PJ.

"You were just stalking me for the part. You knew where I was staying. You wanted the part."

"Yes, I wanted the part, Frankie. Every actor in Hollywood would kill for a role like this. But that doesn't mean we weren't real."

Piercing me with her stare, she remains silent, and I feel the overwhelming need to fill that space, the same way I currently have a need to obliterate blankness on my apartment's walls.

"Yes, Sebastian mentioned to me that you were staying at the Casa del Mar. But I ran into you running on the beach. I wasn't waiting there hoping you were a runner and that you would run past me. That happened by chance, Frankie. And then when you mentioned at breakfast that you were staying there, it would have totally creeped you out if I had said, yeah, I know that."

"Well, it creeped me out when I found out."

"I know. And I'm sorry."

"And the Golden Globes?"

That one surprises me. Where did that come from? "I didn't even know you were going to be there. But I will admit something to you. I saw you enter with Dailey right before the taping started. And it definitely got under my skin. I knew he wanted the role and you were there as his date. So, yeah, it got to me. When I saw you leave on a break, I presumed you were going to the ladies' room, so I went out to the foyer hoping to run into you. I was looking for you. And I was glad you were there. I was just pissed that you were there with him."

"Why were you pissed?"

"Because you weren't there with me. And because he was most likely going to be Griffin Chase and that dream was going to die for me." Reaching out, I bring another spoon of ice cream to her lips and she parts them for me. The move once again destroying me as I focus on her lips, remembering what they feel like against mine, knowing what they taste like with lemon ice cream on them.

"Did you and Eva set me up that night?"

Wow. This is worse than I thought. This is what's been going through her head. "No. I had no idea I was going to see you that night." I put the half-eaten ice cream container down on the coffee table and look back up at her. "Now, let me ask you something. Are you involved with Dailey?"

Her reaction is immediate. Shaking her head, she looks pained by the question.

"He was here with you, Frankie. Here, in Rockport."

"He was down in Texas rescuing horses that were injured and abandoned in the floods we had down here in the last hurricane. He's rehabilitating them with plans of opening an equine therapy facility for children and adults with disabilities, and for physical rehab for people who've had strokes and stuff."

Wow. I didn't expect that. And I'm sitting here being a douche about the guy and he's a fucking saint.

"He's really a nice guy, Finn," she adds, softly.

"Stop calling me that."

"What would you like for me to call you?"

"Parker. Or PJ, if you're more comfortable with that."

"I'm not comfortable with any of this."

"Do I make you feel uncomfortable?"

"No." She shakes her head. "You don't."

I take that opportunity to pick up the ice cream container and to deliver another scoop of ice cream, enjoying the dab at the corner of her lip, one that I might have intentionally planted there. Putting the spoon back into the container, I reach forward and wipe it with my thumb. I'm surprised as her hand grabs mine, dragging it from her mouth to near her heart.

"You just left." Even I can hear the emotion in my voice. If she ever questioned that I cared, those three words unveiled a pain I've kept hidden, even from myself, by throwing myself into Griffin Chase, the man she's really wanted all along.

"I was mad, and I felt played."

"I didn't play you, Frankie. I swear." My eyes are locked on hers. "I'm not that good an actor." Her slight flinch tells me those words were dead on. She believes this was all an act.

"There was a part of me that knew that our relationship did not begin," she searches for a word, "with the purest of motives. We both came into it driven by things that are not normal. Getting involved was a mistake."

"I'm sorry you feel that way." She still has my hand clenched near her heart and it's not juxtaposing properly with the words coming out of her mouth. "I guess my coming here today was a mistake."

She's shaking her head, and I swear her hand has tightened around mine.

"You're the wordsmith here, not me, so I don't know if I can adequately explain what I'm feeling. You changed my world, Frankie, we both know that. But it's not just this film, which obviously has been life altering, that I'm talking about. It's how you came along and dragged me out of this self-imposed exile, where numb was my savior and darkness my salvation. No one cares in LA. No one actually notices. I didn't notice the nothing I'd become. And then you came along, and one of your front teeth slightly overlaps the other, and you eat cookies, and hate avocado, and you looked at my apartment and said what the fuck is wrong with you that you live this way. And whatever it was that was frozen in me for so long, you melted it. And under my permafrost, the sky was blue, the trees were green, and there was this girl from Houston, Texas, whose touch saved me from my own darkness." I can see her eyes welling. "And then you were gone. And it was all my fault."

Tears are streaming down her cheeks as she shakes her head. "It's not all your fault, PJ. It's not. I set this up for failure as much as you did. Maybe the reason I write is because the only place I can successfully maintain a relationship is in my head. Maybe that's just a better reality for me."

"I don't agree. The reality you and I were living in Santa Monica and Venice was really good. It wasn't make-believe. It wasn't fiction. It was a great freaking reality."

"But Eva..." Her voice trails off and she looks away.

"What about Eva?"

"You and Eva. I saw you on location. Even when the cameras weren't rolling, it was evident that you two are very much involved. That it's not a studio-created romance, but a real one."

So, that's why she left without a word. She thinks I'm with Eva. I wonder if Eva knew she was there that night? I wouldn't put it past her.

"Frankie, I don't know what you saw or what you think is going on between us, but, baby, I would not have driven here to pour my heart out to you knowing you could tell me to take a hike. There is nothing going on between me and Eva. You have wrecked me."

"Not even a drunken fuck?" she jokes between sniffling back tears.

Pulling my hand and hers away from her heart, I yank her toward me, closing the gap between us. "Not even a drunken fuck." I laugh.

"You thought Eva and I were together and scammed you for the parts, didn't you?

"I didn't know. But, yeah, it crossed my mind. It did."

"That didn't happen. Eva and I are not happening. And the only thing I want is for us to figure out our trust issues. Frankie, I want to be sharing my experience making this movie with you. I want us to be doing this together."

When she remains quiet, I fill the silence. "What are you thinking?" I ask. I need something back here before I start blathering even more about missing her.

"I wanted us to be real. I wanted to be your girl."

"We were real. We are real." Slipping a hand around the back of her neck, I pull her face close to mine. "I'm sorry that I wasn't totally honest with you at the beginning. But I really need you to believe everything between us was real and everything I've said is the truth. It hurts not to have you by my side. Please come back with me. Stay with me while we're filming."

"But the studio wants everyone to believe that you and Eva... we all agreed."

"I'll do what the studio wants publicly to make sure this film is a success. But privately, they don't have a say. Only you and I have a say. So, what say you?" I smile at her.

"What say I?" She laughs. "Who is the guy saying all this stuff to me? Wow. Here's what I say. I say if you don't kiss me right here and now, I'm going to die."

"That's my girl." I can feel the smile of her lips against mine as the tip of my tongue swipes the corner of her mouth, nabbing the dot of lemon ice cream she didn't even know was there.

Pulling back from me slightly, she slides both hands along my cheeks, her thumbs caressing the front of my face. Tilting her head to the side, she treats me to a smile, where I get to enjoy that little overlap of her front tooth, which for some reason makes my heart race.

"Parker." She searches my eyes, the realization clear as a bell in hers. And again, this time in a whisper, "Parker."

"I'm right here, baby."

Right where I belong.

Back in your arms again.

And although I didn't read it, this time, in her little notebook, I had left a message for her to find.

I want a next chapter.
I need a next chapter.
I need you.
~Parker

Frankie

"Your friend doesn't take his eyes off you." Maverick whispers in my ear, as he comes up behind me near the back of the tent.

"What?" I turn to him with a smile as the auctioneer at the front continues his rapid-fire spiel ginning up the bids on a weekend yacht trip.

"Your friend." With his head, he motions slightly over his shoulder, "Finn. He never takes his eyes off you. Just watch, he'll be over here in under two minutes when he sees me near you."

The film's staff had more than an inkling about me and Finn once I'd joined them on location, but, as the studio wanted, that was kept close to the vest, as Finn and Eva made their appearances in the lead-up to the film's release.

As if on cue, Finn appears on the other side of me.

"Congratulations, this is quite a success, and what an amazing center you've built." Finn tips his champagne glass toward Mav.

"Thank you. This was a labor of love." He takes a sip from his champagne glass. "I'm hearing amazing things about your performance. Word on the street is *Fleeing an August Moon* is not only going to be a box-office smash, which we already knew it would be, but that it's going to receive critical acclaim. So, congratulations."

"Thank you." Finn is gracious.

"I need to check on..." Maverick doesn't finish his sentence. Leaning down, he whispers, "See," and winks at me as he straightens up, knowing Finn can see his gesture, before he leaves us.

"I don't care what you say, that dude wants to nail you." Finn drains his champagne flute.

Shaking my head, I grapple for a moment with telling him that Maverick spent the night at my house in Rockport. "Come, let's walk around the facility." And although, I want to grab his hand and lead him from the tent, I know I can't publicly touch him yet.

As we head toward the paddock, we pass a small boy on one of the rescue horses being led around the ring, and pause for a few moments to watch him. Next to them walks a woman, signing to the little boy.

"This is so special." I can't help but smile watching this. There is pure joy on the child's face as he follows his instructor's direction.

"Dailey is a good guy," acquiesces Finn.

"Yes, he is." We continue to walk along the post-and-rail fence. To our left, the ocean dominates the vista stretching several hundred feet below. I stop to take in the view and breathe in the comforting scent of salt carried on the breeze.

"So, when he came to see the three horses in Texas," I begin, "that's when he came down to see me in Rockport. We met for dinner at this whiskey and seafood place." I see Jua with another horse at the far end of the paddock and steer Finn in that direction. "It was late, and we'd been drinking, and I didn't want him to get back on the road to drive the four hours back to Houston. So, I invited him to stay at the house."

"He couldn't stay at a hotel?" Finn stares straight ahead as we walk, hands shoved deep into his pockets.

"I'm sure he could have, but I've got extra rooms at the house, so I invited him to stay."

"Why are you telling me this?" He looks over at me.

Stopping, I look up at him and smile. "Because I never want us to be in a position again like we were in the beginning."

"Fair enough." He nods and resumes walking, then stops and turns to look back at me when he realizes I am no longer beside him. "Your feet not working?" His eyebrows raise with a sexy grin.

"Do you want to hear the rest?"

"You don't owe me any explanation. We weren't together."

With a few steps, I close the gap between us and reach out, letting my hand slide down his shirt sleeve until it joins his inside his pocket. Immediately, he twines his fingers with mine.

"Nothing happened, Parker. We were both drunk, went to separate bedrooms, and passed out, and in the morning, he made me eat avocado toast because I'd lost a bet." I can feel my nose scrunch up at just the memory of it. "Seriously, he didn't lay a hand on me."

Squeezing my hand inside his pocket, he laughs. "I'll bet he wanted to."

"Maybe. I don't know."

"I do know." And there it is, that little muscle tick above his jaw.

"I'd just spent months, pretty much alone, and I was seriously questioning whether or not I was actually capable of having a successful relationship with an actual person, someone who doesn't only exist in my head."

"Frankie," he shakes his head, "that's fucked up. You have no idea how easy you are to be in a relationship with, and you are more present than any other woman I've ever been with. You are so easy to be around. I hate when you go back to Texas."

"Well, then, maybe I shouldn't."

"Shouldn't go back?"

"Yeah, look at this." I gesture toward the ocean with my free hand. "I should find a place here."

"I'd like that. A lot." Pulling our hands out of his pocket, he let's go, slinging an arm over my shoulder, and letting out a chuckle as he feels me stiffen. "I'm really kind of over us hiding."

"Just until after release," I sigh, and tentatively put my arm around his waist. This is the first time we've touched one another outside of four walls that contain only us.

"Do you really think the public will care?" he asks.

"I think the studio has done a great job of crafting the fantasy, and I'll be the wicked witch who breaks up the real-life Griffin and Gabriela. People are going to hate me for 'breaking you up'. There's whole online communities shipping you two. There's no way I get out of this without being that evil bitch who stole you away and broke up you two."

"Maybe we're the real Griffin and Gabriela, Frankie. Maybe the story should be that the author found her real-life leading man." Kissing the side of my head, he drops his arm from my shoulders. "Before the studio sues us both for breach of contract."

I follow suit, letting my arm fall to my side.

Soon the charade with Eva will be over and the movie will be out.

"So, house or condo," I ask, as we stand side by side, atop a hill overlooking the Pacific, not touching.

"With your travel schedule, condo would probably be the better choice."

Nudging his pinky finger with mine, I look up at him and smile as we lock fingers.

"You're bad." He gives me that smile. "Don't make me do bad things to you in Dailey's house."

I tighten my pinky around his. "It's not like we haven't done stuff in other people's homes." With a subtle body check, I suggest, "Maybe we should try the barn."

"The barn. You are a dirty girl. I like that." He returns, with a shoulder check.

"It's a Texas thing."

The glints from the afternoon sun along the waves cresting below are enticing. I could gaze at this every day and be happy. Actually, I am happy. Very happy. "If I get a condo or a house out here, up in the hills or down near the beach, will you move in with me?" I blurt out.

"Wow. Expect the unexpected." His clear eyes are piercing.

Was that a good unexpected or a bad unexpected? I'm holding my breath.

"Only if I get control of filling the wall space," he says in the next breath.

"So, that's a yes?"

"When you're not traveling, where are you?" He's giving me a 'C'mon, Frankie' face.

"At your apartment." I smile.

"Mmm-hmm. Yeah. So, I was under the impression we were already living together."

"Oh, you were, huh? Okay." I'm silent for a moment as I continue to take in the vista. "I really like it here with the hills and the ocean. Do you think I'll be able to find a condo or a house up here?"

"If you've got the money..."

"I actually do." I laugh.

"Then, it looks like me and my girl are moving to Malibu."

My girl. My insides still turn into those of a fourteen-year-old every time he says that. We are the love story in this. He was right. The girl who was living in her head and the guy hidden behind a myriad of identities. Who both found that slightly broken together doesn't necessarily have to make a mess, but can end up like two disparate pieces of art hanging next to one another and end up complementing and enhancing the other, forming something so much more complete and balanced.

"Come. There's someone I want to introduce you to." I turn and start walking toward the paddock again. She's drinking from a trough near the barn as we approach the fence. "Jua." Her ears perk as I call out to her. Lifting her head, she gazes at me for a moment, clearly not impressed enough to stop watering. Even from the slight distance I can see how much she's healed since I last saw her.

"What happened to her?" I can see Finn is disturbed by her scarring and loss of hair.

"That's Jua, she's the horse who was a victim of the Camp fire. She was Mav's first adoptee and he nursed her back to health."

"Wow. That's amazing. Actually, everything he's done here is pretty amazing." He gazes over at an older man on horseback in the ring working with his therapist. "Horses in need of care helping people in need of them." Nodding his head, he looks back at me. His eyes looking like a peaceful ocean. "It says a lot about him."

"Yes. It really does."

"Jua, are you ignoring our guests?" Maverick's voice booms as he approaches from behind, standing next to Finn along the railing.

Upon hearing his voice, Jua whinnies, and immediately trots over, halting directly in front of Mav.

"Hey, sweet girl, lots going on today, huh? I know that's not your favorite thing." He pets the side of her muzzle and she responds with a sputtering sound and nuzzles her head to his shoulder.

Both Finn and I make a simultaneous "Aww" sound as we witness this sweet bond.

"Have you said hello to our guests?" Maverick asks the horse. "This is Finn." He introduces him.

Reaching out, Finn puts his palm out flat for her to get his scent. "Hey, Jua. Frankie, has told me all about you. You are one impressive girl." As if knowing she's been complimented, she rewards Finn with a nicker and a sniff to the face as if she's going to kiss him.

"Hmm, should I be jealous?" Mav asks her as she revels in the attention of the two men petting her. "She really likes you."

"Hey, Jua, remember me. It's been a while." As I reach out to pat her neck, the horse swings her head, thrusting my hand out of the way, and baring her teeth in a not-so-friendly smile.

"Whoa, that's not nice. Francesca is our guest." Maverick reprimands her. She seemingly ignores his rebuke and moves her head back and forth between the two men, enjoying all the attention.

She can't really hate me, that was probably just a fluke reaction, right?

Again, I reach over, this time to give her a soft pet on her blonde-colored mane. The sound she makes is not her soft nicker as she swats my hand away hard with her nose and goes back to flirting with the men.

"Wow, she really doesn't like me." I am truly feeling dejected.

"You know she likes to be the only female around," Mav says, his tone apologetic at his horse's less-than-welcoming behavior.

Finn's laugh is snide as he says, "She reminds me of Eva."

Throwing his head back in laughter, Mav lets out a loud bellow. "She does. You are absolutely right, she does."

And with a high five, Finn and Maverick finally find their bond.

Shaking my head, I laugh. "I have a feeling this is going to be the start of a beautiful bromance."

Epilogue

Finn

World Première

"**W**hat time is it?" We have the darkener shades drawn in the bedroom.

"Only 6:30," I tell her. "Go back to sleep. I'm going to go for a quick run, then hop into the shower, before I leave for LAX to get my dad."

"Are you sure you want to take him back to your apartment and not just bring him back here?"

Sitting down on the edge of her side of the bed, I push her messy hair from her face, that sleepy face that starts every day with a smile for me. "No. It'll be good for me to have alone time with him, and it gives you and your mom time without me here. Besides, you'll be busy with hair and make-up stuff."

"That's true, without you here, we'll get to talk about you." Smiling, she wipes the sleep from her eyes. "And Caryn gets here around 2:00 p.m." As she stretches and moans, her tank top rides up her belly. If she does that again, my form of exercise won't be running. "Want me to come running with you?"

"You should rest. It's going to be a long day."

"I'm too excited to rest. I'm nervous and I'm scared. I want everyone to love it, you know?"

"I do know," I assure her.

"I'm glad we're going through this together, Parker. I can't imagine not sharing tonight with you."

With my hand on her cheek, she caresses her face into my palm. *This woman.*

"I can't imagine not sharing every night with you."

"You know what I can't wait for?" She reaches out for my other hand, threading her fingers through mine. "I can't wait to be seen in a restaurant with you."

"Soon, baby."

Sooner than you think.

Bending down, I kiss her softly. "If you're asleep when I get back, I'm not going to wake you. I'll see you later at Grauman's Chinese. We'll wait for you at the start of the red carpet."

"Tell your dad I can't wait to meet him." She's already back on her side, curled up, with her eyes closed.

Gathering up weeks of mostly junk mail from the overflowing mailbox, it feels weird to be walking into my apartment, and even stranger to be doing it with my dad. It feels so small and dark compared to the condo, but the colorfully decorated walls look great, if I say so myself.

"This looks like her," are his first words upon entering the apartment.

"Thanks." I take the remark as a compliment and am happy to have inherited my mother's eye for both color and putting contrasting things together in a way that creates a new and better whole.

"You remind me of her." Walking around, he inspects the bright objects heavily peppering the walls.

"Thank you. I like to think I got the best of both of you." I call over my shoulder as I bring his bags into the bedroom. Standing his suitcase up next to the bed, Frankie's red bodysuit tacked to the wall next to the television, catches my eye. "Oh, shit." I laugh, quickly pulling out the thumbtacks and shoving the tantalizing red lace into a drawer. Looking back at the wall, the big, empty white spot annoys me. It's just wrong. All wrong.

Stepping back out into the living room, I find my dad still inspecting all the objects, lifting an airplane, then a metal sculpture of a dog.

"Make yourself comfortable. Can I get you something to drink? I think there's some bottled water, and maybe a beer or two." I should've thought about coming to stock up before he got here, but with a non-stop press and TV schedule leading up to release, I didn't even think about him staying here with an empty refrigerator.

"I'm fine." His back is still to me and there's something in his stance that makes me immediately feel uneasy. "I'm sorry if I wasn't good to you," he begins. "It's because you are so much like her, and I was so angry that she left us."

"I didn't understand that. All I knew was that you didn't want to have anything to do with me." I grab a bottle of cold water for myself, knowing I need something to hold onto. I knew today would be emotional with the première and all, but this, I did not anticipate.

Turning to me, I can see the weariness in his eyes. This has weighed heavily on him. "I'm sorry. I should have been a better father when you needed me. I should have gotten help." He shakes his head. "I should have gotten help for all of us."

"I felt so guilty. Like it must be all my fault. I must've done something wrong to make you hate me. I tried to run as far away from the pain as I could, and that meant losing myself. So, that's exactly what I did. I reinvented myself and I lost Parker. Parker was not worthy. I buried him six feet under with Mom because I couldn't stand to even look at him."

"But this looks just like him." He gestures to the apartment and its colorful décor.

"It does now. But it took me a long time to find him again. And I needed help to get there. I just didn't know I needed it. I had never consciously realized that creating Finn was a shield so that I would never again hurt the way I did when I lost Mom. And then you."

"The pressure of raising you kids when I didn't know how to even make it through a day was too overwhelming. I couldn't see past my pain to even notice that my kids had no idea how to handle their own grief. Not only was I no help, I made it more painful for you by pushing you away when you needed me, needed family, most."

In the flick of a moment, the searing pain swirling inside me pulls me right back to those first days when I consciously had to tell myself to breathe, to hold it together until night, where under the cover of darkness, I could come undone. I'm amazed at how close to the surface this all simmers.

"I'm sorry, Parker. I'm sorry I was not there for you and your brother and sister when you needed me most."

"Dad, I forgive you. There really isn't a roadmap for grief. She was our glue and we lost our glue." I want him to stop carrying this burden. "She'd be so happy that we're here together tonight."

"How did you find yourself again?"

Just that thought sweeps the hurt away. "This little ball of Texas sunshine showed up in my world. And Finn wasn't going to win her heart. But she let PJ in."

"This is the one you messed up with?"

I nod.

"How'd you get her back?"

"I introduced her to Parker."

Frankie: Just pulling up now. Frankie texts.

Finn: I see you getting out of the limo. Walking toward you. That color. Wow!

Frankie: LOL. I thought scarlet might be apropos.

"And you're in your white tux jacket," she says, approaching, as I bend down to kiss her and her mom, Carol.

"Dad... this is my girl. This is Frankie and her mom, Carol."

"It's so nice to meet you, Mr. Finn." She goes right in for the hug, no handshaking for Frankie Simonelli.

"Kevin. Please call me Kevin." I can tell he's immediately drawn in by her warmth.

"Kevin." She smiles and nods. "Now I see where Parker got his beautiful eyes."

He's already smitten, I can tell.

"Finn. Finn. Where's Eva?" someone calls from the crowd.

"Finn, look over here."

"Marry me, Finn."

"Francesca, I love your books."

"We'll be right back," I tell our parents, and Frankie and I walk quickly over to the rope to sign some autographs and take pictures with fans.

Rejoining our party, I ask, "Dad, would you escort Carol on the red carpet?"

"It would be my pleasure." He extends his arm to Frankie's beaming mother.

"This is so exciting," she says to him, slipping her arm around the crook of his elbow.

"Time to flip the script," I whisper in Frankie's ear as the barrage of flashes begin, and I offer her my arm to start our very public walk together down the red carpet.

First press stop is *Hollywood Hotline*. The reporter looks a little flummoxed at seeing me enter with Frankie.

"That dress is amazing. Who are you wearing?" she asks Frankie, knowing it's easiest for her to recover with a stock question.

"Marino Ray." Frankie smiles, not missing a beat. I know she's making it up, there is no designer named Marino Ray, and she has no clue who designed her dress. It's hard to keep a straight face.

"Does the screenplay follow the storyline from your book, or did the screenwriters take a lot of liberties with the material?"

"All in all, it's pretty faithful. Obviously certain things work better cinematically, so readers seeing the film will see some deviations from the book."

"They always say the book is better than the film. Are you worried?"

"I hope the film is better. I generally hate my books when I'm done writing them."

The reporter's eyes widen. I don't think she knows what to do with Frankie, and gives her a fake smile before turning the microphone on me.

"Where is Eva tonight?"

With a shrug, I conjecture, "I'm sure around here somewhere."

"We thought we'd be seeing you walk the red carpet as a couple as this movie seems to have brought you together."

"No. Eva is not with me. Eva and I dated in the past and have remained the best of friends." Leaning toward the camera and mic, I smile, pausing for effect, and in a conspiratorial tone, I confide, "This is the one." I point to Frankie. "This is the one I love."

The shocked reporter barely misses a beat before shoving the mic in Frankie's face. "Francesca, what do you have to say about what Finn is telling us?"

Looking down at Frankie, our eyes lock. I'm daring her to be bold.

Turning from me to look directly at the camera, she says, "I have to thank Griffin Chase for bringing me Finn Parker."

"That's my girl," I whisper and feel her melt into me.

"I think fans worldwide are going to be surprised when they learn of this," the reporter continues, her tone revealing she's not sure how she feels about our coupling.

"Yes, they are." I flash a smile, knowing every news outlet is going to want the footage I'm about to give them. Sliding my arm from where it's resting on Frankie's shoulder, I reach into the inner breast pocket of my white dinner jacket, and slowly drop to one knee just as my hand closes around the small box. I hear the gasps in the background, but they seem far away, like distant thunder on a muggy, summer night.

"I wish you were scripting this because then I know my words would be perfect." I hear laughs in the background, but all I can see is Frankie chuckle at that statement. "I didn't know how blank the walls of my life were until you showed up with a can of red spray paint in one hand and cobalt blue in the other and dared me to show you who I was. You led my spirit out of the cold with your warmth and your faith in me. I can't imagine any man being more in love with a woman than I am with you. Frankie Simonelli, will you spend forever with me?"

I see the nod first, before her lips even form their silent yes, and as I take her hand, I slowly bring it to my lips to softly lay a kiss before slipping the ring onto her finger. Rising from my knee, I take Frankie in my arms and smile down at her, bending to kiss her for the first time as my fiancée. In the background, flashes and cheers become the special effects and soundtrack to the *Fleeing an August Moon* première's surprise love story.

"I think we just flipped the script," I whisper.

Eva who? The press from tonight is going to be all about Frankie and Finn.

"You certainly know how to write the start of a chapter." She smiles up at me.

I have been holding my breath for the last two hours. Surreal does not even begin to describe watching *Fleeing an August Moon* on the big screen in a packed theater. As hard as I'm trying hard not to pick apart my performance, I'm finding it impossible not to think I should've played this scene or that scene differently, and I'm letting it detract from my ability to just enjoy the greatest night of my life.

But seeing myself up there, with everyone watching, and knowing what I know is going to happen, well, yeah, I'm freaking out. Maybe even more than I was flipping out about asking Frankie to marry me on the red carpet.

I figured she was going to say yes.

But with this, I feel more... exposed. There's no turning back.

Frankie is grasping my hand so tightly that her engagement ring has etched a new groove into my palm.

This is our moment.

The story playing out on this screen before us is now part of an indelible fabric that will always bind us together. No matter what. It is the culmination of two individual dreams intertwining and becoming inseparable.

I glance over at Frankie. She is thoroughly entranced by the images on the screen, images that had previously only been in her head. And here they are, laid bare for all the world to see.

My heart is racing as the film nears the end.

There's no turning back now.

And I feel totally exposed.

The theater is still silent as we see Griffin and Gabriela facing away from us. He holds their infant son in one arm and reaches for Gabriela's hand. As the sun breaks the horizon, we watch them walk toward the light until they are just a speck on the horizon.

There is not a sound in the theater.

And in the sustained silence, the credits begin to role and my hand tightens around Frankie's. She doesn't know.

Directed by Richard Lesser

Based on the book *Fleeing an August Moon* by Francesca Simonelli

Starring:

Parker J. Finn as Griffin Chase

The reaction throughout the audience is audibly discernable as they wonder if this is a mistake.

No mistake.

I can see the glisten of tears as Frankie reads the words on the screen and then turns to me, her smile positively brilliant.

There's no hiding anymore. Not now. Not ever.

Parker J. Finn as Griffin Chase

As the audience rises to their feet, the ring of applause peals through the theater, resounding and resplendent, validating the dreams of all involved, from the woman next to me who gave these characters life, to the editors piecing together the final cut, and every single one of us in between. This is our moment. Right now, right here. This. This is everything we live and work for, all in one single moment. Now.

Finally taking my first breath, as the standing ovation continues, I reach for Frankie, our foreheads touching before my lips find hers, sealing this moment as a memory we had the joy of creating together.

I know there is one true love story in this theater tonight, and it doesn't belong to Gabriela Sotomayer and Griffin Chase or Finn Parker and Eva Armeni.

It's the story of Parker Finn and Frankie Simonelli.

And all the chapters we've already written together.

And all those we've yet to write.

Acknowledgements

To Jake – For sharing your story with me and for inspiring *Fleeing an August Moon*.

To the readers and bloggers of the indie romance community – I am beyond grateful for your continual support and love of the stories I create. You are a dream to write for and I am blessed that you have embraced me and my work.

To the *Reel Love* ARC Team – For your time and support and for sharing in my excitement

To my Rogues – Your support allows me to follow my dream. I will be forever grateful.

To Vi and Penelope – Your friendship and fellowship is such a highlight. I am so lucky to have you two to turn to, bounce things off, laugh with, and just be myself.

To Cleida and Kristen – Your ongoing support and friendship means the world to me. Cleida, thank you for thinking of me every week. Your tireless support is very much appreciated, and Kristen, thank you for helping me get this book into everyone's hands and for making sure nothing fell through the cracks. I feel like I pulled you out of retirement and said, "C'mon, just one more time!" Thank you, both!

To Jena – You did it again! Thank you for your patience and wonderful creativity.

To Scott – Third cover photo together! Definitely a winning combination.

To Elaine – Thank you for ensuring it's all clean, crisp, and beautiful.

To Kahlen – Thank you for dragging me out of my shell. I'm a typical Cancerian, and will hide there, given the chance. Thank you for not letting me do that.

To Mindy – My ride or die, as always. Love you! Read faster!

To Mom – Thank you for everything, always, and the three-day read-aloud sessions. I love you!

To Mark & Max... because I'm not easy. My love, always.

Some beach bars are Famous... Others Iconic...
But there's only one beach bar that is truly Infamous...

Are you ready for a summer at the
Legendary Echo Beach Inn?

**To get a sneak preview
of my next novel, ECHO BEACH, visit...**
http://bit.ly/2RdDF26

Never miss one of my releases
http://bit.ly/JulieARichmanNewsletter
Join me in my private readers' group
http://bit.ly/2RichmansRogues

Other Books by Julie A. Richman

The Needing Moore Series

Searching for Moore (Book 1)
Moore to Lose (Book 2)
Moore than Forever (Book 3)
Needing Moore: The Complete Series

Stand-Alone Novels

Bad Son Rising
Henry's End
Moore than a Feeling
Slave to Love
The Do-Over
Love on the Edge of Time
Reel Love

Come find me

Facebook (http://bit.ly/JARAuthorFB)
Instagram (http://bit.ly/JARINSTA)
BookBub (http://bit.ly/JRichmanBB)
On the Web: www.juliearichman.com
Julie's eMail: julie@juliearichman.com